LETHAL OBJECTION

An Edward Mead Legal Thriller

MICHAEL SWIGER

Cover design by: 100 Covers
Library of Congress Control Number: 2018675309
Printed in the United States of America

To my son, James, whose every smile brings unspeakable joy to my life.

1

Monday, January 25
Cuyahoga County Justice Center
Cleveland, Ohio
8:05 A.M.

Judge Samuel Chesterfield examined the four lawyers standing at attention in front of his antique, Victorian desk. His eyes lingered on Jessica Parris, a narrow-faced woman with an erect torso that she accentuated by throwing back her shoulders. She looked heavier in the hams than he remembered. Her mouth pursed up as if she was about to speak.

"Out with it."

"With all due respect, Your Honor," she said, "shouldn't we let the jury decide?"

"Let them decide?" Chesterfield sank back into his chair and shook his head. "Those idiots weren't smart enough to get out of jury duty."

"But—"

"Silence." He raised his hand as a scrawny stenographer fumbled into the room, tripping over her tripod. "Hold it right there, Edith."

She froze.

"We won't be needing your services."

"But Your Honor," Parris said, "I specifically requested that all meetings be on the record."

"I know full well what your sniveling little motion

1

said." He waved his left hand. "Edith, be gone."

The stenographer backed out and shut the door.

Chesterfield spun around in his high-back, burgundy-leather chair and threw his feet up on the brass and marble credenza. He looked out the window; snow pelted the glass. He addressed the lawyers with his back to them as he had done throughout the trial.

"Well, boys and girls, I hope you're satisfied. Right now, I should be in Bermuda chasing half-naked blondes through the surf in a drunken stupor. But noooo... I'm stuck in Cleveland in the middle of a blizzard, because you idiots couldn't settle this case like real attorneys." He crossed his feet and locked his hands behind his head. "So, since you've wasted my time and jammed up my docket for the rest of the winter, I've decided to return the favor. As soon as I finish giving the jury instructions, the four of you will report to my conference room, where you will remain until the verdict comes in."

"You're sequestering us?" Walter King asked.

Chesterfield spun around and sneered at the fat man with the faint mustache of perspiration over his upper lip. King looked like he had stolen his suit out of a Goodwill box and had his hair cut in the dark by a psychopath with a knife and fork.

"I've instructed my bailiff to station two armed deputies outside the door with orders to arrest anyone attempting to leave without my permission."

"But I've got other commitments, Your Honor," Dr. Chandler Rutledge said, his eyes blinking incessantly behind steel-rimmed glasses.

"I don't give a damn."

Rutledge's face turned scarlet; his eyes looked glassy and inflamed.

"I hope the jury deliberates for a week."

"Don't you think locking us in a conference room may be a slight abuse of discretion?" King asked.

"Keep it up, fat boy, and I'll lock you in the janitor's closet."

"What about lunch, sir?" Jonathan Burton asked.

"Ah, the elder statesman speaks." Chesterfield's eyes traveled up and down the thin, wiry man with hollow cheeks and dark circles under his eyes. "Frankly, John, the four of you can suck the lint off the carpet for all I care; just don't leave the conference room. Understood?"

"Yes, Your Honor," the four said in harmony.

"Good. Now let's get this circus over with."

The lawyers hustled out of the room.

Chesterfield stood and buttoned his black robe. He felt a headache coming on, pressure like an iron ring digging into his forehead. He reached in his top drawer, grabbed a bottle of Valium, then tossed three pills in his mouth. He swallowed them dry as he headed down the narrow, L-shaped corridor connecting his office to the outer conference room. He stopped in the private bathroom midway down the hall and checked himself in the mirror. He ran his hand through his close-cropped, black hair, then leaned closer and examined his bloodshot eyes. He straightened his tie then continued into the conference room where his redheaded bailiff waited at the door.

"Ready, Your Honor?"

Chesterfield nodded.

The bailiff pushed open the door. "All rise! This Court is now in session. The Honorable Judge Samuel Emerson Chesterfield presiding."

Chesterfield entered with his habitual rigid dignity, strutted up the three steps to the bench, then scanned the courtroom. The gallery was empty except for a few reporters milling around in the back. A sketch artist worked furiously at his pad from the front row of the gallery.

"Please be seated." He rapped the gavel, plopped down, then reached for his customary trial beverage - vodka and water. He sloshed a gulp of the burning liquid around his mouth and swallowed. He scanned the jury through watering eyes.

Look at these morons. Maybe if I talk like they are 2-year-olds, they won't screw this up.

He cleared his throat. "Ladies and gentlemen, you've heard the testimony, you've examined the evidence, and now it's time for me to place this case into your capable hands. However, before I do, it's my duty to issue the necessary instructions." He belted back the rest of the vodka.

"As you know, Dr. Thomas Baird is accused of medical malpractice resulting in the wrongful death of Ms. Robin Roget. During your deliberation you must determine whether or not Dr. Baird acted with negligence, and if you find he did, you must then decide if his dereliction was the proximate cause of her death."

Chesterfield poured himself another drink and glared over at Dr. Baird, a middle-aged man with a mouth like a fish. Baird's dull staring eyes were fixed on the floor and glazed over, so that he looked as if he'd just been choked.

Chesterfield transferred his gaze back to the oak-paneled jury box. "Now a word of caution. In a wrongful death case predicated on physician malpractice, the burden of proof falls squarely on the plaintiff. The defense—"

A whimpering sob resonated through the cavernous courtroom. The victim's mother buried her face in her hands. Jessica Parris patted her on the back; Walter King offered a handkerchief.

"The defense has raised the affirmative defense of contributory negligence. Which means if you find that Robin Roget conducted herself below a reasonable measure of care - the standard an ordinarily prudent person would have exercised - and if you find she could have avoided the consequences of the defendant's actions, then you must reduce any damages accordingly.

"Furthermore, if you find Ms. Roget voluntarily exposed herself to the injuries she sustained in a knowing and willful manner, then you must conclude she assumed the risk and disqualify her estate from receiving any compensatory damages. Do you understand these instructions?"

Twelve blank faces nodded their befuddled heads in unison.

"Very well then. The bailiff will escort the jury into the deliberation room, and trial counsel will report to my chambers immediately."

He banged the gavel, bolted down the steps, and disappeared through the oversized oak door. Moments later he stormed into his office, threw his robe on the floor, then made a beeline for his desk. He picked up the flask of vodka and started drinking himself into oblivion.

5:35 P.M.

Bailiff Robert Stanley rippled his fingertips on the table outside the jury deliberation room and leafed through the morning edition of *The Plain Dealer.*

The door behind him swung open, and a scrawny man with a monstrous Adam's apple stepped out. "We've reached a verdict."

"Excellent," Stanley said. "The judge will be pleased."

He guzzled the rest of his lukewarm coffee, walked the short distance to Chesterfield's chambers, then slung open the door. Burton sat next to Jessica Parris at the conference table, wheezing behind his hand. King sat off in the corner with his chin tucked into a generous roll of flesh, working on a laptop computer. Rutledge paced along the far wall of bookshelves, nibbling his lips like a nervous horse.

5

"The verdict is in."

A collective sigh went up.

Stanley walked past the conference table, then down the crooked hallway to Chesterfield's office. The door was cracked open; he knocked then walked in. He saw Chesterfield's legs propped up on the credenza, the rest of the body concealed by the back of the chair. "The verdict's in."

Silence.

"Your Honor," he said a little louder. "The verdict is in."

No answer.

He's probably ripped out of his mind. It wouldn't be the first time.

Stanley tentatively tread across the floor. He stopped short of the desk and braced himself for the verbal onslaught that would surely come after rousing the judge from his inebriated slumber. He took a deep breath through his nose; a sweet, pungent scent gorged his nostrils. He crept around the side of the desk, then recoiled in horror.

Chesterfield's cadaverous head hung at an impossible angle. Red-rimmed eyes bulged out of their sockets. A dagger was buried to the hilt in his throat. A coagulated sheet of crimson draped his chest. His talon-like hands clutched the armrests. Blood trickled on the floor; Stanley heard the drip, drip, drip onto the plush carpet.

2

Cuyahoga County Justice Center
3rd Floor
8:45 P.M.

Special Agent Sarah Riehl sat in one of the two metal folding chairs facing the interrogation room door, tapping a black Paper Mate pen on the stainless steel tabletop. The stench of stale coffee and wet cigarette butts permeated the room. She checked her watch, then spun around to face the wall of mirrors behind her.

"Where is he?" she demanded angrily.

"You've got me," a female voice on the intercom said.

Sarah turned toward the door again. She knew better than to take out her frustration on the agents behind the glass. Just a few months earlier she'd found herself exiled to the booth, spending monotonous hours staring at the recording equipment and closed-circuit monitors. But after two hours and four cups of French Vanilla coffee and three trips to the ladies' room, Sarah Riehl felt frazzled. She startled when the door swung open.

An elderly man shuffled in; he stood motionless with parted lips and eyes strangely bright. His overcoat looked three sizes too big. His hair, white and stringy, had the impression of the tan fedora he carried under his right arm.

"Excuse me, sir," Sarah said. "You can't come in here."

"Why not?"

"This is official government business."

"I should hope so," he said. "I'm the special prosecutor for the Chesterfield murder."

"You?"

"I hope you haven't been waiting long. I just got off the phone with Tony not 30 minutes ago."

"Tony who?"

"Tony Barbour."

"Attorney General Anthony Barbour?"

"Anthony. Tony. I call all my students by their first names. Less formal you know."

"You're a teacher?"

"Law Professor, Case Western."

"I'm Sarah Riehl." She stood and looked down on the diminutive man.

"Edward Mead."

They shook hands; she felt the bones and tendons in his sinewy hand.

"I'm sorry about the misunderstanding, Mr. Mead. I was just... I expected..."

"Someone a little taller," he said with a grin.

"It's just that I... younger... I—"

"No need to explain. I make no apology for my 77 years." He unbuttoned his coat and hung it over the back of his chair. He sat down next to Sarah and crossed his legs; his knees cracked.

She examined him out of the corner of her eye. His face looked round and pale. Tired folds of skin sagged over intelligent blue eyes. A network of wrinkles covered his face. Deep smile lines etched into the corners of his eyes. A broad and weathered Russian nose sat atop flesh-toned lips and a stately chin. He glanced over and caught her studying him. She looked away.

"What do we know so far?" he asked.

"Not much." She rummaged through a yellow legal

pad for her notes. "We've got four suspects, all of them lawyers."

"That's interesting."

"Apparently, Chesterfield ordered our suspects to remain in his conference room until the verdict came in and posted armed deputies at the only entrance."

"Kept the lawyers sequestered, you say."

"That's what his bailiff said."

"Rather odd."

"I thought so too." Something about the old man made her feel uncomfortable. "Anyway, sometime during the day one of the lawyers must've slipped into Chesterfield's office and jammed a letter opener through his throat."

"Grisly."

"Spiked his neck right to the back of the chair."

"And no one noticed a dead man bleeding all over the place?"

"Chesterfield's office is completely out of sight from the conference room. In fact, it's separated by a narrow hallway with a private bathroom midway between the two rooms."

"What about the weapon?" he asked.

"What about it?"

"I'm guessing there's no fingerprints."

"None. But I'm having DNA samples collected from the suspects."

He shook his head.

"You don't agree?"

"The office is probably covered with hair fibers and skin cells from every member of the Cleveland Bar Association, including all four of our suspects."

"What do you suggest?" she asked.

"You held the suspects?"

"Of course."

"Let's have a little chat with them. Maybe one of them will confess."

"Don't you want to see the crime scene first?"

"I'll see it soon enough." He steepled his fingers under his chin.

"Through four different sets of eyes."

3

Edward Mead watched Sarah Riehl scribble a list of questions on her legal pad. He gave her the once-over and guessed her at 5 feet 6 inches and maybe 120 pounds. She flipped her shoulder-length, sandy blonde hair over her shoulder. Hazel, almond-shaped eyes focused on the legal pad. Long black lashes swept the exquisite pallor of her cheeks. Her glossy lips were parted just a little.

She looked exotic and beautiful.

He inhaled through his nose. "Lilacs."

"Excuse me?"

"Your perfume smells like lilacs."

"It's called *Lilies*," she said. "My husband bought it for me."

"Smells like lilacs to me."

She rolled her eyes.

"If you don't mind," he said. "Why don't you take the lead in the questioning, and I'll interrupt as needed."

"Works for me."

"Use your instincts. Each suspect will be different."

"I've done this before."

"Just trying to help."

Mead tapped the toe of his black loafers against the table leg and waited. He glanced at the scuffmarks covering the lime-green tile floor.

A few moments later the door opened, and a tall man wearing a gray pinstriped suit walked in, raking his fingers through a thinning mat of blond hair. He appeared to be in his late 40s, with a long face, and a nose like the beak of a hawk. His light blue eyes darted back and forth between Mead and Riehl from behind steel-rimmed glasses.

"My name is Edward Mead, Special Prosecutor." Mead struggled to his feet, bracing himself on the table and offered his hand. "This is Special Agent Riehl with the FBI."

"I'm Dr. Rutledge — Chandler Rutledge — pleased to meet you both." He shook their hands.

"I was under the impression all our suspects were lawyers."

"I'm a physician who's also a lawyer. Although I do most of my operating in the courtroom these days."

"I see," Mead said. "Please have a seat. We'll try not to keep you long."

They sat down. Mead nodded to Riehl.

"Quite an eventful day, huh, Doc?" she said.

"Not one I'll soon forget."

"I'm not going to beat around the bush here, Doc. Did you kill Judge Chesterfield?"

"I most certainly did not." His eyebrows furrowed together.

"Do you know who did?"

"No."

"Was there ever a time when you were out of the sight of the other suspects?"

"Yes."

Her eyes widened. "You left the conference room?"

"Of course I did. The restroom is in the hall near the judge's office."

"When was the last time you used the restroom?"

"Sometime around lunch."

"Who was the last person to use it before the verdict came in?"

"How should I know?"

"Think. Who was it?"

"I... uh... I don't know. Over the course of nine hours we all made several trips. I wasn't paying that close attention. I didn't know it was going to be important."

"Maybe it would help if you told us what you did throughout the day," Mead said.

"Let me think." He shifted his weight. "I spent most of the morning on my cell phone trying to reschedule meetings, touching base with my office, getting ahold of clients, that sort of thing. In the afternoon I helped myself to the law books and did some research on another case."

"What about lunch?" Riehl asked.

"Sometime late in the morning somebody suggested we pick a restaurant and order out."

"Who suggested?"

"I'm not sure. I believe it was King. Yes, as a matter of fact, it was King. He wanted to order pizza."

"What time?"

"Somewhere around 11:30."

"Did you order pizza?" she asked.

"We argued over three or four different places and couldn't agree. So, we each ordered separately."

"What did you have?"

"A turkey and cheese bagel from the snack shop in the lobby."

"What about the others?"

"I don't know. I wasn't paying that close attention."

"How was it?" Mead asked.

"How was what?"

"Your sandwich."

"It was all right, I guess... how's that relevant?"

"It's not." A crooked smile turned up one corner of Mead's mouth. "I missed dinner and thought about grabbing a bite in the lobby on my way out. But I might stay away from the turkey, though. It gives me gas."

Riehl squinted at Mead. "Do you mind if I continue?"

"Go right ahead."

She shook her head, then glanced at her notes. "Let me see... where was I? Okay, Dr. Rutledge, what were the others doing throughout the day?"

"The morning is a bit hazy for me, but I believe everyone made a few calls at one time or another. King went off to a corner and set up his laptop. As I recall he pretty much spent the entire day at his computer, when he wasn't eating. I'm pretty sure Burton and Parris chatted for most of the morning. After lunch Burton went to the restroom then came back, slouched over the table, and took a nap. After he woke up, he used the restroom again, then made a few calls." Mead listened intently, while Riehl took copious notes.

"Parris and King whispered to one another for awhile after lunch, then she excused herself and went to the restroom. When she returned, she spent most of the afternoon writing something longhand."

"Do you have any idea what she wrote?" Riehl asked.

"Haven't a clue."

"Please continue."

"If I'm not mistaken, she got up and used the restroom just before Burton woke up. King stayed glued to his computer for long stretches all afternoon. Occasionally he walked over to the water cooler. I believe he went to the restroom three or four times. And now that I think about it, King was the last one to use the restroom."

"Are you sure it was King?" she asked.

"Positive." Rutledge cracked his knuckles.

"Did you know Judge Chesterfield before this case?"

"By reputation, not personally."

"Did you have any contact with him apart from the trial?"

"No."

"Why did Chesterfield detain the four of you after the trial?"

"I have no idea. The man was a megalomaniac."

"Would you be willing to take a polygraph test?"

"I most certainly would. I've nothing to hide."

"Very good. Thank you for your cooperation. Is there anything else you can tell us that may aid in the investigation?"

Rutledge paused, bit his bottom lip, then dusted the elbow of his coat. "Not that I can think of, at least not at this point. With all the excitement I may be missing something obvious."

Riehl reached inside her purse and pulled out a business card. "I'll be getting in touch with you over the next couple of days. If you think of something, anything at all, call me day or night. Of course, you know that as a suspect in a murder investigation you can't leave the state."

"Of course."

Riehl turned to Mead. "Do you have any more questions?"

"Just a couple. Dr. Rutledge, are you right- or left-handed?"

"Right."

"I see. And you said earlier you didn't know who killed Chesterfield."

"That's correct."

"Then who do you think killed him?"

"I already told you, I don't know."

"I'm not asking what you know, I want your opinion."

"If you're looking for my best guess, I'd have to say King."

"Why King?"

"Chesterfield brutalized the guy."

"How'd he treat the rest of you?"

"He was rude to all of us, but King caught it the worst. And aside from that, King strikes me as someone a bit unstable."

"Unstable?" Mead asked.

"Apparently, you haven't met him yet."

"No. You're the first suspect we've interviewed."

"You'll see. I'll leave it at that." Rutledge blinked a few times. "Is there anything else?"

"One last question," Mead said. "What do you think the verdict is?"

"I have no idea."

"You must have some feel for how it went."

"I was told the verdict is sealed."

"It is."

"Then I couldn't venture a guess. Juries are fickle. Is there anything else?"

"Not right now," Mead said. "You're free to go."

4

S arah Riehl watched Rutledge stand, button his double-breasted coat, and walk out. As soon as the door closed, she looked over her shoulder at the wall of mirrors. "Send in the next suspect."

"Will do," the woman on the intercom said.

Riehl turned to face Mead. "So, what do you think of the good doctor?"

"I'd like to reserve my opinion till the end."

"Well, he maintained good eye contact, and he didn't stammer over his words." She slid off her left shoe and scratched her heel. She adjusted her sock, then slid her shoe back on. "Overall, I'd say he told the truth."

"Our suspects are professional litigators, Ms. Riehl."

"So?"

"So, they know how to lie."

"He agreed to a polygraph."

"They all will."

"What makes you so sure?" she asked.

"Lawyers live in a world of semantics."

"I don't follow you."

"If the polygraph examiner asks, 'Did you murder Chesterfield?' our culprit could answer no without registering a deception."

"How's that possible?"

"Because he's thinking to himself, I didn't murder the

17

guy; I killed him."

"That's a reach, don't you think?"

"It's been my job for the better part of 50 years to teach lawyers how to think."

"A liar is a liar."

"I'm simply suggesting the normal rules won't apply in this case."

"One of them is a murderer," she said with a sarcastic, angry tone. "Anyone capable of running a letter opener through someone's throat is going to stick out like a sore thumb."

"We'll see."

The door opened, and a man about 6 feet tall with a thinning patch of iron-gray hair walked in wearing a navy blue three-button suit. Drooping lids slightly curtained his steel-blue eyes. Pasty skin covered sunken cheeks. Saliva stood at the corners of his thin lips. He appeared to be around 60. His drawn face stretched into a smile when he looked at Mead.

"Professor, what are you doing here?"

Mead struggled to his feet and warmly clasped the outstretched hand. "Tony asked me to handle this case, since it involved a sitting judge. I had no idea you were one of the suspects."

"Ah, but the honorable Mr. Barbour did."

"I suppose he did."

Riehl cleared her throat.

"I'm sorry. Jonathan, this is Agent Riehl, FBI."

"You two know each other?" she asked.

"Jonathan is a former student and an old friend."

"Small world."

They sat down.

"I'm sorry about Victoria," Jonathan Burton said. "I was out of town on business the week she passed. I didn't find out until I got back, or I would've been at the funeral. I didn't know she was ill."

"Breast cancer."

"Cancer... huh." A look of pain covered his face. "I'm sorry, Professor."

"I'm sorry too," Riehl said.

Mead's eyes misted; he wiped his forehead with his veined hand. "Well, let's get started."

Riehl consulted the yellow legal pad. "Mr. Burton, did you kill Judge Chesterfield?"

"I did not."

"Do you know who did?"

"I do not."

"Were you ever alone with Chesterfield during the course of the day?"

"I had no cause to be."

"But you did use his private restroom?"

"Of course I did, but I wouldn't call that being alone with the guy. The facilities are in the hall outside his office."

"Mr. Burton, did you have any contact with Judge Chesterfield outside of this case?"

"I saw him periodically at various legal functions, and I golfed with him at a fundraiser last summer. But we weren't close, if that's what you're getting at."

"What was your impression of Chesterfield?"

"He was a pompous ass."

"But that's no reason to kill him."

"I didn't say it was."

"Did you notice any odd or stressful behavior from your colleagues during the day?"

"Not that I recall."

Riehl flipped through the legal pad and stopped at the page from the Rutledge interview.

"Would you be willing to take a polygraph?"

"Yes, I would."

"Well, that may be necessary." She glanced over at Mead. He stared straight ahead as if deep in thought.

"By the way, are you left- or right-handed?"

"Right-handed."

"Please describe how everyone passed their time throughout the day."

"That's a pretty broad question."

"I'm not looking for minutiae. Just give me a basic sketch."

"Let me think here." Burton wiped his mouth with a handkerchief, seeming to suppress a cough. "As I recall, I spent most of the morning chatting with Ms. Parris. I believe Mr. King sat off in the corner working at his computer. And I'm pretty sure Mr. Rutledge spent most of the morning pacing near the door talking on the phone."

"Did anyone leave the room during the morning hours?"

"I can't be certain, but I don't believe anyone did."

"What about—"

"Wait a minute. Mr. Rutledge did."

"Dr. Rutledge left the room?"

"Yes, I believe he excused himself and used the facilities after we ordered lunch."

"Did anyone else use the restroom after lunch?"

"To be perfectly honest with you, I really can't say. I must've dozed off. I get tired easily these days. It seems like I closed my eyes for only a few minutes, but the next thing I knew it was late in the day. Although I'm pretty sure we all used the facilities as the day wore on."

"From the time you woke up, did Dr. Rutledge use the restroom?"

"Let me think." Burton looked at the floor and massaged the back of his neck. "I really can't say for sure. He may not have. I can't be sure, though. I'm sorry."

"That's all right, Mr. Burton. It's been a very long day. I just have a couple more questions. Do you recall who was the last person to leave the room?"

"I believe it was Mr. King. It seems to me he used the

facilities a couple of times before the verdict came in."

"What do you think the verdict is?"

"I won."

"And when you say you won..."

"The defense won."

"What makes you think that?"

"I've been in this business a long time. In malpractice cases the verdict usually hinges on the expert witness. Ours was better. Ms. Parris tried to compensate by some trick tactic, but I think it made the jury feel sorry for my guy. I'd be surprised if the verdict came back against me."

Riehl made a note of that. "Who do you think most likely killed Chesterfield?"

He shook his head. "I really couldn't say."

"Thanks for your time, Mr. Burton. You've been most helpful. Before we close, is there anything else you'd like to add that would be helpful to this investigation?"

"You may want to look into the bailiff who discovered the body. He was in a great position to do it himself and shift the blame to one of us."

"Thanks for the suggestion. We'll look into him." She tapped her pen on the legal pad. "That's all the questions I have for you right now. I'll be getting in touch with you over the next several days. Here's my card. You're free to go unless Mr. Mead has any additional questions."

She glanced over at Mead, who sat motionless with his lips parted, eyes staring off into space.

"Mr. Mead?" She reached over and touched his arm.

"Huh... what? What was the question?"

"Do you have anything further for Mr. Burton?"

"Just a couple of questions." Mead rubbed his thumb and forefinger across his eyes. "What do you think the verdict is?"

Burton's eyebrows raised. "Professor Mead, I've already answered that question."

"You did? What about your views on who the killer

might be?"

"I've answered that one too."

Mead's face flushed. "That'll be all then. You're free to go."

Burton pulled up his sleeve and checked his stainless steel watch.

"I can't believe I've been here for 15 hours."

"That's an unusual watch," Sarah said.

"Professor Mead bought it for me as a wedding gift. It runs off the body's thermal energy. No batteries."

5

A re you feeling all right?" Sarah Riehl asked after Burton left the room.

"I'm fine, I'm fine," Mead said.

"Because if you're not up to it we could call it a—"

"I said I'm fine."

"If you say so."

Riehl pretended to review her notes, not wanting to make eye contact with her elderly colleague. Before today she had endured 11 years with the Cleveland Police Department, then nine years of peon assignments with the Bureau. Now when the case finally arrived that would catapult her through the glass ceiling, they paired her with a shriveled-up, senile has-been; he even smelled old.

She scrutinized him out of the corner of her eye. Ropy, knotted veins covered the backs of his hands. A simple gold band, timeworn and scarred, wrapped around the ring finger on his left hand. She envisioned her career, her very future resting in those tired, withered hands, and her stomach twisted.

Mercifully the door opened and suspect number three walked in. The woman was petite, maybe 5-foot-3, and wore a blue, ankle-length silk dress. Her dark blonde hair bounced with each step; a few wisps hung down over her temples. She squinted her fawn-colored eyes at the wall mirrors, then sat down and crossed her arms. Her expression was hard and cynical.

"I certainly hope you don't think I had anything to do with this... this... unseemly business."

"My name is Sarah Riehl, FBI. This is Prosecutor Mead."

"I didn't catch your name," Mead said.

"That's because I didn't give it."

"Lose the attitude," Sarah said. "I expect your utmost cooperation. Understood?"

"Jessica Parris."

"That's better. Now, Ms. Parris, did you kill Judge Chesterfield?"

"No."

"Do you know who did?"

"No, but I know who killed Jimmy Hoffa."

"Cute. Who do you think killed him?"

"I'm not going to answer that."

"Why not? Do you have something to hide?"

"I'm not hiding anything. But even if I suspected someone - which I don't - but even if I did, I wouldn't tell you. I may end up representing whomever you charge."

"Or you may get charged yourself."

"What's stopping you?"

"Don't play games with me; I'm not in the mood. I can hold you up to—"

"Seventy-two hours," Parris said, examining her rings.

"You're not helping your cause here."

"I'll be most happy to answer any fact-based questions you have, but I won't sit here and slander my colleagues."

"If I may," Mead said. "Ms. Parris, what did you have for lunch?" Sarah rolled her eyes.

"I ordered a chef's salad from San Souci."

"What did the others have?"

"I don't see where this is leading..."

"Humor an old man."

"It's your circus. Mr. Burton had a Bouillabaisse; we ordered together. Mr. King ordered pizza from the Rascal

House, and Rutledge had some sort of bagel sandwich."

"Did everyone eat what they ordered?"

"I guess so."

"I see. And which weighs more - a pound of lead or a pound of gold?"

"What?"

"It's a simple question."

"I'm not answering that."

Sarah shook her head. "Ms. Parris, did you leave the conference room during the course of the day?"

"Only to use the powder room."

"The judge's private restroom?"

"He wouldn't let us go anywhere else."

"During any of these trips to the restroom, did you happen to enter the judge's office?"

"No."

"For any reason whatsoever?"

"Why? Did someone say I did?"

"No—"

"Because if they did, they were lying." She folded and unfolded her arms, then folded them again.

"Could you describe for us in general terms what everyone did throughout the day?"

"Mr. Burton and I talked for the better part of the morning."

"What did you talk about?"

"We talked about killing Chesterfield; what do you think we talked about?"

"Answer the question," Sarah said.

"We discussed the case... what we thought the verdict might be. We talked, you know, like adults."

"And what did you decide the verdict would be?" Mead asked.

"That I probably lost. I had a good case but didn't have the resources to take on a governmentally subsidized multi-million-dollar industry."

"So, with more money you think you would've won?"

"Without a doubt. But don't get me wrong, I haven't conceded this case yet. The jury could easily have seen things my way. But I've got to hand it to Mr. Burton; he's a good lawyer."

"Yes, he is," Mead said.

The furnace kicked on. Forced air whirled through the overhead vent.

"What did everyone do in the afternoon?" Sarah asked.

"After lunch Mr. Burton put his head down on the table and took a nap. I don't think he was feeling very well."

"What about the other two?"

"King set up shop at the far end of the room nearest the water cooler. Every time I noticed him, he was either banging away at his computer or eating something."

"And Rutledge?"

"Rutledge talked on his cell phone - probably till the battery went dead - then pulled a few books off the shelf and spent the afternoon reading."

"Who was the last person to leave the room?"

Parris crossed her legs and adjusted her dress over her knee. "If I'm not mistaken, Mr. King used the powder room just before the verdict came in."

"Was he acting different or odd when he came back?"

"No."

"Did you know Chesterfield before this case?"

"Yes."

"How?"

"I was his clerk for about three years when I first graduated law school."

"You were," Sarah said, raising her eyebrows and looking at Mead; he nodded. "That's quite a coincidence. And how would you describe the nature of the relationship?"

"We had a professional working relationship."

"What do you mean by that?"

"I mean we worked together professionally. What do you think I meant?"

"Did your professional relationship ever have occasion to turn personal?"

"What part of my answer didn't you understand?"

Wham!

Sarah slammed her open palm against the table. "I'm tired of playing verbal gymnastics with you. Did you have a personal relationship with Chesterfield or not?"

"We dated briefly."

"Define briefly."

"A few months. It was no big deal. It didn't work out."

"Is that why you found another job?"

"No."

"Why did you leave?"

"There's not much money in clerking."

"Would you be willing to take a polygraph?"

"Bring it on. I've nothing to hide."

"During the course of your dating, did he ever become abusive?"

"No."

"How about verbally?"

"He verbally abused everyone. That's what made him Chesterfield."

"Did you have contact with him between the time you broke up and the time this case began?"

"No, I practiced out-of-state for a few years. In fact, I went straight from working for him to being an associate of Chandler, Rodney & Robbins in New York."

"Ms. Parris, are you right- or left-handed?" Mead asked.

"Left-handed."

"Getting back to Chesterfield," Sarah said. "Did you harbor any ill feelings toward him over the breakup?"

"That was seven years ago. I haven't given him a

second thought in years."

Sarah scribbled a note on her legal pad. "What's your association with Mr. King?"

"I hired him to do some research."

"Why him?"

"Because he is extremely diligent and extremely cheap."

"Those two qualities don't usually go together in this profession," Mead said, reaching down and manually crossing his legs. He winced.

"Mr. King is... how should I say... a bit high-strung," Parris said. "He's not the type of guy you'd find trying a case to a jury."

"I see."

"And have you ever worked with King before?"

"No, I haven't." She looked at her watch. "Is this going to take much longer? I've been here since first thing this morning."

"It will last as long as I say it lasts," Sarah said.

Mead reached over and touched her arm. "This is a good time to break. I don't have anything else."

"There are a few points I'd like to follow-up on." Sarah tossed her card on the table. It slid into Parris' lap. "I'll be getting in touch with you soon - very soon."

6

Mead watched Jessica Parris walk away with her shoulders back and head held high. She slammed the door behind her.

"You two seemed to hit it off," Mead said.

"She's hiding something."

"We all are."

"If she didn't do it, she knows who did."

"I wouldn't jump to any conclusions just yet." He stroked his chin with his thumb and forefinger. "She may naturally have an abrasive personality."

"I'm telling you; she knows something. And I guarantee I'll find out what it is."

The door swung open, and in lumbered suspect number four. He appeared to be about 6 feet tall and around 300 pounds. He moved with a slight, almost imperceptible limp. His rumpled sport coat gathered in a heap behind his shoulders. The top of his white shirt was unbuttoned, and a green tie hung like a hangman's noose around his bloated neck. A thick mop of disheveled red hair crowned his pudgy face. He could have been 40 or maybe 27. His brown eyes shifted from Sarah to the mirrored wall to Mead to Sarah and back to the mirrored wall again.

"I'm Special Agent Sarah Riehl, FBI. This is Prosecutor Mead. Have a seat."

King plopped down; the chair squeaked in protest.

"Mr. King, it's late, and we've all had a long day, so I'm going to cut to the chase here. Did you kill Judge Chesterfield?"

"Who... who said I killed Chesterfield?"

"No, no, I'm asking - did you kill Chesterfield?"

"Did Rutledge tell you I did? He never liked me."

"I'm not telling you; I'm asking you. Did you kill Chesterfield?"

"I didn't kill anyone, honest." A thin layer of perspiration glistened on his forehead.

"Do you know who did?"

"I didn't see anything."

"Who do you think killed him?"

"I don't know, I don't know. Maybe he killed himself."

"That's absurd," Sarah said. "No one stabs himself in the neck."

"He... he... he was a mean-spirited man," King wiped his shiny forehead with his sleeve. "He may have done it just to set me up. He was vindictive that way."

"Why would Chesterfield want to set you up?"

"He despised me, looked down on me. He would ruin me if he could."

Riehl looked over at Mead; he raised an eyebrow. "Mr. King, were you alone with Chesterfield at any time today?"

"No, never."

"Did you use his private restroom?"

"Yeah, but everyone else did too. I wasn't the only one."

"Were you the last one to use the restroom before Chesterfield was found dead?"

"Who made me the pisser police?"

"Don't get smart; I'm really not in the mood."

"Sorry." He rubbed his fat, freckled hands together. "I was only joking."

"Were you or were you not the last person to use the

restroom before the verdict came in?"

"I may have been. There wasn't a hall pass or anything."

"Mr. King," Mead said. "Are you the heaviest suspect in this case?"

"I... uh... suppose so."

"And would you attribute that to your weight?"

"Yeah, I guess so... you lost me there."

"Are you right- or left-handed?"

"Right-handed."

Sarah shook her head and smirked at Mead. "Mr. King, describe what you and the others were doing in the conference room during the morning hours."

"I spent pretty much the entire day on my laptop."

"Doing what?"

"I was working on a few things." Large beads of sweat formed on his upper lip and reappeared on his forehead.

"What were you working on, Mr. King?"

"A few personal things, private things."

"You realize that your computer is in the evidence vault as we speak."

"All right. I played video games."

"Video games?" Her lips stretched into a smile. "What kind of video games?"

"Death Grip."

She rolled her eyes. "What is Death Grip?"

"It's awesome. You're an assassin, and you rack up points stalking and killing different victims. It's the next best thing to virtual reality."

"An assassin? You've got to be kidding me. You mean to tell me you spent the day killing cartoon action figures?"

"It's just a game."

"What about the others?"

"They didn't play."

"No, I mean, what were they doing?"

"Jessica spent the morning talking to Burton. Can you believe it? He's the enemy. And they even ordered lunch together. Rutledge acted all high and mighty, prancing around with his cell phone. Like I've never used a cell phone before. And no one wanted to order pizza with me, so I had to eat by myself."

"What did Rutledge order for lunch?" Mead asked.

"He ordered some sort of sandwich. He took it out of the bag but didn't even touch it. And do you think he'd offer it to me? No. I would have asked him for it if he wasn't such an—"

"Did anyone act unusual during the day?"

"I thought it strange that Jessica spent so much time with Burton. And they were friendly and everything. I'm not saying that Jessica had anything to do with Chesterfield getting killed. If anyone did, it would have to be Rutledge."

"Why do you say that?" Mead asked.

"It couldn't have been Jessica; she's too pretty to be involved in something like that. And Burton—"

"Wait a minute," Sarah said. "What does Ms. Parris' being pretty have to do with who killed Chesterfield?"

"I didn't say she was pretty."

"You did."

"I didn't."

"This is being recorded." She looked over his shoulder at the mirrored wall. "I could have the boys in the booth play it back for you."

King dug into his pocket and pulled out a handkerchief. He mopped his brow. "What I meant to say is she's too sweet a person to do something so violent."

"And what about Burton?"

"I don't think so. Chesterfield didn't mess with him too much, and he seemed so tired all the time. And I didn't do it. I mean, no one said I did... right? So that leaves Rutledge, unless Chesterfield killed himself - which you don't think he did - so it must have been Rutledge."

"What was your impression of Chesterfield?"

"Cruel, cold-blooded. He was vicious."

She leaned forward. "Did you ever think about killing him?"

"I... uh... it wouldn't have bothered me much if someone... you know... but I didn't."

"But you did think about it?"

Enormous balls of sweat ran down his face. "Probably his own mother thought about it - if he had a mother." King blurted out a breathy, forced laugh. "You really had to know him."

"What do you think the verdict is in the wrongful death case?" Mead asked.

"I think we lost. Things didn't go well. Chesterfield made sure of that."

"Getting back to the events of the afternoon," Sarah said. "While you were playing video games, what were the others doing?"

"I was really into the game, so I didn't pay much attention to the others. But whenever I took a break to get some water or go to the can, Jessica did a lot of writing, and it looked like Burton took a nap or something. He looked ill for most of the trial."

"What about Rutledge?"

"I couldn't say for sure. We pretty much ignored each other as much as possible."

Sarah looked at her watch. "Let's wrap it up for now. It's very late. Thank you very much for your cooperation, Mr. King. Here's my card. I'll be in touch within the next few days to arrange a polygraph."

"Polygraph? Who said anything about a polygraph?"

"All the others agreed. You don't have a problem with it, do you?"

"No... I'll... I'll take the test."

"Very good. You're free to go unless Mr. Mead has

something else to ask you."

Mead looked at his watch: 10:37 p.m. "Not at this time. You're free to go."

King stood and shook his left leg as if it had fallen asleep. He headed for the door with a pronounced limp. He wiped his forehead on the back of his sleeve and didn't look back. The door banged shut.

"What do you think of Mr. King?" Sarah asked.

"He's wound up tighter than a Hong Kong wristwatch."

"He stuttered and stammered like we'd caught him red-handed. He had guilt written all over his face."

"It looked like sweat to me."

They laughed.

"It sounds to me like King and/or Parris thought they lost the case and decided to take their frustrations out on Chesterfield," Sarah said as she was gathering her things.

"I think it's been a long day, and I still have to visit my wife. Why don't we call it a night and meet in the morning for breakfast?"

"Sounds good to me. Where do you want to meet?"

"Where do you live?"

"Out in Willoughby."

"I'm over in Shaker. Are you familiar with Tommy's in Coventry?"

"Sure, the best vegetarian food in Cleveland," she said. "What time?"

"Let's make it nine."

"I'll see you there." She grabbed her legal pad and was about to stuff it into her bag.

"Before you go, I'd like to borrow a piece of paper if I may?"

She ripped off a sheet and handed it to him. He took a pen from his shirt pocket and wrote a single sentence in the middle of the page. He folded the paper in half, then in half again. He slid it back to Riehl.

"Would you be so kind as to sign and date this for me?"

"What is it?"

"It's just an observation."

"Can I read it?"

"Not till the case is over."

"Why not?"

"It could influence you."

"Then why do you want me to sign it?"

"To authenticate it."

"This is weird."

"Humor an old man."

She scribbled her signature on the paper and slid it back to him.

7

Edward Mead drove his midnight-blue Lincoln Continental out of the parking garage across the street from the Justice Center, made his way down Ontario Avenue to East Ninth Street, then headed east on Euclid Avenue. He motored past the Cleveland Playhouse, flooded in white light. He thought of all the plays and musicals he and Victoria had seen there over the years. Oh, how she loved it when the *Broadway* shows came to town. *Phantom of the Opera* was her favorite; he always loved *Les Misérables*. Just last year they had flown up to Toronto to see the *Phantom* — one last time.

He continued past the sprawling, mirrored complex of the Cleveland Clinic, where Victoria was first diagnosed with breast cancer. Why didn't they catch it sooner? How could it have spread so fast? Why didn't she complain about it? She didn't have to be so brave.

Mead stopped at the intersection of Euclid and Martin Luther King Jr. Drive. The majestic Severance Hall stood ahead on the left, home of the world-renowned Cleveland Orchestra. The palatial limestone structure overlooked Wade Lagoon. He and Victoria were season ticket holders for 52 years, center section on the left aisle, seats 1 and 2. They hadn't missed a performance since her father passed in 1968. What would he do with the tickets now? He could never sit next to Victoria's empty red velvet seat.

He didn't see the light turn green. The car behind him tooted its horn. He stepped on the accelerator and entered University Circle, the heart of Case Western Reserve University. The mammoth University Hospital stood on the right, where he took Victoria for a second opinion and those worthless experimental treatments. How come nothing worked?

The Thwing Center, to the left, buzzed with activity. They had met on this very campus shortly after he began teaching law, when she was a second-year nursing student. How many excruciating commencement speeches had they endured together on this campus? How many hours had they spent walking around the reflecting pool in front of the Cleveland Museum of Art? And how many strolls had they taken through the Botanical Gardens, talking about life and the future and all the children they ended up never having?

The car rolled past the Euclid Tavern. To his right East 123rd Street met Euclid Avenue and provided a rear entrance to Murray Hill, Cleveland's Little Italy. He smiled, remembering the tiny 3 room apartment with the leaky roof they first rented after the wedding. It wasn't much, but it was enough. And all those late night drives to Presti's Bakery. She loved those wonderful glazed doughnuts fresh out of the oven.

The Lincoln sped past the Rapid Transit station and pulled up to the soaring wrought iron gates of Lake View Cemetery. He always thought the cemetery seemed so out of place here in the midst of the decaying urban sprawl. He knew Cleveland history; he had lived through 77 years of it. When he was a boy this cemetery bordered the famed "Millionaire's Row" homes of the Cleveland industrial barons since the advent of the Industrial Revolution. Now the only mansions still standing were boarded-up ruins. The rest had long since collided with the wrecking ball and been replaced by government housing projects. He shook his head.

Entropy is so cruel... to both buildings and people.

The gatekeeper, bundled up in a goose down parka, must have recognized the car. He shuffled out and opened the gates without asking for identification. Mead steered past the gatehouse. Up ahead on the right he saw the silhouette of President Garfield's tomb and memorial house. Massive oaks encircled the medieval looking tower; swaying branches partially obstructed his view. He negotiated the narrow, winding path past John D. Rockefeller's grave with its headstone, a 100-foot tall replica of the Washington Monument.

I wonder how much old John D. left behind? All of it, I guess.

The car drove over a slight grade and down to a section of private mausoleums. He stopped the car, turned off the ignition then stepped out. Knifing pain stabbed his knees as the frigid January wind whipped around his spindly legs. The frozen turf crunched underfoot with each unbalanced step he took toward the marble edifice. He took off his leather gloves and fumbled through his key ring in the moonlight. The oversized bronze key was easy to find. He stepped into the shadow of Victoria's new home. His hands trembled as he searched for the lock. He found it, and the door opened with a whine.

He walked inside. Moonlight forced its way through the circular stained glass window, washing the crypt in a pale red glow. He eased up to Victoria's vault and rubbed his bare hand against ice cold marble until he found the chiseled engraving of her name.

At 11:42 p.m. on January 25, Edward Mead wept.

8

Edward Mead walked down the newly widened sidewalk beside Coventry Road, marveling at all the renovation since his last trip to the village. Something in the brisk, pine scented air enlivened his step. He strolled past Hunan's Oriental Restaurant - Victoria thought they made the best Szechuan food in Cleveland - then stopped in front of Mac's Paperbacks. He looked through the window at the mounds of books and thought about all the money he'd spent here over the past 20 years, a small fortune. He continued up the street to Tommy's.

He pulled open the door with great effort; a whoosh of frigid air announced his arrival. His eyes adjusted to the light as he looked around the restaurant. The hardwood floors, wooden tables, and horizontal oak paneling gave the place a cozy feel.

"Over here, Professor Mead."

Sarah Riehl waved from the wooden bench lining the far wall in the front, right-hand corner of the restaurant, her papers strewn across the small square table. She wore her blonde hair pulled back in a ponytail. A single rogue ringlet hung down across her temple. Her hazel eyes looked surprisingly alert for this time of the morning.

"Good morning, Ms. Riehl."

"Morning."

"Sorry I'm late." He pulled off his gloves and stretched out his hand. "I'll never get used to living alone." They shook hands.

He removed his fedora and ran his crooked fingers through his thin white hair. He caught his reflection in the window. A spattering of tiny, red veins covered his cheeks. A small piece of blood-saturated toilet paper stuck to his face just below his left ear. Puffy discoloration ringed his tired eyes.

How did I get so old?

The waitress came over and took their orders, then hurried away.

"After you left last night, I interviewed the bailiff," Sarah said.

"What did he have to say?"

"Basically, he walked into the office like he had done a thousand times before to announce the verdict. He said it looked like Chesterfield was sleeping with his feet propped up on the credenza, but he really couldn't tell because the back of the chair faced the door and obstructed his view of Chesterfield's upper body. Anyway, the bailiff yells, 'The verdict is in,' and when he didn't get a response, he walked around the desk—"

"And found Chesterfield spiked to his chair."

"Exactly," she said.

"Sounds plausible."

"And the coroner's office faxed over a copy of the post-mortem first thing this morning. It seems Chesterfield bought the farm sometime between noon and two."

"What time did the bailiff find him?"

"After five."

"I guess we can rule him out."

"That's what I thought."

"Did you bring a copy of the autopsy?"

"It's here somewhere." She riffled through the papers

on the table, then handed him the report.

He reached into his shirt pocket, pulled out a small pair of round-lens reading glasses, and placed them on the end of his nose.

"It says here an 8-inch blade entered the neck 2 inches below the mandible on the left side of the esophagus at a sharp, downward angle. It missed the jugular vein, but pierced the larynx, severed the spine, then exited between the C4 and C5 vertebrae at the base of the neck."

"He couldn't move or cry out."

"Quite a piece of work." He removed his glasses.

"I'm thinking a spontaneous crime of passion or maybe a crime of opportunity?"

"Or made to look that way."

The waitress returned and slid a frothy mug of café mocha along with a chocolate chip muffin in front of Sarah. She placed a steaming cup of black coffee in front of Mead. He bent over and took a deep whiff of the rich aroma.

"It smells good."

"The coroner said Chesterfield's blood alcohol level was three times the legal limit."

"I didn't see that in the report."

"The coroner said the higher-ups instructed him to leave it out of the official report, you know, for the media." She shrugged.

"So, he was smashed."

"Probably never saw it coming."

"If the weapon entered from the left at a downward angle," he pantomimed the motion with his pen, "then the assailant must've been right-handed. If my recollection serves me correctly, only Ms. Parris claimed to be left-handed."

"But what if she came up directly from behind the chair and reached around with the letter opener?"

"She would've been stabbing in the blind," Mead

reasoned.

"So."

He raised one eyebrow.

"I'm not saying she did it, only that she could have," Sarah defended.

"So how would you rank the suspects?"

She sipped her mocha. "Obviously, King has to be the prime. The guy was practically bouncing off the walls."

"Indeed."

"And he's the only one to flinch at the polygraph." She took a bite of the muffin; a chunk fell on her lap. "Parris comes next. She's hiding something. If she didn't do it, she was in on it."

He shook his head.

"You don't agree?"

"Whoever did it, acted alone."

"Why do you say that?"

"Call it a hunch."

"What if Parris and King planned it ahead of time?"

"They had no way of knowing Chesterfield was going to detain them all day."

"Maybe they were all in on it together."

"They couldn't agree on where to order lunch, so I can't see them agreeing on a murder."

"Maybe the bickering about lunch was a part of the cover story."

"You really believe four people can keep a secret?"

"Why not?" she said.

"Four can only keep a secret when three are dead."

"That may be, but I'm not ruling out anything at this point." She held the cup up to her lips, pulled it away, blew on it, tried again. "Dr. Rutledge would come next, with Burton last."

"I can vouch for Burton; he's no killer."

"You seem sure about that."

"Quite sure, but I still want complete workups on

all four backgrounds: financial records, phone bills, the whole shootin' match - and that goes for Burton as well. No special treatment. And once the preliminary work is done, start digging deeper, one by one."

"Starting with King?"

"Starting with Rutledge."

"Why not King?"

"Start with the least likely suspect and work backward. The sooner we eliminate those who didn't do it, the more time and energy we can spend on the actual killer."

"What about Burton?"

"What about him?"

"I thought he's the least likely suspect."

"I'll handle him personally."

"No special treatment, huh?"

Mead picked up the coffee, spilling some into the saucer.

"What about the polygraphs?" she asked.

"Not yet, let them simmer awhile."

"And what will you be doing while I'm running all over God's green earth?"

"I'm having a stenographer put a rush on the trial transcription." He set the cup down; his hand trembled. "Something happened during the trial that triggered this mess, and the transcript is the key. I also plan on paying our suspects a personal call on their turf."

He reached for his coffee and knocked it over, spilling it across a pile of Sarah's paperwork. "Sorry. My dexterity isn't what it used to be." He sopped up the mess with his napkin.

"Can I ask you a question?"

"Certainly."

"When was the last time you prosecuted a case?"

Mead paused and looked up from the coffee-stained napkin. "Twenty-two years ago."

A long pregnant pause hung in the air before she said, "That's a long time."

"What's your point?"

"This is a big case."

"And..."

"Let's be honest, you're not exactly young, and your behavior last night was... was... well, out there. I mean you zoned out for who knows how long during the Burton interview. This case is incredibly important to me and—"

"I may be a little unorthodox, but there is indeed a method to my madness."

"I sure hope so."

"I've been a little preoccupied since my wife passed."

"How long ago did she die?"

He looked down, waited a few seconds, and raised his head. "Eight days ago."

9

Edward Mead walked out of Tommy's, made a right, and tucked his chin against his chest. The winter wind whistled along the storefronts. He mindlessly put one foot in front of the other, fighting the urge to cry. When he finally looked up, he found himself on Euclid Heights Boulevard in front of the Grog Shop, formerly Arabica's coffeehouse. He thought of the countless nights he and Victoria spent here snacking on fresh-baked pastries, sipping exotic coffee, and listening to aspiring poets, musicians and intellectuals flaunt their wares on the small wooden stage. Now the place was a rock music club. *Why did things have to change?*

He turned around and backtracked to Tommy's, feeling more and more frustrated with each step. He goose-necked up and down the street, and his frustration turned to fear; he couldn't find his Lincoln. He shuffled between two parked cars and crossed Coventry Road in front of the Big Fun nostalgic toy store, its red and white awning flapping in the steady breeze.

Nothing looked familiar. Fear escalated to panic.

"I must be losing my mind," he mumbled, his breath visible in the biting air.

He attempted to re-cross Coventry. A car screeched to a stop inches from his legs. He froze. The heat from the engine engulfed him.

The driver thrust her head out the window. "What on earth are you doing?"

He didn't respond.

"Are you blind or... Professor Mead?"

His eyes grew wide; his cheeks flushed. "Ms. Riehl?"

"Are you all right?"

"I'm fine." He walked around to the driver-side window.

"Do you need a ride somewhere?"

"No, I'm just getting some fresh air."

"Are you sure you're all right?"

"Fine, fine."

"All right."

He stepped aside, and she drove off.

The surge of adrenalin sparked his memory. He walked down Coventry to Famous Dave's Sub Shop and found his car parked on the street where he'd left it.

Didn't I look here already? Maybe not. It didn't matter.

He had an appointment to keep. He drove himself to the courthouse feeling embarrassed, angry with himself, and insecure.

Is it true the short-term memory is the first thing to go?

He parked his car on the street in front of the Justice Center and took the elevator to the 2nd floor. He walked into the Clerk of Courts office and asked for the transcripts from the Chesterfield trial. A smart young woman with a lavish application of rouge handed him a brown envelope of loose-leaf papers. Only a small portion of the stenography tape had been transcribed; it would take at least a week to complete the task.

Mead took the bundle and headed for the Sears Library on the Science and Engineering quad at Case Western Reserve University. Over the years he'd discovered the reading rooms at the Sears Library were the best place for a law professor to get away to read without being disturbed. He parked his car in the Cedar Avenue faculty parking lot and took the elevator to the top floor. The elevator doors opened to the familiar musty scent; dust mites feasted on the volumes relegated obsolete. He felt strangely akin to these relics.

Recently he managed to find solitude amid the labyrinth of shelves. He meandered to his customary corner table overlooking the brick-paved quad. He sat down, opened the package, and began to read. The events played out in his imagination as if he was a spectator in the gallery....

"All rise: Hear ye, hear ye, hear ye! This Court is now in session. The Honorable Judge Samuel Emerson Chesterfield presiding."

Chesterfield strolled through the oak-paneled door, carrying his 5-foot-10-inch frame ramrod-straight. The fluorescent light shimmered off his thick, black hair. His hazel eyes burned with anger.

He climbed the three steps to the bench and rapped the gavel.

"Be seated."

He surveyed the modern-looking courtroom. The walls were lined with vertical oak slats offset with recesses of walnut. The seats in the gallery gradually sloped from back-to-front like a movie theater; few spectators were in attendance. The jury box sat on the right side of the room nearest the witness stand. The jurors fidgeted, looking cramped and uncomfortable.

"Good morning, ladies and gentlemen," Chesterfield said. "Now that you've been sworn in, and we've dispensed with the preliminaries, we shall proceed with opening remarks. Keep in mind that nothing said by either attorney is considered evidence. Since the burden of proof is on the plaintiff in a civil case, Ms. Parris will speak first." He looked over at the plaintiff's table. "You may proceed."

"Thank you, Your Honor," Parris said.

The petite blonde stood, buttoned her gray wool blazer, and approached the jury box, being careful to make eye contact with those in the front row.

"Ladies and gentlemen, my name is Jessica Parris, and I represent the plaintiff - the estate of Robin Roget. Robin won't be joining us today, or any other day for that matter, because she's dead. She died at the hands of that man."

Parris spun and pointed at Dr. Baird. He slouched and averted his eyes to the floor.

"This is not a murder trial. The State of Ohio in its infinite wisdom has decided not to press charges against the good doctor, and for the life of me, I can't figure out why not. But that's beside the point. You're here today for another reason; you must determine whether or not the defendant caused the wrongful death of Robin Roget by his medical malpractice."

She paced along the jury box, allowing her French manicured hand to slide along the brass railing. "My opening remarks will be brief. The facts in this case are very simple: one, Robin Roget was a beautiful, perfectly healthy, 22-year-old woman when she walked into Dr. Baird's clinic for a simple, out-patient operation; two, Dr. Baird horrendously botched that routine procedure; three, Dr. Baird negligently failed to notify Robin that anything went wrong or that her life was in danger; four, Dr. Baird maliciously failed to perform or recommend any medical treatment following surgery; five, Dr. Baird knowingly and willfully released Robin from his clinic in a dangerously unstable condition; and six, Robin Roget died less than 18 hours later as a direct result of Dr. Baird's egregious malpractice."

She paused to allow the silence to drive her words into the jury's collective subconscious.

"While this case focuses on two people, Robin Roget

and Dr. Baird, it will impact many more. A wrongful death always leaves a trail of destruction in its wake, especially when the victim is struck down in the prime of her life. Robin Roget has left behind a grieving mother who is sitting behind me at the plaintiff's table. She will suffer the pangs of this loss for the rest of her life. But that's not all. Robin also left behind two small children who depended on her exclusively for their financial and emotional support: Lovell, age 2, and Rachel, age 3. Right now, these children are much too young to understand exactly what happened. All they know is that Mommy isn't coming home anymore. It's impossible to measure the irreparable psychological damage these children have sustained. They will be scarred for life.

"Ladies and gentlemen, your job here is rather straightforward. You must find Dr. Thomas Baird guilty of medical malpractice and compensate those tragically left behind by Robin Roget's wrongful death. It's the only fair and merciful thing to do. Thank you for your time and consideration."

Jessica Parris walked back to the plaintiff's table and sat down next to Walter King. He patted her on the back.

"The defense may proceed with opening remarks," Chesterfield said.

"Thank you, sir." Jonathan Burton stood and nodded to the judge and then to Jessica Parris. His steps toward the jury box were slow and deliberate, the sound of his black wingtips on the hardwood floor echoing throughout the room.

"Good morning, ladies and gentlemen of the jury. I'm Jonathan Burton, and I along with Dr. Chandler Rutledge represent Dr. Thomas Baird. As you may expect, the story I'm about to tell you is somewhat different from the version you've just heard. I don't mean to imply that Ms. Parris has lied to you; she has not. However, when facts are presented outside their proper context, they tend to lose their meaning. For example, let's consider the case of The United States versus Kirby."

He clasped his hands behind his back and paced in front of the jury box. "Mr. Kirby was charged with four counts of willfully obstructing the passage of the United States mail; he was accused of detaining Mr. Farris, a mail carrier who was actively engaged in the performance of his job.

"We all know the mail must go through. So, when charged with these crimes, Kirby confessed to not only detaining the mailman, but to binding and gagging the man for several hours. There you have it - a confession - case closed, right? Not so fast. The story doesn't end there. As it turns out, the mail carrier was wanted for murder, and at the time of the incident Kirby was the county sheriff. By arresting the mail carrier, Sheriff Kirby may have interfered with the delivery of the mail, but he was only doing his duty.

"You see, the story needed to be told in its proper context before the correct conclusion could be drawn. And just like the intent of the law in the Kirby case was not to prevent a law enforcement officer from arresting a murderer who happened to be a mailman, so the intent of the wrongful death law is not to penalize a law-abiding doctor for unusual and unforeseen consequences brought on in no small part by the patient's own negligence."

Burton stepped up against the railing and leaned slightly into the jury box. "Let's review the facts as presented by Ms. Parris and see how they hold up under the microscope of context. First of all, the defense will stipulate that Robin Roget was a beautiful, 22-year-old woman when she entered Dr. Baird's clinic. But she wasn't technically healthy. It seems that Ms. Roget was suffering from gonorrhea and syphilis - a fact she neglected to share with Dr. Baird, and a fact Ms. Parris conveniently omitted.

"The defense will also stipulate that Ms. Roget financially supported her children. After all, she was an all-nude dancer at the Wild Pony Saloon. I understand such dancers can generate an impressive income with tips for... shall we say... special favors. But as for the amount of emotional support she offered her children, the defense has its doubts about that.

"Ms. Parris referred to the surgery in question as a simple, outpatient procedure. I prefer to call it what it is - abortion. In fact, Ms. Roget's third abortion in as many years. The story is starting to sound a little different now, isn't it? You see, this case is not quite as simple as Ms. Parris would have you believe."

Burton wiped the back of his hand across his clammy forehead.

"A wrongful death case predicated on physician malpractice is usually the most complicated case that can be tried to a jury. Aside from all the technical mumbo-jumbo you'll hear from the medical experts, there are also some pretty delicate legal principles you'll be forced to grapple with. For instance, in a case such as this the law does not allow you to presume negligence on the doctor's part simply because an injury has occurred. The burden of proof is on the plaintiff to show by a preponderance of the evidence that Ms. Roget was injured by the specific negligence of the defendant, and that such negligence resulted in her death. In other words, just because Ms. Roget sustained an injury, you cannot automatically conclude that my client is at fault."

"Another principle you'll be hearing quite a bit about in this trial is that of contributory negligence. You'll be asked to sort through all the nitty-gritty details and determine if and how much of Ms. Roget's injuries were the result of her own irresponsibility. The law requires a patient to use such care as would be exercised by an ordinarily prudent person under similar circumstances. The defense will present conclusive evidence that Ms. Roget demonstrated a clear pattern of reckless behavior and gross neglect for her own health and safety.

"Lastly, the defense will offer the principle of assumption of risk. Basically, you will be asked to determine whether or not Ms. Roget was aware of the possible dangers and complications surrounding the abortion, and if so, did she knowingly accept them. To this end, the defense will present a waiver signed by Ms. Roget verifying she completely accepted any and all risk associated with the operation. The defense will also present a second document signed by Ms. Roget agreeing that in the event of a complication she would not sue or seek legal recourse."

Burton stepped away from the jury box and put his hands in his pockets. "As Judge Chesterfield has said, the plaintiff will be the first to present its case. And as you've already discovered, facts are not always what they seem. There is a proverb in the Bible that says, 'He who states his case first seems right until his rival comes and cross-examines him.' I want you to keep this piece of wisdom in mind as Ms. Parris presents her case against my client. Thank you."

10

Edward Mead felt the presence of another body hovering nearby. The faint aroma of lilacs flitted under his nose. He looked up from the transcript.

"Good afternoon, Professor," Sarah Riehl said with a smile. "Sorry to interrupt."

"No, no, it's no bother. I was just... uh... how did you find me here?"

"I'm an FBI agent. It's my job to find people who don't want to be found."

"You called my secretary?"

"You'd better believe it."

"Where are my manners?" He struggled to his feet. "Have a seat."

She sat down on the orange vinyl chair and placed her bag on the metal table. "Man, it smells like mildew up here."

"It's not me. It smelled that way when I got here."

"I didn't mean to imply—"

"I know, I'm only joking."

She smiled. "Find anything interesting in the transcripts?"

"Not yet. This is just the opening remarks. Both sides are drawing lines in the sand."

"Any impressions so far?"

"Only that Jonathan Burton is a better lawyer than

Jessica Parris." He sat back and stretched. "What about you?"

"I spent the entire day tied into the FBI mainframe at Quantico, and I've extracted every piece of electronic information available on Dr. Chandler Rutledge."

"Very good, Sarah. May I call you Sarah?"

"Sure."

"I'm guessing the doctor is clean."

"Squeaky. Not so much as a speeding ticket." She dug through her bag and pulled out a report and handed it to him. "It's all there. He was born and raised in Elyria, Ohio. Both his parents were doctors. He graduated from Elyria High at the top of his class and went on to The Ohio State University. He studied biology and pre-med. He graduated *magna cum laude* and went on to medical school at Wright State University, where he specialized in obstetrics and gynecology." Mead sneezed.

"God bless you."

"Thanks." He blew his nose into his handkerchief.

"Following med school, he married a woman named Ruth Goldburg; she comes from old money. No kids. They're still married. After ten years at the Cleveland Clinic, he went to law school at Cleveland State and specialized in medical malpractice. He seems to have developed a reputation for being one of the best in the area. No criminal background, no juvenile record. He's basically a productive citizen."

"I wonder what prompted his career change."

"It's hard to tell."

"What about his finances?" Mead asked as he flipped through the report.

"Everything is in good order. The IRS audited him three years ago, and they discovered they actually owed him money."

"What are these complaints with the Ohio Medical Board?"

"Malpractice claims. He was cleared of any wrongdoing."

"What kind of malpractice?"

"Abortion related."

"Doesn't that strike you as significant?"

"Why would it?"

He picked up the transcript. "This is an abortion malpractice trial."

"I wasn't aware of that. Still, from what I understand, these guys do literally thousands of abortions a year. The sheer numbers dictate at least a couple of oddball cases."

"I see."

"You see what?"

"He's desensitized to killing."

"Oh, come on—"

"Abortion is rationalized murder."

Her eyes narrowed. "Let's keep political ideology out of this, shall we?"

"I'm merely pointing out the obvious. The man is trained to look at the human body clinically. And if he's done a number of abortions, at least in his own mind he doesn't see anything wrong with taking lives for money."

"Aborting a glob of cells and killing a grown man are two entirely different things."

"I agree. The grown man is a much larger glob of cells."

She rolled her eyes.

"The autopsy pointed to an almost surgically precise wound," Mead said.

"But any puncture to the neck is bound to hit something vital."

"Perhaps."

"Besides, Rutledge doesn't have a motive."

"That we know of."

"You think he did it?" Sarah asked.

"I'm not saying anything of the kind. But I would like to pay the good doctor a house call before I cross him off my list. Do you have his address?"

"It's on the front page there. He lives out in Pepper Pike."

"Oh, yes, here it is."

"If it's all the same to you," Sarah said, "I'd like to shift my attention to King or Parris."

"Start with Parris."

"Very good." She nodded, licking her dry lips. "What time should I check in tomorrow?"

"Give me a call around 5 o'clock."

"After all the phones I've tapped over the years, I don't feel comfortable discussing sensitive matters over the information superhighway. Maybe we should meet someplace instead."

"When's good for you?"

She flipped through her datebook. "I'm meeting my husband at 6:30. How about we make it 4:45?"

He looked down at his wedding band and twisted it around his crooked finger, staring at his distorted image in the gold.

"Professor Mead?"

No answer.

"Professor Mead?" she said louder.

He shook his head. "I'm sorry. You were saying?"

"Where would you like to meet?"

"I have to run down to the Justice Center to pick up more of the transcription. Let's make it someplace downtown."

"How about my office at the Federal Building?"

"Sounds good," he said.

"Your wife?"

"What about my wife?"

"You were thinking about her just then?"

"I think about her always."

"It's none of my business, but maybe it would help if you took off your ring?"

"I can't."

"Is it stuck?"

"No, I made a vow before God that we would stay married till death."

"With all due respect, Professor, your wife is dead."

He raised his eyes, slowly, painfully; he spoke in short, quick gasps that betrayed deep emotion. "Yes, but I'm not."

11

S arah Riehl pulled in the driveway behind her husband's gray and red Dodge Intrepid. It felt good to be home. They had lived on Mentor Avenue since their marriage 16 years earlier. She had fallen in love with the red-brick, ranch home and could picture the place filled with kids, but it wasn't meant to be.

She climbed out of her car. The streetlight on the corner cast bluish-pink shadows on the unbroken carpet of white. Flecks of snow drifted to the ground. Her husband's footprints were barely visible in the light dusting that covered the walkway leading to the front door. She looked up at the sky. Dark, ominous clouds obscured the moon. It wouldn't be long before Cleveland was pelted with another heavy snowfall. She cautiously made her way to the front door. The juniper tree standing in front of the bay window to the left of the front door creaked and swayed in the breeze.

She stopped at the door, slid her hand in the mailbox, and pulled out another stack of bills. Jerking open the door, she stepped into the foyer and dropped the mail on the table in the corner. She took off her coat. She could smell bean soup wafting from the kitchen.

"Honey, I'm home."

She kicked off her shoes. The plush carpeting felt

wonderful after a long day on her feet. She collapsed on the couch and propped her feet up on the glass coffee table, nudging the candle centerpiece with her big toe. She stared at the floral-pattern wallpaper on the far wall near the bedroom hall.

I really need to replace that stuff.

Doug Riehl, a tall, handsome, swarthy fellow dressed in a flannel shirt and pair of tan corduroy pants, walked in from the kitchen. His shoulder-length hair was pulled back in a ridiculous ponytail. His gentle brown eyes were nearly hidden behind a heavy brow-line. A large nose and thin lips filled out his oblong face. He was a couple years younger than her - a point he didn't let her forget.

"How's my little sleuth today?" He snuggled up next to her on the couch. "Catch any bad guys?"

"Not lately."

"How's your grandfather holding up?"

Sarah smiled. Edward Mead did pose a striking resemblance to her maternal grandfather.

"At times he's bright and lucid, and at other times he's out there in *Never Never Land*."

"Maybe he's got Alzheimer's."

"I wouldn't put it past him. It's painful to watch him slip in and out."

He raised a questioning eyebrow at her.

"Doug, the man actually asked a suspect, 'Which weighs more - a pound of gold or a pound of lead?'"

"No kidding. What did the suspect say?"

"She didn't."

"Interesting question."

"It's ridiculous. They weigh the same."

"No, they don't."

"Of course they do."

"The standard measure for lead is 7,000 grains per pound. Gold is measured in Troy weight: 5,700 and some odd grains per pound. Lead is definitely heavier."

"Are you sure?"

"I'm a metallurgist," he said in a condescending tone.

"It's still a bizarre question."

"I think it was kind of clever."

"Come on now," she said.

"Didn't you say he just lost his wife?"

"Yeah."

"Well, cut him a little slack. That's got to be hard on the old guy." He put his arm around her and gave her a squeeze. "You'd better never die on me."

"I won't."

"Better not, or I'll come and do nasty stuff to your grave."

She jabbed an elbow into his ribs. "I'm trying to be serious here."

"I know, I'm sorry."

"Even if he is crazy, I'm stuck with him. The guy was handpicked by Attorney General Barbour."

"That doesn't mean you can't work it through proper channels. If he can't handle the job, he's got to go."

"Come on, Doug, he was picked for a reason. I've done some digging and found out that Barbour and Burton were roommates at law school. Maybe Barbour picked Mead to protect Burton."

"Or bury him."

"Mead has made it clear that he'll personally deal with Burton. What's that tell you?"

"Do you think this Burton guy did it?"

"No."

"Then what's the big deal?"

"I don't know. I feel like I'm walking through a minefield here."

"What're you going to do?"

"Something... nothing... I don't know. Maybe I should be investigating Mead along with the rest of them."

"So, investigate him."

Lake View Cemetery
6:35 P.M.

Salt-stained streaks lined Edward Mead's numb cheeks. He pressed his lips against Victoria's nameplate and kissed her good night. He stepped back and shivered. A ball of something fell off the end of his nose. He stepped out of the mausoleum, locked the door, and turned toward his car. The bone-colored moonlight peered through the clouds and cast a stark glow over the grounds. He took small, careful steps through the crusted snow. His feet didn't seem to be responding to his neurological commands. It felt like heavy weights were strapped to his ankles. Possibly the 45 minutes of standing on the icy marble floor had something to do with it.

He inched closer toward his car. The tip of his right shoe caught something buried in the snow. The 77-year-old man lunged face first toward the crystallized ground. He thrust his arms forward just in time to keep his face from slamming into the ice. The jarring impact shot bolts of searing pain through his brittle arms and knees. He held himself perfectly still; his breath billowed in the frigid air.

"How did I get so old?"

His mind raced back through decades of time. It had been over 50 years since his body last smashed to the frozen turf, but then it was with the aid of a 220-pound Villanova linebacker.

Edward Mead had been an All-American tailback at Rutgers. His piston-like, high-knee running style earned him the nickname Crazy Legs. Back then his body was muscular and chiseled and solid as New England granite. With a football tucked under his arm, he could run all over the field without batting an eye. His every darting cut, or slashing spin was pure fluidity and grace.

The legs that once carried him to a national rushing title now betrayed him. He tried to stand, and his feet slipped; he sprawled out face first in the snow.

"Somebody please shoot me," he cried out.

With his bare hands stinging in the snow, he crawled the remaining 15 yards to his car; his arthritic knees screamed with each stride. He braced himself on the front fender and staggered to his feet. A miserable cold and damp sensation surrounded his legs. He looked down to see his brown suit pants matted to his legs by slushy snow.

"What else can go wrong?"

12

C handler and Ruth Rutledge lived on an elegant 40-acre estate in Pepper Pike. A quarter mile-long drive, hand-paved with brick, snaked through dense woods and looped around in front of the multi-gabled mansion. The estate had been in the Goldburg family for years, a wedding present to Ruth from her parents. The deed remained in the possession of the Goldburg Trust.

Chandler and Ruth were not a happy couple, but they both had what they wanted - social acceptability. Close friends likened their marriage to a business partnership. They lived separate lives with little contact or affection between them.

Dr. Rutledge spent most evenings alone in his study, and tonight was no exception. He reclined behind his desk and absently looked around the room. Floor-to-ceiling oak shelves lined the walls and held numerous collectibles - everything from ancient, leather-bound volumes to tribal fertility statues. An Oriental rug partially covered the mahogany parquet floor. To the right of his desk stood a Dutch silver spirit case with a siphon of soda water and several large cut-glass tumblers on a marqueterie table. His desk, loaded with the latest modern computer gadgetry, looked oddly out of place in this makeshift museum.

With medical malpractice cases now in vogue, Rutledge found himself dreadfully overworked, yet oddly short on cash. As he pored over his computer screen, his concentration diminished. He needed a little something to recharge his batteries, so he slid open his top desk drawer and reverently removed an heirloom wooden box. He flipped open the lid, and his pulse quickened at the sight of row upon row of tiny glass vials filled with precisely one gram each of pharmaceutical grade cocaine. He emptied one of the containers onto a mirror, manipulated the powder into four thick lines with a razor blade, then inserted a small glass tube into his nose and snorted. His eyes squinted shut then blinked rapidly. Ruth's shadow in the hall outside the door caught his attention. He shoved his treasure back into the drawer, just as she walked in.

"What is it?" he asked.

"There's someone here to see you."

Ruth Goldburg Rutledge was one of those tall lean greyhound women who looked good in tweeds. She wore her hair parted in the middle and pinned tightly in a bun, accentuating her high forehead. There was an arrogant beauty about her face.

"Tell Dr. Douglas to go home and take some tranquilizers," Rutledge said. "There's nothing I can do until they make a settlement offer."

"It's not George."

"Who is it then?"

"Someone named Mead."

"Mead? I don't know any Meads." He dabbed at his nose. "Is he an older gentleman, kind of small?"

"Yes, he is."

"Show him right in."

"Who is he?"

"He's the independent counsel handling the

Chesterfield murder."

"What's he want with you?"

"I'm sure it's nothing."

"Obviously it's something, or he wouldn't have driven all the way out here from God knows where."

"I'm not in the mood to play sixty questions with you. Show him in."

Ruth disappeared and a few moments later returned with a disheveled Edward Mead, his tan overcoat rumpled and stained with ice and mud.

"This is somewhat of a surprise, Mr. Mead. You're lucky to have caught me at home."

"Nice house."

"Thanks."

"Sorry to barge in unannounced. I just need to ask you a few questions."

"Ask away. Anything I can do to help." Rutledge motioned with his arm toward a hard-backed chair near his desk. "Have a seat."

"Thank you."

"What can I do for you?"

"Dr. Rutledge, would you please describe Judge Chesterfield's office for me?"

"You mean the physical layout?"

"Precisely."

"Well, when you first walk in from the hall, there's an antique French desk off to the left. King Louis XIII, I believe. Probably a knockoff. Behind the desk is a brass-and-marble credenza." Rutledge adjusted his glasses on the bridge of his beak-like nose and blinked his eyes in rapid succession. "Across from the desk on the right side of the office is an off-white couch and matching chair. High-quality. On the wall opposite is an alcove filled with bookshelves."

"What kind of books?"

"Ohio State Reporters, I believe, and others."

"And what about his desk?"

"I said it was a knockoff."

"No, I mean what was on it?"

"He had a computer. I believe it was on the right side, your left if you're facing the desk. And a nameplate."

"Very good sir. Is there anything else you recall about the office or desk?"

"Not that I remember."

"Did you happen to notice a letter opener?"

"No."

"Dr. Rutledge, would you say you have an abnormally large bladder?"

"Excuse me?"

"Your bladder, is it large?"

"No."

"Do you have any bladder problems?"

"What does my urinary tract have to do with this investigation?"

"Nothing, per se."

"Then why do you want to know?"

"Call it peripheral."

"No, there's nothing wrong with my bladder, but thanks for asking."

"Dr. Rutledge, how is it you came to work with Jonathan Burton on this case?"

"In all modesty, I'm the best in the business. All the big cases gravitate to my door."

"So, he sought you out?"

"You could say that."

"I see." A strand of hair fell down in Mead's right eye. He brushed it aside. "Tell me, Doctor, what made you leave the medical profession and take up law?"

"That's a good question. I guess it was a matter of pressure."

"I wouldn't think a surgeon would have problems with pressure."

"Let me put it this way. If a lawyer makes a mistake, his client can appeal. If a surgeon makes a mistake, his patient ends up dead."

"I see. So those malpractice complaints levied against you at the Medical Board drove you from the profession."

"Absolutely not." Rutledge bolted forward in his chair. "I was exonerated of those malicious accusations."

"Abortion-related, weren't they?"

"What's your point?"

"The Chesterfield case was also abortion-related."

"And?"

"Obviously, abortion is an issue you've been involved in over the years."

"I have."

"Do you think it's wrong?"

"It's legal."

"That's not what I asked."

"It's a medical procedure sanctioned by the United States Supreme Court."

"Indeed. But you agree it's the taking of human life?"

"Do you think I'm an idiot?" Rutledge said, blinking incessantly. "Of course, it destroys human life, but it's for a justifiable reason."

"Really?" Mead smiled a bitter smile, which only lifted one corner of his mouth. "Do you like antiques?"

"Antiques?"

"You know, really old stuff that people collect."

"I know what antiques are. And, yes, I'm a collector, but I don't see the relevance."

"I noticed that you have several valuable items laying around." He pointed to the shelf just to the left of Rutledge. "Take that silver snuffbox for instance. How do you go about finding something like that?"

"One develops an eye over time. The snuffbox is an interesting story. Ruth and I were attending an estate sale, the Wellingtons over in Chesterland. On the initial walk-through, I spotted that little gem tucked away on the top shelf of an old hutch. It was tarnished and covered with dust and obviously hadn't been touched in years. No one else even noticed the hutch, let alone the snuffbox. If you know what you're looking for, things like this sort of jump right out at you."

"I've never had such an eye."

"It's a gift."

"Indeed. Well, I've taken up enough of your time." Mead stood and slid his hand into his front pocket. "One last question. Do you like riddles?"

"I guess so. Why?"

"I have two coins in my pocket that amount to 30 cents. One of them is not a nickel. Tell me the denominations of the two coins."

"With all due respect, sir, this is absurd."

"Humor an old man."

Rutledge shook his head. "You say you have two coins in your pocket that equal 30 cents and one of them isn't a nickel?"

"Correct."

"If one isn't a nickel, it's impossible to have 30 cents."

"I beg to differ."

"Show me the coins."

Mead pulled his fisted hand out of his pocket and opened his palm, revealing a quarter and a nickel.

"You said one of the coins wasn't a nickel."

"Indeed. And the one that's not a nickel is a quarter."

13

A cloudless, copper-green sky gleamed overhead. Edward and Victoria Mead rode hand-in-hand in the backseat of their realtor's 1947 Packard convertible through the streets of Shaker Heights. Edward gazed at his wife, her long fawn-colored tresses whipping in the wind.

Such a beautiful woman.

He kissed her on the cheek. She turned and leaned her face so close to his that he could see the extraordinary structure of her irises, a multitude of colored streaks and flecks, her pupils enlarged. His heart took off at a gallop. He kissed her again; he couldn't help himself. Could anyone on earth be happier?

The car turned off of Northfield Road onto Van Aken Boulevard and stopped in front of a two story brick colonial. A large magnolia tree in bloom partially obscured the left side of the house. Tulips lined the walkway leading to the front door. Purple geraniums filled the flower boxes below each of the four second-story windows facing the street.

Victoria squeezed his arm. Her eyes grew wide, and her face barely contained her excitement.

Edward tilted his head and whispered in her ear, "Try not to act interested, and maybe he'll come down on the price."

No use. Victoria shot out of the car and dashed into the front yard like a kid at Christmas.

"It's perfect! It's perfect!"

"So much for restraint." He watched his enraptured wife bounding toward the front door and glanced over at the grinning realtor, no doubt already spending his commission. "I guess we'll take it."

He ran to meet her and swooped her off her feet. He carried her over the threshold. She threw her arms around his neck; they kissed.

"Welcome home," he said.

"I love you."

They kissed again.

Ring!

Ring!

Ring!

Edward Mead opened his eyes. The double-bell alarm clock sounded its 7:00 a.m. warning.

"It was just a dream."

He rolled over to turn off the alarm; biting pain shot through his right shoulder; he crumpled back to the mattress. It felt like someone had slipped into his bedroom and beat every inch of his body with a baseball bat. His back ached; his shoulders, knees and hips were locked into contorted positions. How could one fall cause so much pain?

With great effort he straightened out his tangled limbs and sat up on the edge of the queen sized bed. He attempted to stand; muscles rebelled; both thighs cramped. He stumbled back to the bed writhing in pain. This was not going to be a good day.

It took the better part of two hours for Mead to go through his morning ritual: shower, shave and coffee. Only sheer determination got him behind the wheel of his Lincoln. He drove downtown, fighting muscle spasms in his neck and back.

He limped through the corridors of the Justice Center en route to the Clerk of Courts office. He picked up the next bundle of transcripts, then headed to his top floor hideaway at Sears Library.

Twenty minutes later he settled down at his usual table feeling light-headed and nauseous. Bright spots danced in front of his eyes. He took a few deep breaths and began to read. His temporal afflictions faded away as he became just another spectator in the back of the courtroom....

"Ms. Parris, you may call your first witness," Chesterfield said, while pouring himself a tall glass of vodka and water.

"Thank you, Your Honor. The plaintiff calls Dr. Nicholas McCorkle to the stand."

A short, dumpy man in a gray herringbone suit stood at the rear of the courtroom, then walked down the center aisle carrying a manila folder under his left arm. His stringy, black hair looked wet and lay plastered to his scalp by some sort of hair gel. Wrinkled bags hung beneath his blue eyes. He stroked his bushy mustache as he climbed the steps to the witness stand. He sat on the edge of the seat with his back stiff and his body rigid. The uniformed bailiff carried the courtroom Bible over to him.

"Raise your right hand and place your left on the Bible. Do you swear to tell the truth, the whole truth, and nothing but the truth, so help you God?"

"I do."

"You may be seated."

Jessica Parris stood, adjusted her calf-length, navy blue skirt, then walked to the examiners' podium directly in front of the witness stand.

"Good morning, Doctor."

"Morning."

"Would you please state your name and occupation for the record?"

"Dr. Nicholas McCorkle, forensic pathologist."

"And where are you presently employed?"

"Cuyahoga County Coroner's office."

"How long have you worked there?"

"Fifteen years."

"Were you on duty the morning Robin Roget's body arrived at the county morgue?"

"I was."

"And did you conduct the autopsy?"

"I did."

"Please describe for the jury what you found?"

McCorkle opened the file and reviewed its contents. "As to the external examination, the deceased was a 22-year-old, Caucasian female, 5-feet-4-inches tall and weighing 127 pounds. Muscle tone above average. No sign of trauma to the head, upper torso, or limbs. Discoloration and swelling observed in the lower abdomen and genitalia. The internal exams showed the heart and lung sacs filled with serous fluid."

"Please define serous fluid."

"Serous membranes line the closed body cavity and secrete a fluid. Whenever the body cavity is violated, this fluid mixes with the blood and causes vascular congestion. This is precisely what I found in Ms. Roget's heart, lungs and kidneys."

"Is that dangerous?"

"Lethal."

"Please continue."

"The vagina was packed with gauze. The uterus was boggy with the placenta still attached and it contained approximately 50 cc of brownish-red, purulent and foul smelling—"

"Excuse me, Doctor," Parris said. "Could you define

purulent for the jury?"

"A pus-like secretion present during infection."

"Please continue."

"The left ovary and fallopian tube had been removed. A large rupture was present at the base of the uterus through which approximately 14 inches of small intestine had been pulled into the vaginal cavity."

"And the cause of death?"

"Septicemia due to incomplete abortion."

"I'm sorry to keep interrupting, but could you please define septicemia?"

"Septicemia is a systemic disease caused by a pathogenic organism or its toxins in the bloodstream."

"Could you try that, one more time, in layman's terms?"

"Basically, the dismembered fetus caused poisonous toxins to invade the bloodstream, which choked off the vital organs and ultimately led to Ms. Roget's death."

"Did you say dismembered fetus?"

"I did."

"Would you care to elaborate on that, Doctor?"

"The examination of the abdomen revealed approximately 75 cc of blood in the body cavity as well as the head and torso of the fetus." Murmuring rippled through the jury box.

"Are you saying, Doctor, that the defendant left the aborted baby inside Robin's body?"

"That's correct."

"Isn't that prima facie evidence of malpractice?"

"Objection!" Burton shouted. "That's for the jury to decide."

"Sustained."

"But Your Honor—"

"What part of sustained don't you understand? Now ask another question."

"Yes, Your Honor." She turned back to the witness

stand. "Is it standard procedure for a doctor to leave a rotting carcass of an aborted baby inside—"

"Objection!" Burton yelled. "Inflammatory."

"Sustained."

"I'll rephrase the question," she said. "Is it common for fetal parts to be left inside following an abortion?"

"I'm not an abortionist, but I understand that retained fetal material is not too uncommon - maybe the skull or some other bony matter. But in the case at hand, half a body was shoved through the floor of the uterus and thrust into the abdomen. That's unusual any way you slice it."

"How much force is necessary to do this kind of damage?"

"A great deal of force."

Jessica Parris walked back to the plaintiff's table and picked up a stack of photographs mounted on green backing. "Your Honor, the plaintiff would like to enter the autopsy photographs into evidence."

"Objection," Burton said, half-standing. "The photos are inflammatory. The defense will stipulate that Ms. Roget is dead."

"Bring the pictures to the bench," Chesterfield said.

Parris handed the stack to Chesterfield and stood at attention while he flipped through them.

"I'll allow the pictures."

"Thank you, Your Honor."

He handed them back to her, and she relayed them to the jury foreman. She stepped back to watch the expressions on the jurors' faces contort as the images were passed around. Satisfied they were universally disgusted, Parris continued.

"Doctor, would you please describe the condition of the fetus removed from Ms. Roget's abdomen?"

"Both his arms had been ripped off. The heart and some ribs were torn out of the chest cavity. The head was intact with the exception of a missing left ear. Judging from the skeletal development, I approximated the gestation age at 24 weeks."

"The baby was 6 months old?"

"Correct."

"So, in your expert opinion, Robin Roget died as the direct result of the defendant's botched abortion."

"Correct."

"And in all the years you've practiced pathology, have you ever seen such a heinous mutilation?"

"Objection!" Burton shouted while springing to his feet.

"Sustained."

"I have no further questions." She returned to her seat, then whispered into Walter King's ear. He jotted down a note.

"Mr. Burton," Chesterfield said. "Does the defense wish to cross-examine the witness?"

"We do, sir. Dr. Rutledge will conduct the cross for the defense."

"The witness is yours, Mr. Rutledge."

"That's Doctor Rutledge, Your Honor."

Chesterfield's eyebrows contracted into a tight squint. "Mister Rutledge, do you see any nurses or patients or X-ray machines lying around my courtroom?"

"No, Your Honor."

"Do you see any operating tables around here, Mister Rutledge?"

"No, Your Honor."

"Then as long as you're in my courtroom you will be addressed as Mister Rutledge. Is that clear?"

"Yes, Your Honor."

"Now that we've got that straight, you may proceed."

Rutledge slid his steel-rimmed glasses up the bridge of his nose with his index finger, then blinked his eyes twice in an exaggerated fashion before walking to the podium.

"Dr. McCorkle, in the course of your work as a coroner, how many times have you ruled septicemia to be the cause of death?"

"I couldn't venture a guess."

"A handful?"

"Dozens."

"So, you're no stranger to such a finding?"

"No."

"And you ran the whole battery of lab tests?"

"The standard protocol."

"And did the blood test reveal the presence of any venereal diseases?"

"Yes."

"Which one?"

"Two actually - an active case of gonorrhea as well as stage one syphilis."

"Gonorrhea and syphilis," Rutledge said, raising his eyebrows. "An impressive combination. It seems Ms. Roget wasn't the kind of girl you take home to Mother."

"Objection!" Parris shouted.

"Sustained," Chesterfield said. "Mr. Rutledge, you're on thin ice. You may proceed... cautiously."

"Doctor, would you say these venereal diseases contributed to the post-operative complications?"

"Objection!" Parris shouted. "Argumentative."

"Your Honor," Rutledge said, "the witness is a professional pathologist. He's more than qualified to offer such an opinion. Besides, he's the man who determined the cause of death."

"Objection overruled. The witness may answer the question."

"It's hard to say with any precision what part the venereal diseases may have played."

"But would you agree that anytime a person contracts gonorrhea and/or syphilis, the immune system is greatly compromised?"

"Yes, of course. But I—"

"Thank you, Doctor. So, it's possible that the gonorrhea and syphilis contributed in some way to Ms. Roget's death?"

"I didn't—"

"Yes or no, Doctor?"

"I guess it's possible."

"Is it probable?"

"That's not what I ruled."

"But probable nonetheless?"

"Possible, I guess."

Rutledge turned to Chesterfield. "I have no further questions." Rutledge sat down and cracked his knuckles.

"Ms. Parris, would the plaintiff like to redirect the witness?" Chesterfield asked.

"Just one question, Your Honor."

"Proceed."

She stood in front of her chair. "Dr. McCorkle, in your professional opinion, even if Ms. Roget didn't have any venereal diseases, would she still have died from the complications and injuries sustained in the botched abortion?"

"Yes."

"I have no further questions."

14

Sarah Riehl spent the day prying into the life of Jessica Parris from the comfort of her computer console. The fruits of her labor filled her computer screen. She read over the information one last time before printing out the dossier.

Jessica was born in Euclid, Ohio, to Joseph and Nancy Duncan. Joseph died in Vietnam when Jessica was only two. Six years later Nancy remarried, this time to a drug-abusing alcoholic named Dirk Murphy. Three months later, after neighbors complained of abuse and neglect, the Cuyahoga County Board of Children's Services stepped in and placed Jessica in temporary custody. Medical tests confirmed sexual assault and sodomy.

Jessica bounced around several foster homes before being adopted by Mr. and Mrs. Thomas Parris, who provided a stable home in the Collinwood neighborhood of Cleveland. Jessica attended Collinwood High; her grades were average.

During her sophomore year at Cleveland State, her adopted father, Thomas Parris, suddenly died of a massive heart attack. The loss catapulted Jessica into her studies. She graduated with honors with a degree in Political Science and studied law at Capital University, where she graduated near the top of her class.

Following law school Jessica took a law clerk position with Judge Chesterfield before accepting a position at the Chandler, Rodney & Robbins law firm in New York. For three years Jessica blossomed in New York. Her income shot up into the high six figures, and she rented a posh Manhattan apartment. Then all traceable records abruptly ceased for a period of 18 months: no business transactions, no credit cards, no tax returns, no financial records of any kind. She simply stepped off the planet, and then after 18 months reemerged without missing a beat. All her records continued as before with no apparent explanation for the missing 18 months.

A year after the paper trail resurfaced, Jessica returned to the Cleveland area and bought a home in Parma. She rented a small suite of offices at the Burgess Building on West Sixth Street and went into practice for herself.

Sarah Riehl double-clicked the mouse and printed the file. She leaned back in her chair and waited for the printer to spit out the report. The 18-month gap bothered her. She pondered it for a moment, then decided to pay Jessica Parris a visit.

It took only 15 minutes to negotiate the pre-rush hour traffic over to West Sixth Street. Sarah parked her car and entered the lobby. She took the elevator to the 5th floor and found Parris' meagerly furnished suite. Nothing hung on the white walls in the reception area except an autographed photo of Supreme Court Justice Ruth Bader Ginsburg. Three tacky blue chairs stood against the right-hand wall and clashed terribly with the plush red carpeting. A large fern sat on a small table next to the chairs.

Sarah walked up to the desk where a teenaged receptionist chatted away on the phone, completely oblivious to her presence.

"Excuse me - is this Jessica Parris' office?"

The young brunette looked up and nodded while continuing to gab.

"Is she in?"

An annoyed expression crossed the receptionist's face. She held up a finger, whispered something into the phone, then hung up. "Is she expecting you?"

"No, she isn't."

"Then you'll have to come back when you make an appointment."

"Here's my appointment." Sarah flashed her badge. "Tell her Special Agent Riehl is here from the FBI."

The receptionist's eyes grew wide. She scurried back to the door directly behind her desk and pushed it open.

Sarah could see Jessica Parris typing at a computer, the monitor surrounded by yellow sticky-notes. Parris nodded to the receptionist, then started straightening out the mounds of paperwork on her cluttered desk.

The receptionist returned. "Go on in."

Sarah walked in.

Parris stood and stretched out her hand. "Ms. Riehl, I've been expecting you. Allow me to clear off a place for you to sit."

"Don't bother. I'll only need a couple moments of your time." Sarah closed the door. "Is this a bad time?"

"I do have a pressing engagement in a few moments, but I'll make time for you."

"Thank you, I'll try to be brief."

"I want to apologize for being so defensive with you the other night," Parris said, while tossing a coffee-stained Styrofoam cup into the trash can next to her desk. "I hope I didn't give you the wrong impression."

"I'm sure it was an upsetting day for everyone."

"So, what can I do for you?"

"I've been doing some routine background checks - not just on you, but on all the suspects."

"Uh huh."

"And there seems to be some sort of anomaly in your record."

"Anomaly?"

"There's an unusually large gap in your documentation. Everything just stopped about three years after you moved to New York. I was hoping you could shed some light on that for me."

Parris shook her head. "A gap, you say. I don't... uh... that's odd."

"Did you leave the country or move out of state for a while? Anything like that?"

"I spent a month in Europe on sabbatical, but that wouldn't account for the whole year and a half."

"How did you know how long the gap was?"

"You said so."

"No I didn't."

"Sure you did."

"I most certainly did not."

Silence.

"Have you ever used an alias?" Sarah asked.

"No."

"Are you sure?"

Muscles tightened across Parris' forehead. "Did someone say I did?"

"No."

"If they did, they were lying."

"No one said you did; I'm just kicking around some possibilities."

"I'm sure I don't know why this... what did you call it?"

"Anomaly."

"Yes, why this anomaly in my records occurred. I'm sure there's a perfectly good explanation."

"Uh huh."

"Probably a computer glitch."

"Yeah, probably," Sarah said.

Parris smiled, brushed a wisp of blonde hair from her

eye, then looked at her watch. "Is there anything else?"

"Ms. Parris, you admitted to having a relationship with Judge Chesterfield while you were his clerk, did you not?"

"That was a long time ago."

"Did he make any unwanted sexual advances during this latest trial?"

"No."

"Did the two of you rekindle any—"

"Absolutely not."

"You understand I have to ask."

"Look here," Parris said, her voice rising an octave. "When I got out of law school, I was naïve and impressed with power. Chesterfield cared little for my feelings... or anyone else's as far as that goes. And I'm not the kind of person to make the same mistake twice."

"I understand."

"I'm kind of in a hurry here, so if there's nothing further...."

"Just one more question."

Parris checked her watch. "Ask."

"During our initial interview you weren't willing to say who you thought killed Chesterfield. Now that you've had a few days to think about it, have you changed your mind?"

"As I said, I was a nervous wreck on Monday. I just wanted to get it over with and go take a shower. But now that I've had the chance to reflect a little, I would have to say—"

The door swung open and pinned Sarah to the wall behind it.

"Are you ready for dinner, Sweetie?" the male voice said.

Sarah peered out from behind the door.

Parris looked strained; she raised a hand and shook her head. "I'm uh... I'm kind of in the middle of something."

The door closed, and the gentleman walked into the office, unaware of the woman behind the door.

"You said you'd be ready by 5 o'clock. I've got tickets to the Playhouse."

Sarah Riehl emerged from behind the door. The man stepped back with a look of disbelief. Sarah offered her hand.

"Jonathan Burton, funny seeing you here."

15

Icy air whistled through the windowsill as Edward Mead leaned forward in his favorite *La-Z-Boy* chair and adjusted the ice bags over his swollen, aching knees. He grimaced, then eased back. The furnace kicked on with a bang. The curtains in front of the bay window fluttered against the baby grand piano.

He stared open-mouthed at the television, trying to sort out the flood of information Sarah had dumped on him at their meeting. In the background Andre Bernier announced the temperature outside had dropped to a frigid 9 degrees Fahrenheit, 20 below with the windchill. A winter storm warning was in effect for the entire viewing area, with the snowbelt getting the worst of it.

Mead panned his eyes across the living room and thought about the day Victoria first started decorating the place, and the argument they'd had over the $18 per gallon, dusty-rose paint for the walls. But he had to admit, the color blended nicely with the pale gray carpeting after all.

The doorbell rang. A groan slipped through his lips as he unlimbered his legs and shuffled to the door.

"Jonathan, so good of you to come on such short notice."

"Are you kidding me? You left a dozen messages on my

voicemail."

They shook hands.

"Come in. You're letting all the warm air out."

Burton stepped in and took off his hat and coat. "It smells like Bengay in here."

"It comes with getting old."

Mead plodded back to the recliner and replaced the ice bags on his knees. Burton sat on the end of the couch nearest the chair. Mead examined Burton's face in the light from the brass lamp on the end table. Burton's lips looked thin and colorless; his skin appeared more peaked than usual. He coughed behind his hand.

"Are you still smoking?" Mead asked.

"I quit three months ago."

"Good for you."

"Doctor's orders, you know." Burton crossed his legs. "What's with the ice packs?"

"I fell."

"Let me see."

"It's nothing."

"Let me see."

Mead removed the ice and pulled up the legs of his red silk pajamas, revealing badly bruised and swollen knees.

"Professor, that looks terrible."

"It's nothing."

"You should see a doctor."

"I bruise easily these days."

"That's more than bruising. You probably tore something."

"Jonathan, I didn't ask you here to talk about my legs. What do you think you're doing, dating a murder suspect in my investigation?"

"I'm a murder suspect in your investigation."

"You know what I mean." He rolled his pajamas back down and gently replaced the ice bags. "You've got to be the only lawyer on the planet to be brilliant at work and stupid in your personal life."

"What about Bill Clinton?"

"I'm not in the mood, Jonathan."

"It's a harmless fling."

"Your last two flings became wives three and four."

"That's not fair."

"How long ago did this fling start?"

"A couple weeks ago."

"During the trial?"

"Yep."

"You didn't consider that a conflict of interest?"

"It's not that big a deal."

"If she killed Chesterfield it is. Ever heard of guilt by association?"

"In all fairness, I had no way of knowing Chesterfield was going to come up dead when we started dating."

"But Ms. Parris may have."

"Jessica isn't like that. She doesn't have it in her."

"You've known her for a few weeks, and you're ready to vouch for her character?"

"I know her better than you do."

"I'm sure you do." Mead slammed his hand on the armrest. An ice bag dropped to the floor. Both men reached for it, and they cracked heads.

"Leave it to you to complicate things." Mead snatched the bag from Burton. "If you want to be a suspect, I'll treat you like a suspect. Describe Chesterfield's office."

"Are you serious?"

"You bet I'm serious."

"You've known me for 30 years."

"Answer the question."

"I can't believe this." Burton scratched his ear, a grave look in his eyes. "He had a fancy desk. Behind it and at the far end there were some bookshelves. He had the obligatory leather chair and couch. And he had a brass coat rack. There... are you satisfied? Oh yeah, and he had a framed copy of *Cleveland Magazine* hanging on the wall with his picture on the cover.

"What about the desk?"

"If you mean, did I see the letter opener, yes I did. You couldn't miss it. He kept the thing right next to his nameplate. It looked like an antique dagger or something."

"Do you know your girlfriend used to clerk for Chesterfield?"

"She mentioned it."

"Did she mention they had an affair?"

Burton frowned.

"Does that concern you?" Mead asked.

"Should it?"

"It concerns me."

"I'm a big boy."

"Jonathan, I can't go into detail, but from what Riehl told me today, your girlfriend is carrying around some serious emotional baggage."

"Look, Professor, I'm not fooling myself here. I'm 56; she's 35. This won't last more than a few months - trust me."

"So, you intend to keep seeing her?"

"It's only physical."

"And that makes it better?"

"It does to me."

"Sometimes you make about as much sense as a kamikaze pilot wearing a bicycle helmet."

"We are just a couple of lonely people meeting each other's needs."

"I understand lonely."

Awkward silence.

"How are you holding up?" Burton asked.

"I'm surviving."

"I can't imagine what you—"

"No, you can't. Everything in this house reminds

me of her. Every piece of furniture has a thousand memories embedded in it. I haven't touched anything. I want everything to be just the way her hands left them. I haven't even washed her pillowcase." He took a deep breath. "I can still smell her hair on it."

Mead pointed toward the piano. His eyes latched onto the carpet underneath the bench. "That's where I found her, all twisted up under the piano. She must have collapsed and hit her head on the keyboard." He raised his hand to his temple. "She had a knot on the side of her head, and her dentures got knocked out. I don't know how long she had been lying there before I came home... she was cold. I called 9-1-1, but it was no use... she was gone."

Tears trickled down the grooves in Mead's weathered face. "I tried to pick her up. I wanted to get her to the couch. I couldn't lift her. I tried... I tried, but I couldn't lift her. How did I get so weak?"

Burton offered his handkerchief.

"I put her teeth back in and tried to fix her hair. You know how she had to look just so. She would have been mad if I let strangers see her that way."

"I'm sorry, Professor."

"I miss her so much it hurts to breathe. There are times when I'm driving, I get the urge to slam my car into a bridge abutment just to get it over with."

"Professor—"

"She was my best friend. She was all I had."

Silence.

"Tonight is the first night since she died that I didn't go see her."

"She wouldn't want you out in the middle of a blizzard."

"It's not for her, it's for me." He blew his nose.

"Can I get you anything?" Burton asked.

"Maybe some water."

"Coming right up."

Burton hustled into the kitchen and returned a couple minutes later with a glass of water.

"Thanks." He took a sip.

"No problem."

"I've been reading through the transcripts," Mead said, feeling the need to change the subject.

"What did you think of my opening remarks?"

"They were stronger than your girlfriend's."

"How far did you get?"

"I'm just now up to the coroner's testimony."

"And..."

"The facts are pretty grisly, and they're not on your side."

"We tried a good case."

"Rutledge handled himself pretty well, that is, if the jury followed him."

"If you're only up to the coroner, then you've not seen the best of him yet."

"He seems like a pretty smart guy - a little nervous, though."

"You mean the blinking thing?"

"It's hard to miss."

"He does that whenever he's worked up. But don't let that fool you; Rutledge is sharp as a whip."

"Do you think he did it?"

"Killed Chesterfield? No."

"Why not?"

"He doesn't have the stomach for something like that. Besides, he'd never do anything to tarnish the family name. His wife would have him killed."

"How was it you came to work with him?" Mead asked.

"The owners of the abortion clinic sent him. Insisted on him, actually. He's apparently on retainer with them."

"Hmmm... that's odd."

"That he's on retainer?"

"No, that you didn't solicit him."

"Why is that odd?"
"He said you did."

16

Before falling asleep that night, Edward Mead had comforted himself with the belief that it was physically impossible for his body to hurt any more than it already did. However, when the alarm clock blared to life, he instantly realized his mistake. The pain declared itself first as a murmur, then a whine and a moan, and finally to a scream. He worked his way to the edge of the bed and tried to stand, but his legs wouldn't straighten. He took a few uncertain steps, then stumbled toward the window and braced himself on the ledge.

He pushed back the curtain and looked out. The first rays of dawn streamed in upon Van Aken Boulevard and glittered off the fresh blanket of white. Snow blowers were out in force. Up and down the street people brushed off cars and scraped windshields. The sheer brightness of the cloudless sky and brilliant new day seemed to invite activity. It was an invitation Edward Mead respectfully declined.

He staggered back to the edge of the bed, picked up the phone and called the courthouse. He requested they send the day's transcription to his house by courier. An hour later he plunged his crippled body into the steaming whirlpool bath with the transcription in hand....

"Ms. Parris, you may call your next witness," Chesterfield said.

"Thank you, Your Honor. The plaintiff calls Indigo Robinson."

"Objection," Burton said, half-standing. "The defense deposed Ms. Robinson. She isn't a material witness, and her testimony is irrelevant."

"Your Honor, Ms. Robinson is a former patient of Dr. Baird. She has credible—"

"Silence!" Chesterfield shouted. "Ten-minute recess. Counsel in my chambers - now!"

He slammed the gavel, traipsed down the steps behind the bench, and disappeared into his chambers. He was already seated with his back to the door, his feet cocked on the credenza, when the four lawyers and stenographer assembled at attention.

"You idiots sicken me with all this frivolous bantering, like someone actually gives a rip about this case."

"With all due respect," Walter King said, "the Roget family deserves their day in court and—"

"Shut up, fat boy." Chesterfield looked over his shoulder. "I'm surprised you managed to gimp your big butt cheeks in here with the rest of these rectal irritants."

A pink blush started below King's collar and worked up his face, as if somebody were filling a wineglass.

"As far as the objection over this Robinson woman goes, I'll let her testify."

"But sir," Rutledge said, "she'll inflame the jury."

"I thought we had an understanding. You don't piss me off, and I won't throw you in jail."

"Sorry, Your Honor."

"I own you."

"Sorry, Your Honor."

"Now, as I was saying. I'll let her testify on camera after clearing the jury."

"Thank you, sir," Burton said.

"Does the plaintiff intend to call any more prior patients?"

"Just one more," Parris said. "And maybe one of Baird's former employees."

"Are they all women?"

"Yes, Your Honor."

"They'll all testify on camera. If anything these skanks have to say is useful, I'll let the jury see the video."

"Skanks," Parris said. "Is that necessary?"

"Did I just hear flatulence or was that Parris running off at the mouth?" Chesterfield burst into a stream of profanity peppered with unusual combinations of four-letter words. "Besides, Parris, I didn't call you a skank. Although, as I recall, you did spend a fair amount of time on your back around here."

Her eyes narrowed; her face contorted; she slid her hands up and down her hips.

"Now get back in there, and let's get this farce over with."

The group reassembled in the courtroom. A bailiff ushered the jury into the deliberation room, while another set up a video camera directly in front of the witness stand. Parris stepped up to the podium and again called Indigo Robinson. An attractive black woman stood in the front row behind the plaintiff's table and made her way to the stand.

Indigo Robinson was not tall, but seemed to be, so proudly erect did she hold her slender figure. Although not a large woman, she had sumptuous breasts. Her hair, braided and beaded in cornrows, dangled around her shoulders and rattled with each step. She wore a yellow pantsuit and low-cut top that showed an excessive amount of cleavage.

Chesterfield leered over the bench and got himself an eyeful.

The bailiff administered the oath, and Parris began.

"Please state your name for the record."

"Indigo Robinson."

"And are you familiar with Dr. Baird?"

"Yeah."

"Is he in the courtroom?"

"Yeah."

"Please point to him."

She stood, rolled her eyes, and pointed at Baird.

"Let the record show that the witness identified the defendant," Chesterfield said while pouring himself another drink.

"And for what reason did you go to see Dr. Baird?"

"I needed an abortion."

"Ms. Robinson, explain with as much detail as possible what happened the day you went into the defendant's clinic for the abortion."

"Girl, the place wuz off-the-hook. Dirty, nasty, and smellin' bad like I don't know what. I could tell all they wanted wuz my money."

"Objection," Burton said.

"Sustained. Ms. Robinson, stick to the facts."

"What happened after they took your money?" Parris asked.

"After I gave 'em my cheese, they made me sign a bunch of papers."

"What kind of papers?"

"Papers sayin' how safe it be and papers sayin' I can't sue."

"Waiver forms."

"Yeah."

"Go on."

"This nurse takes me in a room and tells me to get buck-naked, and she hands me this paper thang to put on. There was blood on the walls. That's when he comes in." She pointed to Baird. "Drunken piece of—"

"Objection," Burton shouted. "Witness is making

unsubstantiated attacks against my client."

"Sustained."

"Ms. Robinson, what makes you think the defendant had been drinking?"

"I smelt it."

"Please continue."

"He put me up on the table and starts pokin' and proddin' and then all a sudden - wham - it felt like he jammed his fist up in me."

"And what did you do?"

"I started screamin' like a m—"

"Excuse me, and what did the doctor do?"

"Girl, dude be trippin'." She swiveled her head side-to-side, Egyptian style. "He wuz like, 'Stop screamin' cuz you scarin' the patients.' And I'm like, 'forget that.' Then he up and bounces."

"He left you in the middle of the procedure?"

"Girl, please. He came back talkin' bout I wuz wastin' his time and carryin' on."

"But he did finish the abortion?"

"Yeah, he finish all right. He comes in and starts stabbin' me with somethin'... hurt real bad too. I think it wuz on purpose if you ask me."

"Objection!"

"Sustained," Chesterfield said. "Ms. Robinson, keep your opinions to yourself."

"Whatever."

"So what did you do when he hurt you?"

"Kicked him."

"You kicked him?"

"Got him good too."

"What did the defendant do?"

"He start cussin' and strapped my legs in those thangs."

"The stirrups."

"Yeah, them thangs. Anyways, he takes care his

business and bounced. An hour later I kep on bleedin' and bleedin'. Nurse gonna tell me it's all normal like I stupid or somethin'. By the time I get home, I got blood sloshin' all in my shoes."

"Then what did you do?"

"I started feelin' all dizzy and weak and somethin' be kickin'."

"Excuse me, what do you mean by kicking?"

"You know, stankin'."

"A bad odor."

"Girl, kickin' like Jackie Chan. So, I pulled down my panties and a lump of doo-doo falls out."

"I'm sorry to keep interrupting you, but doo-doo?"

"You know, dukie, crap—"

"Feces?"

"Yeah, I gots feces comin' out my vagina."

Murmuring swept the courtroom.

"Order!" Chesterfield banged his gavel. "I will have order!"

"Then what happened?"

"I freaked. I called 9-1-1, and they took me to the Emergency Room at Metro. The next thing I know they sayin' I got a hole in my vagina and in my rectum and they got to operate."

"Did they operate?"

"Yeah."

"And all that damage was the result of Dr. Baird's botched operation?"

"Think I ain't?"

"I've got no further questions." Parris walked back to her seat with a smug, satisfied look.

"Does the defense wish to cross-examine the witness?" Chesterfield asked, his eyes glassy.

"Yes, sir." Jonathan Burton stood, walked to the podium, and started coughing. He held up his index finger until the fit subsided. "Ms. Robinson, you have no doubt been through a terrible ordeal. And I don't think anyone in this courtroom today doesn't feel sorry for you. I know I do."

"I ain't lookin' for no pity."

"Nevertheless, you've been through a lot. So how does that make you feel toward Dr. Baird?"

"You kiddin' me? I want to scratch his eyes out. Nearly kilt me, tearin' my insides up."

"Pretty angry, huh?"

"Said I wuz, and I meant it."

"Mad enough to lie about it?"

"Objection!" Parris shouted.

"I withdraw the question. Ms. Robinson, how many previous abortions did you have prior to this incident?"

"Three."

"And who performed those abortions?"

"He did." She pointed at Baird.

"Any problem with those earlier procedures?"

"No."

"I see. And how close did Dr. Baird come to your face during the most recent procedure?"

"I don't know."

"Take a guess?"

"Three or four feet, I guess."

"Ms. Robinson, do you have an above average sense of smell?"

"No."

"But at three or four feet, in a room you described as somewhat odorous, you were somehow able to detect alcohol on Dr. Baird's breath. How do you explain that?"

"I know what I smelt." She crossed her arms, pushing her ample bosoms together.

Chesterfield's eyes nearly popped out of his head.

"Are you sure that's not the anger talking?"

"Objection!"

"Question withdrawn." Burton scratched his eyebrow.

"Assuming Dr. Baird had been drinking, why did you allow him to operate on you?"

"They said it was safer than going to the dentist."

"Would you allow a drunken dentist to pull your tooth?"

"No."

"Of course not, no sensible person would. Yet you allowed Dr. Baird to operate on you?"

"Yeah."

"See, I have a problem with that. Because if you knew he was drunk and still allowed him to operate on you, under the law you assumed the risk of injury; and I think you're too smart for that. So the only other option is that Dr. Baird wasn't drinking?"

"He wuz drunk."

"If he was and you let him operate on you, I guess that makes you just plain stupid."

"Objection!" Parris shouted. "Please sanction him, Your Honor."

"Tone it down, Mr. Burton."

"Yes, sir." He turned back toward the witness. "Let me switch gears here. Did you know Robin Roget before her death?"

"Yeah."

"How did you know her?"

"We worked together."

"And what kind of work do you do?"

"Dancer."

"Exotic dancing?"

"Yeah."

"Where do you dance?"

"Wild Pony Saloon in Brookpark."

"Isn't that an all-nude establishment?"

"Yeah."

"Ever do sexual favors for money?"

"Objection!" Parris sprang out of her chair.

"Overruled. The witness will answer the question."

"Have you ever slept with men for money?" Burton asked.

Robinson squirmed.

"Ms. Robinson, lying under oath is a crime. You could go to jail for perjury. So, I will ask you again, have you ever had sex with men in exchange for money?"

"Maybe a couple times, but I ain't no hoe."

"Did Ms. Roget have sex with men for money?"

"How should I know? I ain't no pimp."

"Were you present when Ms. Roget went in for her abortion?"

"No."

"Did you see her at any time that day?"

"No."

"So, let me get this straight. You're an all-nude dancer who's had four abortions, you've admitted to prostitution, and you weren't a witness to any of the events surrounding the death of Robin Roget. Is that correct?"

"You make it sounds like—"

"Yes or no?"

"Well, yeah."

"So, in other words, you have nothing relevant to say about this case."

"Objection!"

"I withdraw the question. I have nothing further for this witness."

Burton returned to his seat and whispered something in Dr. Baird's ear. Baird nodded.

"Does the plaintiff wish to re-direct the witness?" Chesterfield asked.

"You bet I do, Your Honor." Parris bolted to the podium. "Ms. Robinson, before you went into Dr. Baird's clinic, did you have a three-inch laceration in your vagina?"

"No."

"How about a rupture in your uterus? Did you have that before Dr. Baird operated on you?"

"No."

"Did you happen to notice any fecal matter falling out of your vagina or notice your rectum ripped open before the good doctor got ahold of you?"

"No."

"But you did after you left his clinic?"

"I said I did, and I meant it."

"I have no further questions."

17

Shaker Heights, Ohio
4:30 P.M.

Sarah Riehl steered her hunter-green Saturn onto the unplowed drive; the snow crunched under her tires. She stepped on the brake, and the car slid to a stop just inches from the garage door. She checked the address on the paper she held in her gloved hand, and then glanced at the house number.

"This must be the place."

She wrapped a black cashmere scarf around her neck, grabbed her briefcase, then pushed open the car door. The frosty air watered her eyes. She gingerly stepped along the snow-covered walk toward the front door. The house was dark except for a light in an upstairs window. Icicles hung down from the edge of the gutter and reflected the pink glow from the setting sun.

She stumbled over the welcome mat buried in the snow and dropped her briefcase. She brushed it off, knocked on the door, then jammed her hands deep into her pockets and rocked from foot to foot trying to stay warm. Several minutes passed before Mead opened the door. His face looked puffy and pale; his cardigan sweater was misbuttoned. She wondered if he'd been drinking.

"I'm sorry to keep you waiting," he said. "I'm not moving too briskly these days."

"No, no. I'm sorry to barge in on you like this,

Professor, but I came across something that needs your immediate attention."

"It's no bother at all; please come in."

"Are you feeling okay?" She pulled the door closed behind her. "Your secretary said you called in sick."

"I'm fine, feeling a lot better, actually."

He took her wool trench coat and hung it on the brass rack in the corner of the foyer, then escorted her to the sofa. He eased down in the recliner. "So, what can I do for you?"

"I spent the day digging into the wonderful world of Walter King. And some of this stuff gave me the willies." She reached into her bag and pulled out a manila folder. "Walter King is an abortion survivor."

"Say what?"

"He wasn't supposed to be born. His mother tried to abort him."

"That can't be good for the self-esteem."

"The doctor screwed up, and King came out nearly intact."

"Nearly?"

"His left leg got ripped off from below the knee during the abortion."

"I bet that hurt."

"He wears a prosthetic."

"That explains the peculiar walk."

"He spent his adolescent years bouncing from institution to institution. When he turned 12, he was sent to the Cuyahoga Hills Juvenile Detention Center. And get this. He stabbed a boy with a pencil - in the neck."

"No kidding." He stroked the white stubble on his chin. "What brought that on?"

"The file didn't say."

"Something provoked him."

"His conduct evaluations were riddled with the same word - incorrigible. It appears that young Mr. King didn't play well with the other children."

"How did he get from reform school to law school?"

"After he turned 18, a retired pastor took him in and apparently turned him around. King went to Lorain County Community College and then on to law school at Cleveland State."

"I know a couple professors there."

"King had the lowest LSAT scores of any student ever accepted at Cleveland State. He finished dead last in his class, then failed the Bar exam three times before squeaking by on the skin of his teeth."

"At least he passed."

Sarah flipped through the file. "He works at the Public Defender's Office doing mostly research work. The only other thing I could find is that he belongs to several pro-life groups, which is not surprising considering his brush with death."

"It sounds like Mr. King has experienced a lot of frustration and rejection in his short life," Mead said. "That makes for a volatile combination. And from what I've read so far in the transcripts, Chesterfield provoked him every chance he got."

"I sent his laptop to our computer lab at the Federal Building. He played a game called Death Grip the day Chesterfield was killed."

"I believe he mentioned that during the initial interview."

"But he didn't mention the game is a simulator used by the Special Forces to desensitize the soldiers to killing. The graphics are exceptionally realistic. And according to the boys in the lab, King's weapon of choice was the stiletto." Mead raised his eyebrows.

"They even managed to review the last program King ran. It seems he simulated the assassination of a South American leader. In the game he sneaked up on the president of Bolivia - who was working at his desk, by the way - and slit his throat."

"Disturbing coincidence."

"That's exactly why I'm here. I think King should be upgraded to the prime suspect, and I'd like to have his phones tapped."

"I'll get the court order first thing in the morning."

"Thanks."

"What I'd like you to do, Sarah, is track down this kid King stabbed and find out everything about the incident: was it premeditated, spontaneous, *yada yada yada*. You know the drill."

"Will do."

"But don't drop the ball on Parris."

"Oh, believe me, I won't. She's gotten deep under my skin."

"Speaking of the lovely Ms. Parris, I had Jonathan Burton over last night."

"What'd he have to say?"

"Well, he was very forthcoming, as I expected." Mead crossed his legs, winced, then uncrossed them. "He said he's been dating her since weeks before the murder, and he's emphatic she didn't do it."

"Do you believe him?"

"I believe he believes her. But Jonathan has a history of monumentally bad decisions regarding women."

"I know a lot of guys like that."

"He says it's just a fling."

"A fling, huh? You should've seen the way he looked at her when he didn't know I was behind the door. You can tell a lot by the way a man looks at a woman."

Mead's eyes crinkled with a secret amusement.

"What is it?" she asked.

"I remember shortly after Victoria and I were married; I remember it like yesterday. I came home from work, and I just looked at her. I didn't say a word; I just looked at her and smiled. Finally, she asked me, 'Why do you look at me like that?' 'Like what?' I said. 'Can't a man look at his wife?' She said, 'Of course, but not the way you do, as though you were thinking of something funny.' And I said, 'I can't help it. Every time I look at you it makes me feel so good inside, I just want to laugh.'"

He glanced over at the piano and whispered, "She was so beautiful."

18

Parma, Ohio
7:06 P.M.

Jessica Parris crept in behind the living room curtains and peered out the picture window at the driveway. Nobody there... still. Everything in the four-gabled, brick Tudor smelled lemony fresh; the only thing missing was the guest of honor.

She couldn't help but think about several other nights just like this one, nights when the candles burned down to nubs and one plate of food went uneaten. The corridors of her mind were littered with the debris and carnage of relationships gone bad. Sure, everything would go all right at first during the getting-to-know-you phase, but as soon as things started to get serious, her men got going. Why did she always attract the type of guy who wanted to hit and run? But this time it was different. Much different. This time...

A jet-black Mercedes 250 SL pulled into the drive. Jonathan Burton climbed out, and the wind whipped through his thinning crop of iron-gray hair. His gray wool overcoat tangled around his legs. He straightened the coat and tucked his maroon scarf around his neck. He walked carefully over the icy sidewalk.

Jessica ran to the door and opened it before the bell rang. She flung herself into his arms. "Jonathan, I was beginning to worry you changed your mind."

"I got hung up at the office." His voice sounded hoarse.

"You're not getting tired of me already, are you?"

"Don't be silly."

He stepped inside. She took his coat and scarf and hung them in the closet, then led him by the hand through the living room and into the dining room. A tongue of fire flickered from the tapered candle in the center of the table. Shadows danced on the wall. Beads of condensation ran down the side of the stainless steel ice bucket and soaked into the red tablecloth. A brass corkscrew jutted out the top of a bottle of white Chardonnay.

"It smells wonderful in here," he said. "What is that?"

"Roast duck, marinated in raspberry sauce."

"Impressive. What's the occasion?"

"Jonathan!" She pouted her lower lip. "Today's our anniversary."

"It hasn't been a year."

"One month."

"Oh... I... uh..."

"It's no biggie. Why don't you pour the wine, and I'll go get dinner."

"Sure."

He watched her disappear down the hall. Her curly blonde hair bounced over her shoulders. The cable-knit turtleneck and black stretch-pants accentuated her petite, yet curvaceous figure. He popped the cork from the wine bottle and passed it under his nose.

A few minutes later Jessica returned carrying a silver platter; she set it gently on the table. Steam wafted off the duck, filling the air with its sweet aroma. She stepped back to admire her handiwork; Jonathan looked up to admire her.

"You look incredible tonight," he said.

"You don't think this outfit makes me look fat?"

"Of course not."

"If it does, I'll change."

"You look great."

"You really think so?"

He coughed a deep, congestive cough.

"Are you okay?" she asked.

"It's just a cold or something. Really nothing to worry about."

Jessica grabbed the carving fork and thrust it into the duck. A stream of juice squirted out and hit Jonathan in the face.

He flinched.

She giggled.

"Good shot." He wiped his cheek with a napkin.

"Sorry."

"Don't worry about it."

She clenched the carving knife in her left hand and held it up to the candle. A glint of light sparkled off the blade. She smiled at him then plunged the knife into the duck. She hacked off a chunk of white meat and placed it on his plate.

"I was over at Professor Mead's house last night," Jonathan said.

"He invited you?"

"More like a summons. I knew it was coming after we got busted at your office."

"What did he say?"

Jonathan took a bite of duck; his face relaxed. "This is delicious."

"What'd he say? What'd he say?"

"Just that it was stupid for me to be seeing you during the investigation."

"What'd you say?"

"That it was none of his business."

"And..."

"And if he didn't like it, we would waste him just like we did Chesterfield."

108

"Jonathan, you didn't!"

"No—"

"Don't even joke like that."

He smirked. "Calm down."

"That's easy for you to say. They're digging into me like I was Lee Harvey Oswald or something."

"Don't you think you're overreacting?"

"That Riehl woman hates me."

"Ah, come on."

"She does, and she'd set me up if she could."

"Now you sound paranoid."

"This whole thing creeps me out." She rubbed one elbow, then folded and unfolded her thin arms in constant motion. "And I don't mind saying that your senile buddy makes me nervous."

"You've nothing to worry about. That is, unless you did it."

"Jonathan!"

He chuckled.

"That's not funny."

"Sure it is, and by the way, Professor Mead certainly isn't senile."

"Then he must be crazy. He actually told me turkey gave him gas. What's up with that?"

"When ordinary mortals don't comprehend a genius, they get even by calling him crazy."

"What's that supposed to mean?"

"Have you ever taken a course in forensic profiling?"

"Yeah, sure."

"Mead wrote the book on it."

"So, he knows about it."

"No. He literally wrote the first textbook on it. He practically invented the field."

"Probably a hundred years ago."

"I'll let you in on something else. He's got the most prodigious memory I've ever seen. He has total conversational recall. I'll bet he didn't even take notes when he interviewed you."

"So?"

"He's got the whole dialogue memorized."

She shook her head. "It looked to me like he wasn't paying attention."

"He has been a little out of sorts since his wife died, but I promise you, the dog can still hunt."

"He still makes me nervous."

"It wouldn't surprise me if he already knows who did it."

"Did he tell you that last night?" She gave him a sharp glance over her wine glass.

"No, no, he wouldn't tell me if he did. He asked about us, and then rambled on about his wife. The death of a spouse tends to make one ponder mortality."

"Not always." She tipped back her glass, then took her first bite of food.

"A lot of things do," he said.

"What?"

"Make us think about mortality."

The conversation trailed off. Large flakes of snow ricocheted off the window. The flickering candle reflected off the glass china cabinet behind Jessica's left shoulder. The ticking of the grandfather clock seemed to grow louder.

Burton turned his attention to the duck. He cut off a chunk and sopped it in the purple marinade pooling along the rim of his plate. The food was delicious; the atmosphere felt like obligation. *But what the heck? It isn't a real relationship - only simple carnal gratification and nothing more. And that body of hers is addicting.* He smirked at his thought, then caught himself staring at her breasts. He looked up, and their eyes met. She smiled.

Jonathan looks weary, she thought. *He is a bit older and works such long hours, but that will change if all goes as planned. He's no Tom Cruise, but he's established and gentle, and he's not running anywhere. He seems so different from all the rest. And I know he won't hurt me. What could it hurt to ask?*

"How do you think things are going?"

"It's the best duck I've ever had."

"I meant with us."

"Oh." He took a gulp of wine. "Things are going... uh... swell."

"But what about me?"

"You look beautiful."

"But do you love me?"

He felt an invisible noose tighten around his neck, and a little voice in the back of his mind told him to run.

19

Friday, January 29
Shaker Heights, Ohio
8:10 A.M.

E dward Mead rolled out of bed feeling invigorated for the first time since Victoria died. He flipped on the weather band radio on the nightstand. A blustery, Arctic cold front had swept down from Canada and engulfed the greater Cleveland area in a painful stranglehold of sub-zero temperatures. The windchill factor flirted with 15 below.

He slid his feet into his leather slippers and walked over to the closet. He pulled out a blue pinstriped suit, grabbed a starched, white shirt, and wrapped a yellow paisley tie around the hanger. He shuffled back to the bed and sat on the corner. He pulled his pajama bottoms down around his ankles and examined his knees. The swelling had subsided, and the bruises looked more green than black. Healing came slowly these days. He wiggled into his suit pants and felt a bulge in the front pocket. He reached in and pulled out a folded-up playbill for *Les Misérables*. It must have been there for months, but he remembered the night well. Such a marvelous performance, and Victoria had the time of her life. She seemed to be in remission.

He finished dressing, then drove down to the Federal Courthouse and secured a wiretap order for Walter King's phones. Next, he drove over to Cleveland-Marshall College of Law. He had been a guest lecturer there countless times over the years and developed a few friendships on the faculty. He parked his car on Euclid Avenue in front of the Rascal House Pizza Parlor. He walked across the campus and found the office of his old friend John Ligon. Ligon taught courtroom tactics and oratory, a required class for all students. Walter King would have had to pass under Ligon's watchful eye at one time or another.

Mead knocked on the door.

"Come in."

He pushed open the door and walked into a veritable pigsty. Law books were piled and strewn and tossed everywhere. Stacks of files covered the desk and spilt over onto the dusty, tile floor. Crumpled paper wads filled the wastebasket to overflowing. John Ligon sat proudly behind his fire hazard. He sported a huge body, a bushy goatee, and a natural frown.

"Good to see you, Professor Mead. How long has it been?"

"Too long, my friend."

"How are you?"

Mead pondered the question. "I'm older than I used to be, but God willing, I'm not as young as I'm going to be."

"I see you haven't changed a bit."

"I'm afraid this isn't a social call, John." Mead cleared off a chair and sat down. "A former student of yours is a suspect in the Chesterfield murder."

Ligon's eyes widened. "They've kept that case awfully quiet."

"Gag order."

"How'd you get roped into that mess?"

"It's a long story."

"So, which of my former students is the lucky man?"

"Walter King. Do you remember him?"

"King... King, that's a fairly common name. How long

ago did he graduate?"

"Three years."

"Fat kid, walk with a limp?" Ligon said.

"That's him."

"I do remember him. He moved with the grace of a startled bird. What do you want to know?"

"Anything really. Background, personality quirks, that sort of thing."

"He was the absolute worst student I ever had. He stammered and spit and struggled and sweated. If he ever had to speak at a real trial, I'm sure he'd flood the place."

"That's him."

"But I'll say this much for him: no matter what proposition I assigned him, old King would hang on till he got it."

"Tenacious?"

"Let me put it this way. If King was a dog, and he bit you, not only would you have to kill him, but you'd have to break his dead jaw to get him off of you."

"That's surprising."

Ligon sneezed and wiped his nose on the back of his sleeve. "He wasn't the sharpest tool in the shed, if you know what I mean. But don't get me wrong; he's no babbling idiot. He struck me as a man whose mind was unbroken."

"What about friends?"

"None that I could speak of. No one really talked to him. He came across as always preoccupied, like he would stop breathing if he didn't concentrate on it." Ligon dug into his left nostril with the tip of his thumb.

"Did you know Chesterfield?" Mead asked.

"Not really. Though I heard he was a real ball-buster. I guess King figured he needed a good killing."

"So, you think King is capable of murder?"

"Under the right circumstances about anyone is capable of murder. I just don't think King would need as much prompting as others."

"Unstable?"

"He struck me as the kind of guy who would wake up one day, strap on an AK-47, and kill everyone in a 7-Eleven because his Slurpy didn't have enough cherry flavoring."

"Seriously."

"I'm serious as a heart attack. You kick a dog long enough, and one day he's going to bite back. I don't know what King went through growing up, but his ego seems to have taken a few too many mule kicks along the way."

"I appreciate your time, John." Mead checked his watch. "I've got to get going."

"I'm a little disappointed, Edward."

"Why?"

"We've been friends for how long?"

"Twenty years."

"Every time you come here you give me one of those corny riddles. And today, no riddle. What gives?"

"I've not been myself lately." Mead closed his eyes and rubbed his forehead. "Two fathers and two sons go fishing, and everyone caught a fish. At the end of the day they went home with three fish. How is that possible?"

Ligon scratched his head. "One of them caught a fish and let it go, and the next man caught the same fish."

"Nope, each caught his own."

"Did one of them let his fish go?"

"They all kept what they caught."

"Then I don't know."

"The answer is simple - three men went fishing."

"But you said two fathers and two sons went. Two and two equals four in my book."

"Two fathers and two sons did go: a grandfather, a son and a grandson. Get it? One of them was both a father and a son."

"That's a trick question."

"You asked for it."

"Get out of here."

"Sometimes the obvious lives right below the surface."

20

Cleveland, Ohio
10:30 A.M.

E dward Mead pulled his car into the McDonald's drive-thru on Euclid Avenue and ordered an Egg McMuffin and a cup of black coffee. He nibbled on breakfast while driving over to the Justice Center to pick up the last bit of transcription for the week. Twenty minutes later he settled into his hideaway on the top floor of Sears Library and began to read....

"Ms. Parris, you may call your next witness," Judge Chesterfield said.

"Your Honor, the plaintiff calls Belinda Nathanson."

An attractive woman stood up three rows behind the plaintiff's table. Long, black hair cascaded midway down her back. Her round face appeared a bit too large for her petite body. She wore a tan turtleneck beneath a black blazer and matching skirt. A string of pearls swiveled around her neck and rattled with each step as she walked between the video camera and empty jury box. She took a seat on the witness stand and adjusted the microphone to her mouth.

A uniformed bailiff administered the oath, then returned to his position next to the chamber door.

"Please state your name and occupation for the record," Parris asked.

"My name is Belinda Nathanson, and I'm a physical therapist." Her voice sounded soft and throaty.

"And are you familiar with the defendant, Dr. Baird?"

"I am."

"Is he in the courtroom today?"

"He is."

"Would you point to him please?"

The witness squinted her eyes and pointed to Baird. The doctor dropped his gaze to the floor.

"Let the record reflect the witness has made a positive identification of the defendant," Chesterfield said.

"Ms. Nathanson, how did you become acquainted with Dr. Baird?"

"I went to his clinic for an abortion."

"And how long ago was that?"

"Three years ago."

"Please tell us about your experience with Dr. Baird." Parris placed her elbow on the podium and leaned her chin on the palm of her hand.

"Well, as I said, I went to Dr. Baird's clinic for an abortion. I signed the waivers and paid the fee. The receptionist prepped me for surgery - the receptionist, mind you. Then Dr. Baird came in and put me to sleep. The next thing I know I'm waking up in recovery, and the nurse tells me I'm free to go."

"And did everything go well?"

"I thought so, but when my period didn't come a month later, I got worried, so I called the clinic."

"What'd they say?"

"They said it was like nothing to worry about, you know, this sort of thing happens all the time. So, I didn't give it another thought till about a week later when I felt the baby kick."

"You felt the baby kick?"

"Yeah."

"What did you do then?"

"I went down to the clinic. They gave me the runaround and said I couldn't see the doctor. But I was like, 'I'm not leaving' until I see him, and I'm not afraid to make a scene. So finally, I got to see him."

"What'd he say?"

"At first he's like, 'You must've got pregnant again.' Which was impossible since I hadn't had sex in three months. Then he's like, 'Maybe it was a twin,' and we missed one."

"Did you believe him?"

"He wasn't very convincing."

"What was your mindset at the time?"

"Stressed out. I mean, I thought it was all over with. I felt terribly guilty about the first abortion, and now I've got to have another one? I didn't want to be pregnant. I mean, I did in a way, but my boyfriend was like, 'No way.' And I didn't want to lose him... I was trying to finish college. I just wanted it to be over."

"What happened next?"

"Dr. Baird said he had to charge me for the second abortion. Can you imagine that? He's going to charge again, and to top it off he says it's going to cost me extra due to the baby being bigger now. Then he showed me a diagram, and how he'd have to cut the baby up in sections and all." She gestured her hands in a slicing movement.

"Did you pay the additional fee?"

"What else could I do? I was like, let's get it over with. I paid the fee and went in for the abortion. But this time when I woke up in recovery, I knew something was wrong."

"How did you know?"

"I felt all weak and clammy. I was bleeding pretty bad down there. The nurse told me to squeeze my thighs together and to clench my... my... you know. When I did a gush of blood came out. Beth starts flipping out."

"Excuse me," Parris said. "Sorry to interrupt, but who's

this Beth?"

"Beth Bolavara. She's my best friend; she drove me to the clinic, and thank God she was there, or they would've let me bleed to death."

"Objection," Burton said. "Conjecture."

"Sustained." Chesterfield shifted in his leather chair. "The last statement will be stricken from the videotape. Bailiff, make a note of the tape counter. Ms. Parris, ask another question."

"Ms. Nathanson, what happened after the first gush of blood came out?"

"Beth and the nurses tried to move me, but another gush came out and I fainted. Beth insisted they take me to a hospital. She said—"

"Objection," Burton said. "Hearsay. If the witness fainted, she couldn't possibly know what was said."

"Sustained."

"What happened next?" Parris asked.

"Well, Dr. Baird refused to send me to a hospital. Instead, he performed a D & C to stop the bleeding, but it didn't work. When I came to the second time, I heard Beth shouting for someone to call an ambulance. They refused; said they wouldn't as long as there were protesters out front; said the sight of an ambulance would whip them into a frenzy."

"Let me get this straight." Parris looked over her shoulder at the slouching doctor. "You asked for emergency treatment, and the good doctor refused?"

"That's correct. Beth ended up taking me to the hospital in her car."

"Were you conscious?"

"I drifted in and out, but I was mostly awake."

"Were you in a lot of pain?"

"I can't even begin to tell you."

"What happened next?"

"Beth tried to keep me calm, but we both got scared

when I started passing clots." Tears welled up in her eyes.

"Go on."

"At first the clots were small, but by the time we got to the hospital they were the size of golf balls. Beth ran inside, and all I could think about was the mess I was making in her car. A few minutes later she runs out with a nurse and a wheelchair. They opened the car door and helped me up, but when I took the first step another gush of blood came out and..." Tears trickled down her face.

"Take your time."

"And... and... half my baby fell out."

Murmuring ripped through the gallery.

"Objection," Burton said, rising to his feet.

"Shut up and sit down," Chesterfield said. "I want to hear the rest of this."

"Thank you, Your Honor." Parris turned back to the witness.

"What did you do?"

"I freaked. I could see his little eyes... little arms... all mangled... looked like he was eaten by a dog." She took a deep breath and wiped her eyes on her sleeve.

"Do you want to take a break?"

"I'm all right."

"Are you sure?"

"Yeah."

"All right, what happened next?"

"They rushed me inside. The Emergency Room doctor took my temperature. It was 105. They rushed me straight to the operating room. The surgeon later told me he repaired multiple lacerations in my uterus and vagina. He said I also had a large rupture in my small intestine, and he had to remove a section of my bowel."

"I know this may sound like a foolish question, but did you have these injuries before you went in to see Dr. Baird?"

"Of course not."

"Did you notify Dr. Baird of the damages he caused you?"

"I tried to, but the receptionist never let me talk to him. When I told her the part about my baby falling out in the parking lot, she said, 'You wanted a dead baby, and you got a dead baby; what's the big deal?'"

"Have you experienced any emotional difficulties?"

"I've been in therapy ever since. They diagnosed me with Post Traumatic Stress Disorder." Pain draped her face. She wrung her hands. "I have nightmares. I'm withdrawn. Kind of funny, I guess. I had the abortion because I wanted to keep my boyfriend, and now I may never be in another relationship again. I'm damaged goods."

"What do you mean by that?"

"I can't have kids."

"One last question. Why didn't you sue Dr. Baird?"

"I didn't think I could."

"Why?"

"I signed a waiver that said if anything went wrong, I wouldn't sue the doctor or the clinic."

"You didn't know the waiver was illegal?"

"By the time I discussed my case with a lawyer, the statute of limitations had run out."

"Your Honor," Parris said as she walked back to the plaintiff's table, "I'd like to enter Ms. Nathanson's waiver into the record as Exhibit A. I'd further like to enter an identical waiver signed by Robin Roget as Exhibit B."

"So noted," Chesterfield said.

Parris handed the waivers to the bailiff, who then placed them on the evidence table.

"I have no further questions, Your Honor." Parris walked back to her seat.

"Does the defense wish to cross-examine the witness?" Burton and Rutledge exchanged hushed whispers.

"I said, does the defense wish to cross-examine the witness? Don't make me repeat myself again."

"Mr. Rutledge will conduct the cross," Burton said.

"Get on with it."

Rutledge made his way to the podium, his heavy soles thumping against the hardwood floor. He adjusted his glasses, then studied the witness for a few moments.

"Get on with it," Chesterfield said.

"May I approach the bench for a side bar?"

"Approach."

Burton stood up.

Rutledge looked over at him, shook his head, then said, "Alone please."

Burton sat down.

Rutledge walked up to the side of the bench.

Chesterfield turned off his microphone and leaned over. The two men whispered for a few moments, then Rutledge returned to the podium. He cracked his knuckles and said, "The defense has no questions for this witness."

21

S arah Riehl drove west on I-90 into the blinding glare of the setting sun. She flipped down the visor; it offered no relief. She groped around the front seat for her sunglasses, then realized they were already perched on her nose.

Some days you just can't win.

She peered out over Lake Erie; a dense cloudbank crept in from the north. Arctic air and warm lake water meant only one thing - snow - and lots of it.

She thought back over the day. It had been pretty busy for a Friday. She turned in her first report in the Chesterfield case, then drove over to the Cuyahoga Hills Detention Center in search of the young man King had stabbed years before. Three hours in the musty records office yielded the name Paul Booth. The files showed Booth was released from the Detention Center on his 18th birthday, three years after the stabbing.

With name and Social Security number in hand, a simple check of the FBI's database at Quantico revealed that Paul Booth had served two years in the Army and received an OTH discharge - other than honorable discharge. A year later he was arrested on the West Side of Cleveland for a string of burglaries. He plea-bargained for a 5-year sentence. She next searched the Ohio

Department of Rehabilitation and Correction computer database and discovered Booth had only eight months remaining on his sentence and was presently housed in the minimum-security facility in Grafton, Ohio.

Sarah turned off I-90 and went south on Route 83. With the sun out of her eyes, she loosened her grip on the wheel and flipped up the visor. Over the years she had visited many state and federal correctional facilities, but this was her first trip to a minimum-security work farm.

A single fence surrounded the ancient brick building; it looked more like an old schoolhouse than a prison. She parked her car as close as possible to the front gate and checked her face in the mirror. The elements had taken a toll on her shoulder-length, sandy hair. She ran a brush through it, but only managed to generate static electricity. She applied a coat of balm to her chapped lips, grabbed her soft leather case, and braced herself for the cold.

She pushed open the door and stepped out. The wind whipped across the open farmland and pinned her against the car. She fought the polar blast and ran to the gate. She pressed the intercom button, but nothing happened. She shook the fence; nothing happened. She tried the intercom again, and the gate buzzed open.

She scampered up the steps, the salt crunching underfoot, and walked through the metal detector and into the entrance area. An old, white-haired guard dressed in a crumpled gray uniform sat reading a book at the main desk. He didn't look up until Sarah knocked on the counter a few inches from his head.

"Excuse me, I'm here to see inmate Booth."

"Visiting hours ended at three."

"I'm not a visitor."

"Then you'll have to leave."

"I'm with the FBI."

"Did you call me a liar?"

"No, I said I'm with the FBI."

"Call the FBI for all I care, but visiting hours are over, and you'll have to leave."

"Are you deaf or just stupid?" She pulled out her badge. "I'm here to interview inmate Booth. There should be a gate pass for me."

"You don't have to get all testy about it."

He led her to a small room filled with broken chairs. The smell immediately seized her - a strong, heavy, warm odor, a combination of wet wool and vinegar. A flimsy table barely fit in the cluttered cubicle.

She sat on one of the cloth-covered chairs and felt a damp sensation on the back of her legs. A few moments later a thin man dressed in tan pants and shirt walked in. His fierce, bulldog face was covered in badly pocked skin and framed in a tangle of black hair. What appeared to be the tooth of a comb jutted through his left earlobe.

"Mr. Booth, I presume."

"Who wants to know?"

"I'm Special Agent Riehl, FBI." She stood and stretched out her hand.

He offered a firm shake, then sat down. "Am I in trouble here or what?"

"I just need some information on an assault—"

"Whoa there, lady, I'm no snitch."

"No, no, you don't understand, an assault on you."

"Say what?" His forehead wrinkled. "Ain't no one assaulted me. I take care of my business. Believe that."

"The incident I'm referring to took place about ten years ago at Cuyahoga Hills, a stabbing. Do you know what I'm talking about?"

"Yeah. Getting shanked ain't something you forget with the quickness."

"Do you remember the man's name who stabbed you?"

"Yeah, some fat psycho named King."

"What do you remember about Mr. King?" she asked.

"I remember he stuck me."

"Anything else?"

"Not really."

"Why'd he stab you?"

"How should I know? He got me when I was sleeping."

"Sleeping, you say." She scribbled a note.

"Hey, ain't there a statute of limitations on old cases like this?"

"It's seven years."

"Then why you asking me about some drama that jumped off ten years ago?"

"King's a suspect in another case."

"So, this ain't about me?"

"Not exactly."

"Then what's in it for me?"

"Absolutely nothing."

"Why should I help you?"

"Because it's the right thing to do."

"I don't roll like that."

"And you might be helping us put King in the electric chair. A little delayed justice if you will." She glanced down at his hands. The letters L-O-V-E were tattooed across the knuckles of his right hand and H-A-T-E tattooed on his left.

"Some get-back, huh. I'm down with that. Will I get to watch him fry?"

"No."

"Can't have everything. What do you want to know?"

"What made him do it?"

"I don't know. Dude was tore up from the floor up."

"Excuse me?"

"Everybody cracked on him, you know, being fat and missing a foot and all. He caught the blues over the boot thing he wore too. I guess he got tired of it and bugged out."

"Why you?"

"I don't know. Maybe he saw me as the ringleader."

"Were you?"

"Probably."

"Can you think of any other reason why he attacked you?"

"He may have been trying to get a rep off me."

"I don't follow."

"In the joint, if you whoop up on one of the tougher guys, it makes the chicken-hawks think twice about messing with you."

"But you can't think of anything specific that may have provoked him. A fight or something like that?"

"Nope."

"And you say he stabbed you in your sleep?"

"Yeah. The coward got me up around the neck. Liked to take my head off." He pulled back his shirt collar and showed her a jagged, raised scar about 5 inches long.

"Did he have any friends I could talk to who might know what he was thinking?"

"You kidding? He was the lamest dude I ever seen. Straight loner and a flip artist."

"What do you mean by 'flip artist'?"

"Unpredictable. You know, one minute quiet and the next he's wigging out. Dude's lucky no one capped him already."

A beeping went off in Sarah's briefcase. She dug through the bag and grabbed her cell phone. She retrieved the text message from the FBI headquarters.

The tiny digital screen read: There will be an attempt on Professor Mead's life tonight. Return to Cleveland at once.

22

E dward Mead's stomach knotted a little as he dressed for his first visit with Victoria since injuring his knees; in a way it felt like a first date. He prided himself over the years in looking his best for his wife, and just because her body lost its vigor didn't mean she deserved any less now.

He climbed into his car and turned the ignition; his breath fogged the windows. He backed out of the drive, went down Van Aken Boulevard, made a right on Northfield Road, then another right on Warrensville Center Road. Large snowflakes swirled and drifted and splattered against the windshield. The weatherman called for snow squalls later in the evening, but it looked like the storm didn't intend to wait. The closer he got to the lake, the more constant the snowfall. No matter. He hadn't seen his wife in three days, and it would take a bullet to stop him from seeing her tonight.

By the time he reached Euclid Avenue and the huge wrought-iron gates of Lake View Cemetery, the flurries had turned into a wall of white. The wipers labored to slash aside the accumulating flakes. He stepped on the brake, the tires locked, and the car slid to where the gate should have been.

"That's odd."

The gate was open and the guardhouse empty. He lightly pressed his foot on the accelerator and prodded the car along the winding road. The wind buffeted and whipped against the car, forcing it to drift to the left. The muscles in his neck and shoulders tightened. He struggled to keep the car from slipping off the pavement. Thankfully, fresh tire tracks marked the route toward Victoria's mausoleum.

The darkness and snowfall reduced the visibility to just a few feet. The beam from the headlights simply bounced off the falling snow. He struggled and strained to locate a landmark. He tugged the wheel a little too sharply to the right, and the car lurched into a slow spin. He frantically turned the steering wheel into the rotation, and the car straightened. In spite of the cold, beads of sweat appeared on his forehead. He mopped his brow with a handkerchief then continued to his destination.

Mead shoved open the door and started to step out. Then he stopped, reached over to the passenger seat, and grabbed a metal-tipped walking stick. There would be no repeat performance of the other night. He cautiously stepped out onto the unbroken white blanket, leaning into a strong headwind. The freezing wind clawed at his arthritic knees, sending a shiver through his body. He took his time crossing the 20 yards, probing each step with the cane.

The marble mausoleum provided some relief from the driving wind. Mead brushed a few strands of white hair off his forehead. Something caught his attention out of the corner of his eye. A silhouette of a man standing off in the distance. Mead squinted in that direction. Nothing. It vanished. Probably just his 77-year-old eyes playing tricks on him. He turned his attention to the door, fumbled with the keys, then stepped in.

"Hello, precious. Sorry I haven't made it in a few days. I had a bit of an accident. No big deal, I made it tonight." He patted the marker. "Lord knows I've missed you. I didn't think it was possible to hurt this much. I guess I always thought I'd go first, so I loved you as though you'd never die. And now I don't know how to live without you; you were my second self. I always believed our two souls had been one, living in two bodies. Now, life scares me... how do I live with only half a soul?"

Tears welled up in his tired eyes.

"Things around the house have been a little confusing lately. You know how I am with tunnel thinking. And between missing you and focusing on this case, it's a miracle I haven't burned the house down... at least not yet." He chuckled. "The other day I wet my hair in the morning and forgot to comb it. I didn't realize it until about noon when a couple of students stopped by my office. You should've seen it; my white hair standing up on end. The kids probably thought I'd lost my mind."

He turned up the narrow collar on his wool overcoat. "If I knew you were going to leave me in the middle of winter, I would've had a heater and some lights installed in this thing."

He blew his nose in his handkerchief. "I know we had our disagreements over the years, but they were never spiteful. Just honest differences, sort of like when a man differs with himself. And the rare times when things got heated, the making-up always kindled a flame that melted our hearts and welded them into one."

The silence swallowed his words.

"Pastor Koly came to see me again last Sunday. We talked about death. What a surprise, huh? He says death is nothing more than the temporary separation of the body and soul. I don't know. I've decided it's impossible to say exactly what death is. It seems to me when the heart stops beating death steps in. But that doesn't mean we cease to exist. I know as sure as I'm standing here that you're still alive in Heaven. I know it."

He rocked from foot to foot. His expensive walking shoes didn't do much to repel the cold.

"I haven't been to church since the funeral. I just don't feel too spiritual right now. You're in Heaven, and I'm happy for you; I really am. But what about me? I gave you my heart 50 years ago, and you took it with you when you went. You have two, and I have none. All I have left is this broken-down body, and it betrays me every chance it gets. I'm telling you, dear, I'm just waiting to die. I welcome death, but it doesn't come. Why won't God take me so we can be together again?"

He bent over and pressed his head against the cold bronze plate. Tears trickled down his cheeks and dropped to the frozen, marble floor.

"What am I supposed to do now? What was I thinking getting involved in this who-done-it murder mystery? I feel just like I'm in the middle of one of those Michael Swiger novels. I must be losing my mind."

A shadow filled the tiny compartment. Something blocked the feeble stream of reflected moonlight. Mead turned to see the silhouette of a man filling the doorway, ducking his head and shoulders through the door.

23

Anthony J. Celebrezze Federal Building
Cleveland, Ohio
7:10 P.M.

Sarah Riehl knocked on the walnut-paneled door of Cleveland's FBI Director William Kirby.

"Come in."

She pressed open the door and stepped into the spacious office; her feet sunk into the plush, navy blue carpet. The pungent stench of a cigar assaulted her nose. Kirby sat at a small conference table near a wall lined with autographed photos of everyone from President George W. Bush to Winona Ryder.

"Is this someone's idea of a sick joke?" she said, holding up her pager.

"I wish it was." Kirby tamped out the cigar. "The surveillance team taped King soliciting a hit man about an hour ago."

"Who's the hitter?"

"We don't know. The call was traced to a phone booth downtown. The lab is analyzing the tape right now."

"What exactly did King say?"

"It's all right here." He handed her a single sheet of transcription.

She plopped down in the chair next to him, her lips moving as her eyes raced across the page.

King: What took you so long? You aren't backing out on

me, are you?

Mr. X: I ain't backing out on nothing.

King: You owe me.

Mr. X: I said I'd do it, and I meant it.

King: It's got to be tonight.

Mr. X: What's the rush?

King: He's getting too close, that's why. He's rooting into everything. It's only a matter of time until he figures it out.

Mr. X: What about the other one?

King: She's irritating but harmless. It's the old one I'm worried about.

Mr. X: What about the noise? The sound of gunfire tends to disagree with people.

King: I'm out in the country. No one will hear a thing.

Mr. X: You're sure about this?

King: At his age I'm doing him a favor... I'm doing both of us a favor.

Mr. X: Sometimes them old ones will surprise you.

King: Don't worry.

Mr. X: I don't like surprises.

King: Just be here before 8 o'clock.

Mr. X: How you gonna get him there?

King: He'll come if I call.

Mr. X: And if he doesn't?

King: I'll hunt him down and drag him here.

Mr. X: What about the remains?

King: I've already got the hole dug.

Mr. X: When it's done, we're even.

King: You bet we are.

Mr. X: Cool. I'll be there.

King: I'll be waiting.

Sarah shook her head. "Where's Mead now?"

"We don't know," Kirby said. "We sent a team to his house, but there's no sign of him."

"Did you check his office?"

"He's not there."

"What about the library?"

"He's nowhere on campus."

"What about King?"

"He lives out in Kirtland. He wasn't home an hour ago. I've got a squad out there right now."

A young man in shirtsleeves burst through the door. "We've got a match, sir. We've got a match."

"The voiceprint?"

"Yes sir, we've got a match - Thomas Grant. And get this. He's one of King's former clients."

"What kind of case?"

"Shooting."

"That's our man."

"Is the helicopter gassed up?" Sarah asked. "It's already 7:20."

"No can do on the chopper," Kirby said. "It's grounded because of the storm. We're gonna have to drive."

"Let's go. Let's go."

Kirby looked at the two agents seated at the table. "You two hunt down this Grant character. Move heaven and earth but find him." They nodded.

"Riehl, you come with me."

With a snow squall erupting in the skies over Cleveland, the downtown traffic was unusually light. William Kirby drove the 350 horsepower Chevy Caprice while Sarah Riehl fidgeted on the seat next to him. Several inches of slush covered East Ninth Street; it thickened to the consistency of cookie dough on I-90.

Sarah watched Kirby struggle to keep the tires in the narrow troughs left by the previous traffic. Hopefully, the hit man was having equal difficulty with the elements. As they inched closer to the heart of the snowbelt, the visibility diminished to near zero. They passed the exit for Wickliffe, and the tire ruts disappeared. The car drifted one way then the other. The wipers strained to keep the accumulation off the windshield. Both Kirby and Sarah strained their eyes, searching for State Route 306 and the Kirtland exit sign.

"Hang on, Professor," she whispered against the window. Her breath fogged the glass. She wiped it away. "We're coming."

Kirby turned to hear what she said, the car veered toward the right shoulder, side-swiping a ridge of crusted snow. Frozen slush kicked up in the wheel wells; it sounded like the floor was ripping apart. He fought to navigate the car back onto the road.

"Man, driving in this stuff is a nightmare. I don't know how you people do it."

She didn't answer.

The crunching of tires compacting virgin snow droned on as precious minutes ticked away. The whiteout was so thick the headlights did little more than reflect off the swirling snow.

Static crackled over the radio followed by a male voice. "Red leader to unit one, over."

Kirby grabbed the mic. "Go for unit one."

"Sir, we've got a visual on the suspect. He just parked his truck and is heading inside, over."

"Is he alone?"

"Negative. A second man in a trench coat."

"There," Sarah yelled, pointing off to the right. "There's the exit."

"I see it."

The radio crackled. "Request permission to move in, over."

Kirby aimed the car toward the spot he thought the exit ramp should be. The tires dug through the snow and hit a layer of ice covering the pavement. The rear end of the car spun around. The car slid sideways down the ramp. Sarah dug her fingertips into the dashboard, her stomach up in her throat. The car crashed into a snowbank at the bottom of the ramp.

Bang!

The airbags engulfed them in silky billows; white powder filled the car.

"Are you all right?" Kirby asked, as the airbags deflated.

"Yeah, I'm fine."

"I'm sorry. I didn't... we must've hit some ice."

She looked at the digital clock on the dash: 7:55 p.m. "Just get us out of here."

He stepped on the gas, and the drive wheel slipped and spun. He threw the car in reverse and tamped down on the accelerator. The wheels whined; the car rocked. He shifted the gear into drive. The tires dug through the snow and caught the gravel shoulder. The car jerked forward and sped down the ramp.

He snatched the mic. "Unit one to red leader, over."

Static.

"Unit one to red leader, do you copy?"

Static.

"They're not responding."

"Maybe the radio is out."

He slammed the mic against the console.

They raced on in silence.

King's A-Frame home sat 50 yards back off Eagle Road. They turned onto the narrow access drive. Sarah's stomach twisted when she saw the unmarked car parked sideways in the front yard with the engine running and both doors open. Two sets of tracks looped around the sides of the house in a pincer movement.

Kirby slid the car to a stop a few feet behind a red pickup. Sarah kicked open her door and dashed around the right side of the house.

A single shot rang out.

She dropped to her knees.

24

Sarah Riehl lay face down in the snow. The echo from the gunshot reverberated through the countryside.

Boom!

Boom!

She recognized the reverberation of the FBI-issue 9 millimeters returning fire. She felt a burning pain in her hands and looked down. Her hands were buried in the snow. She pulled them out. Goose bumps rippled up her arms. She sprang to her feet and gave herself the onceover. No bullet holes.

She unzipped her black parka and unholstered her .40 caliber Glock, then trudged through the drifting snow toward the backyard. A large oak tree stood just a few feet beyond the corner of the house, its branches slumping under layers of ice and snow. She darted her head around the corner; a wooden shed obstructed her view. Taking a couple of deep breaths, she dove, rolled and popped up behind the tree. She pressed her back against the bark. Her breath billowed in the frigid air. She drew her weapon up to her shoulder and summoned every ounce of courage.

Which way to go?

She lunged around the left side of the tree and pointed

the laser-sighted crosshairs at the first human she saw. A red dot danced around Walter King's right ear. He stood on the back porch under a brass light fixture in front of a sliding glass door. An expression of horrified disbelief shrouded his pale, chubby face. His mouth hung open; his eyes were glazed and fixed off in the distance. Large drops of sweat ran down his forehead.

She panned the gun to the right, following King's line of sight. The red dot stopped on an average-built man wearing a full-length, green trench coat and black combat boots. A 16-gauge shotgun dangled from his right hand.

Thomas Grant, hitman Mr. X.

A couple of feet in front of him, FBI Director William Kirby slid his pistol back into its shoulder holster and shook his head. She shifted her arm to the right, and the laser found two agents with pistols drawn, bearing down on an object a few feet away.

"What kind of hitman are you?" said the taller agent, looking over his shoulder at Grant. "How could you miss at that distance?"

"You're lucky we were here," the second agent said. "He almost got away."

She panned the crosshairs to the dark mass stretched out on the snow. Crimson drops speckled the white blanket between the shooters and their feeble victim. Steam drifted up from the fresh and fatal wounds. A widening arc of blood oozed through the snow, emanating from the twitching form of a 150-pound Doberman Pinscher.

"No way," she whispered, "King set up a hit on his own dog."

25

E dward Mead stood in front of the living room picture window, rippling his fingers on the ledge, waiting for the courier from the Clerk's Office to arrive with the next installment of transcription. He was still irritated by the cemetery gate guard stopping by Victoria's vault last night to make sure he was all right. Mead considered his visits with Victoria sacred, and the last thing he needed during such an emotionally charged moment was the intrusion of a stranger. The hours had passed dreadfully slow over the weekend, all alone in that big empty house. Getting back to work would be a welcome change.

The furnace kicked on, and a rush of air blew up his pant-legs. He looked down to see he was standing over the register. The smell of dust made him fight the urge to sneeze. He pressed his index finger under his nose and tipped his head back, just as a salt-stained, brown car pulled up in the drive. A couple moments later the doorbell rang. He shuffled over, opened the door, and sneezed.

"God bless you," the courier said.

"Thanks."

Mead signed for the sealed envelope, then shut the

door. He settled down into his overstuffed La-Z-Boy with a cup of coffee in one hand and the transcript in the other....

A tiny blonde wearing a pink sweater and matching skirt walked up the center aisle and took the stand. Her short, shapely legs didn't reach the floor.

"Miss, that chair adjusts," Chesterfield said. "It's on rollers."

"Okay, thanks," she said, her voice high-pitched and childlike.

"That microphone adjusts too. Speak up and look directly into the camera, and we'll all be very happy."

"Okay."

Chesterfield flashed a rare smile at the young witness.

"Would you please state your name for the record?" Parris asked.

"Amber Wilson."

"And did you ever work for Dr. Baird?"

"I did."

"And is he in the courtroom today?"

"He is."

"Please point to him."

She darted a tentative finger at Baird, then looked away.

"Let the record show the witness has identified the defendant," Chesterfield said.

"How long did you work for Dr. Baird?" Parris asked.

"Two years."

"What kind of work did you do?"

"I answered phones, did some counseling, that sort of thing."

"By counseling, do you mean crisis counseling?"

"Uh huh."

"Were you trained to do crisis counseling?"

"I was trained to... let me get the phrase right... to

maximize marketing potential of the women who called the clinic."

"That's a mouthful."

"He beat it into our heads."

"That doesn't sound like crisis counseling to me."

"It's not. He gave me a book on using high-pressure sales techniques over the phone."

"Telemarketing?"

"Pretty much. I received a commission on each woman who came in for an abortion at my referral. There was even a bonus on the type of anesthesia I sold. For general anesthesia I got two bucks, 75 cents for Valium, and 25 cents for local."

"Where does the counseling come in?"

"We were trained to listen to whatever the women said when they called, and when they finished talking, we told them abortion is the way to go."

"What if someone calls and just wants a pregnancy test?"

"It doesn't matter what they want. The philosophy is that each woman is potentially worth a certain amount of money. The more women we see, the more money we make."

"Did you do any work directly with the abortions?"

"No. I stayed as far away as possible from that area. Although..."

"Go on."

"Well, one day I did go up to the lab, and saw what looked like a rubber doll on the pathology table. But when I got closer, I realized it was a fetus."

"How did that make you feel?"

"It made me sick. I couldn't believe it looked so real. It had all its fingers and toes, you know, like a baby. I never thought it would look so... so... human."

"Were you involved in disposing of the babies?"

"No. They set it up so most clinic workers never have

to see the babies. It's pretty upsetting."

"Whose job is it to handle the corpses?"

"Generally, they assign one worker to do that. You know, she stores them, sends them to pathology, disposes of them, that sort of stuff."

"So, you've never actually seen an abortion?"

"No. But on killing days, the smell of blood fills the whole clinic."

"Objection," Burton shouted. "The witness is using inflammatory language."

"Overruled."

"Is there a high turnover rate working under those conditions?"

"Oh yeah. The first six months I was there the entire staff turned over twice."

"I'm going to shift gears now and ask you some questions about Dr. Baird. Is that all right?"

"Sure."

"What kind of boss was Dr. Baird?"

"The man's a pig."

"Objection," Burton shouted.

"Sustained," Chesterfield said. "The witness will refrain from such characterizations. Ms. Parris, ask your witness a more specific question."

"Yes, Your Honor. Ms. Wilson, how did Dr. Baird treat you and the other female employees?"

"He was always making sexual remarks. He talked about our legs a lot, and he said he would only hire young girls who wore short skirts."

"How did he treat the patients?"

"Same. He'd say stuff like, 'Take off your pants and spread your legs. You're obviously good at that.' I remember one day he walked out of the recovery room all covered in blood and shouted, 'If you sleazebags wouldn't jump into bed with the first guy who comes along, I wouldn't be in this mess.'"

"Did any of the patients complain?"

"A lot did."

"What types of complaints did you hear?"

"At first it was his rude attitude, but toward the end almost everyone complained about his sadistic behavior."

"Objection," Burton said, half-standing. "The witness is characterizing again."

"Overruled."

"Do you recall any specific incidents?" Parris asked.

"One woman complained that Dr. Baird hurt her so bad she started screaming, and when she didn't stop, he stuffed a tampon in her mouth."

"Was this sort of thing unusual?"

"By the time I quit you could hear all his patients screaming. Some vomited from pain."

"What else did patients complain about?"

"One lady said that he stared between her legs and sang a silly song during the exam."

Chesterfield chuckled.

"During the time you worked for the defendant, did you notice any alcohol abuse?"

"Objection," Burton said. "Relevance."

"I'll allow it," Chesterfield said. "You may answer the question."

"He was smashed almost every day. More than once I'd open up in the morning and find him lying in a puddle of vomit."

"What about drugs?"

"Objection."

"Overruled."

"I've seen him with pot a few times, but he must've been on other stuff. Once I actually had to tell him, 'Look, you don't have any shoes on. Go put some shoes on before you start seeing patients.'"

"Did you condone this behavior?"

"Of course not."

"Why didn't you quit?"

"I tried to. But he threatened to tell the unemployment office I was fired for stealing, so I couldn't get benefits."

"But you ultimately did quit."

"Yeah."

"What made you change your mind?"

"One day a patient's mother came in all angry and upset. She carried a little milk carton, you know, the kind chocolate milk comes in. But it had a tiny fetal head in it. Her daughter passed it after she went home. Well, a couple days later I opened the refrigerator in the break room and found the carton with the head still in it." She closed her eyes and fluttered her eyelids. "The eyes were all bugged out, and he... he had taped a sign to it that said, 'Hi, remember me?'"

"What'd you do?"

"I ran out and never looked back."

"I have no further questions for this witness, Your Honor." Parris walked back to her seat with a determined expression.

"Would you like to cross-examine the witness, Mr. Burton?" Chesterfield asked.

"Just a couple of questions, if I may."

"Proceed."

Burton stood slowly, coughed, and then walked to the podium. His voice sounded hoarse. "Ms. Wilson, were you on duty the day Robin Roget came in for her abortion?"

"No."

"So, you have no direct knowledge of her case?"

"No."

"I see. Ms. Wilson, during the time you worked for my client, did you ever have sex with him?"

"Objection." Parris leapt to her feet. "Relevance."

"Overruled. I'd like to know the answer to that question myself."

"We dated briefly."

"But did you have sex with him, yes or no?"

"Yes."

"I have no further questions."

Chesterfield looked contemptuously at the tiny blonde. "You may step down. Trial counsel will meet in my chambers immediately. Court is in recess."

He rapped the gavel then bolted down the steps and into his chambers. He drained a decanter of vodka into a tall glass while the apprehensive band of lawyers assembled in front of his desk. He belted back the burning liquid, then dropped down in his seat. He turned his back to the group and threw his feet up on the credenza.

"I've made my decision concerning the videotaped testimony. I'm not going to allow it."

A faint smile stretched across Rutledge's normally stoic lips.

"But why not?" Parris asked.

"Did I stutter? What part of *no* don't you understand?"

"But sir," Walter King said, "if you don't give us a reason, it will be impossible to appeal the decision."

"So?"

"That's abuse of discretion."

"What did you say?" Chesterfield spun around, stood up, and jammed his index finger into King's chest. "What did you say, fat boy? Abuse of what? Don't you know, I'll do things to you a farmer wouldn't do to a barnyard animal."

And Chesterfield poured out a volume of profanity that rose to such levels of spontaneity, color, and accomplishment, he would've excited the admiration of the most ardent rap star.

26

Cleveland, Ohio
1:30 P.M.

Walter King stared out the 5th floor office window of 100 Lakeside Place, home of the Cuyahoga County Public Defender's Office. Out on the horizon over Lake Erie, ominous clouds assembled for another assault on the snowbelt. The sun struggled to break through the overcast. A single ray escaped and for a moment sent a blinding glare across the window and illuminated King's tiny cubicle.

He felt safe here in this isolated world. No confrontation, no egotistical judges belittling him in front of his peers, and no rejection. From behind the safety of beige wall dividers, he could peck away at his computer and fight the system that seemed to enjoy crushing little guys like him. He closed his eyes and took in the cacophony of the appellate division. He heard the incessant whirling of the copy machine layered beneath the blaring phones and shouting lawyers. Soft, sweet jazz droned from the ceiling speakers and fought to overcome the din of office noise.

King laced his fingers together behind his head and surveyed his kingdom. Two stacks of folders stood on the left-hand side of the desk, each stack precisely ten folders high. The desk calendar showed no signs of doodling, each deadline and court appearance neatly printed in red ink. A lithograph of John Trumbull's famous painting "The Declaration of Independence" hung above his precious computer. He rolled his chair up to the console and double-clicked the mouse to print an amicus brief he spent the day writing for the Ohio Supreme Court.

Guilt assailed King's conscience, as he thought about Friday night's fiasco and his Doberman. Poor Nero blown to bits by the FBI. He deserved to die with dignity, not hunted around the yard like some rabid wolf. King hated himself for not having the guts to do it himself.

He sensed the presence of someone looking over his shoulder. He turned to see the smiling face of Edward Mead. King stood and stretched out his hand.

"Mr. Mead, I um... I can explain about the dog."

"What dog?"

"I... you know, my dog."

"What are you talking about?"

"I figured after the way they... never mind."

"Is there someplace private we can talk?"

"Yeah, sure. There's a few conference rooms over by the restrooms."

"Lead the way."

The two men walked through the maze of cubicles and filed into a conference room. They sat on opposite sides of the long, rectangular table.

"I'm guessing this isn't a personal call," King said with a forced smile.

"I'm afraid not. But I know you're busy, so I'll try to be brief."

"Take your time."

"Mr. King, please describe Judge Chesterfield's office for me?"

"You want me to tell you what it looked like?"

"Exactly."

"Well, let me think about that. It was bigger than I expected, and he had a real fancy desk and one of those high-backed chairs. You couldn't see his head from behind it. Let me think... there was a brass and marble thing behind the desk."

"A credenza?"

"Yeah, that's it. He used to put his feet up on it all the time." Miniscule drops of perspiration formed on his brow and upper lip.

"Did you notice anything in particular on his desk?"

"He had a computer, Dell, I think, one of the older ones. Let me see, he had a big nameplate, and... oh yeah, he had that dagger-looking thing standing next to it."

"The letter opener?"

"I don't know what it was. I guess you could open letters with it."

"What else do you recall?"

"That's about it."

"Are you sure that's all you remember?"

"Yeah, that's about it."

"Mr. King, did you stab a man named Paul Booth when you were in the Cuyahoga Hills Detention Center?"

"Wow, that's some segue."

"Yes or no, Mr. King?"

"It's not that cut and dried."

"Yes or no."

"Yeah, I stabbed him, but don't you want to hear my side of the story?"

"That's why I'm here."

"This could take awhile."

"I've got all day."

King rubbed his forehead and closed his eyes. "Have you ever lived in an institution, Mr. Mead?"

"No."

"Then you have no idea the kind of torture I've endured, and Cuyahoga Hills was the worst. Just being there was agony enough, but then Booth decided to make my life a living hell. He started turning the other kids against me." King's mouth twitched, and his parched tongue seemed unable to articulate. "I've always been overweight, and he tortured me about that, but he got the biggest laughs messing with me about my leg. I wear a prosthetic."

"What happened?"

"I lost it when I was born."

"How much of your leg is missing?"

"About midway up my shin. See, look here."

He pulled up his pant leg. The flesh-tone molded-plastic met the nub just below the knee.

"How'd that happen?"

"An accident. I don't like to talk about it."

"Fair enough."

"Where was I?"

"Booth."

"That's right. One time I left my leg outside the shower, and Booth stole it. I tried to hop back to my bed, and I fell. Everyone laughed. Then he snatched my towel, and I had to crawl back to my bed naked. They all laughed and laughed." Sweat beaded across his forehead.

"Shoe-bootied. That's what they called me."

"Why's that?"

"The prosthetic had a black shoe on it. But after I outgrew the matching one, they gave me a boot to wear on my good foot. Get it?

Shoe on one foot, boot on the other. Shoe-bootied." Mead nodded.

"After a while Booth wasn't satisfied with humiliating me in front of everyone; he got physical. He and his little buddies started sneaking up on me when I was sleeping. A few of them held me down by the corners of my blanket, while the others stuffed bars of soap in some old socks and beat me with them. They laughed and laughed. I can still hear them cackling like a bunch of hyenas. It got so bad I couldn't sleep at night. I never knew when they'd attack." Great drops of sweat rolled off King's face. He reached in his front pocket for a handkerchief and dabbed his forehead. "I suffer from hyperactive sweat glands. As soon as I get a little tense, look out, I'm flooding the place."

"That's unfortunate for a lawyer."

"Tell me about it." He jammed the handkerchief back into his pocket. "Where was I?"

"You were telling me about how you came to stab Mr. Booth."

"Yeah, that's right, I keep getting sidetracked here. Well, anyway, after one of these blanket parties, Booth yanked me out of bed and shucked my pants down. I thought he'd just take them and throw them in the toilet or something, but the next thing I know he's trying to rape me. I couldn't get him off... I couldn't. I screamed for help, and all they did was laugh. I reached for anything I could get my hands on. I managed to pull the nightstand over and grab a pen. I stuck him wherever I could. I guess I got him in the neck."

"So, you stabbed in self-defense?"

"It was all I could do to stop him."

"I see."

"You don't believe me?"

"Getting back to Judge Chesterfield, I've been reading through the transcripts. He was pretty tough on you."

"We had some issues."

"That's an understatement."

"Chesterfield was a bully. Bullies like to push around those they perceive to be weak. I was an easy target for him."

"Did he make you angry?"

"You've read the transcripts, what do you think?"

"What I think is irrelevant."

"Yeah, he pissed me off. But if you're trying to draw a parallel between Chesterfield and Booth you can forget it. I didn't kill him. I'm a professional, and I handle my problems professionally."

"What does that mean?"

"It means I was going straight to the Bar Association after the trial to see about getting him thrown off the bench."

"Last week I asked you who you thought killed Chesterfield, and you said Rutledge. Do you still think so?"

"I'm not sure. But of the four of us, my money is on Blinky."

"You called Rutledge 'Blinky.'"

"Not to his face."

"I see. Well, thanks for your time, Mr. King. That's all the questions I have for you right now."

"I give you my word, I didn't kill him."

"Thanks for your time."

"You do believe me, don't you?"

Mead jammed his index finger into his right ear and wiggled it around, while making an agonized face.

"Are you all right?" King asked.

"It's nothing. My ear is ringing. Can you hear it?"

"What?"

"Nothing."

Mead attempted to stand, his knees cracked, and he fumbled back down in the chair. He braced his hands against the table and rose on his second attempt. "I stopped by to see an old friend of mine last week," Mead said. "He used to be one of your professors."

"Which one?"

"Professor Ligon."

"I can only imagine what he might have told you."

"Why do you say that?"

"The man hated me. He'd get so mad at me his ears wiggled."

Mead grabbed the knob and pulled the door open a few inches, then closed it again. "One last thing, Mr. King. Do you think Chesterfield fixed the case?"

"I've got my opinion."

"I'm asking your opinion."

"Yeah, I think he threw the case."

"When did you first suspect something was up?"

"I didn't trust him from the beginning, but I got suspicious when he didn't allow the jury to see the video testimony of our witnesses. I mean, that was pretty much our whole case. And he didn't even offer an explanation."

"Thank you, Mr. King. You've been most helpful."

"I'll cooperate all I can."

"Do you like riddles, Mr. King?"

"I don't know, I guess so."

"Here's one for you. What's more powerful than God, more evil than the Devil, rich folks don't have it, but poor people do?"

King placed his hands in front of him on the table and repeated the riddle under his breath. After a few moments he shrugged. "I give up, what is it?"

"Nothing."

27

C handler Rutledge stopped in the restroom outside the suite of offices occupied by Jessica Parris. This was going to be awkward.

He and Parris butted heads throughout the trial. He didn't like her, and she hated his guts. Nevertheless, the circumstances called for unconventional tactics. Gag orders usually held for about a week, which meant the Chesterfield murder was about to explode in the media. Besides, his wife was breathing down his neck for more money, and the sooner the Baird case was settled, the sooner he could cut his losses.

What did his wife do with all the money he gave her? He was afraid to ask in light of his self-medicating expenses. She would never understand how innocently the addiction had started: No-Doze in college, then Speed in medical school. Now an ounce of cocaine a day just to function.

He reached into the breast pocket of his suit coat and pulled out a miniature bottle of Tylenol. He unscrewed the cap, then tapped out a small piece of wire and a plastic straw. Using the wire, he fished out a tiny, rolled up plastic baggie filled with cocaine. He dumped the contents onto the back of his left hand between the thumb and index finger then snorted. He squinted tightly, took off his glasses, then looked in the mirror. His pupils dilated so wide that the blue of his irises nearly disappeared.

"Now I'm ready."

He composed himself, walked out of the restroom, then into Parris' office. A teenaged receptionist chatted away on the phone. He waited for a few moments while she ignored him. He checked his watch, then walked past her.

"Hey, mister, you can't go in there."

"Watch me."

"You're in big trouble, mister."

"Yeah, right."

"Stop!" she screamed.

Parris jerked open the door. "What's going on out here?"

"This guy just barged in."

"Oh, it's you." She looked at Rutledge with a look of disgust. "What do you want?"

"We need to talk."

"Does Jonathan know you're here?"

"I don't represent Mr. Burton." He dabbled his beak-like nose with a handkerchief. "I'm here at Dr. Baird's request."

"Jonathan is the lead counsel."

"My client is aware of - how should I phrase it - your less-than adversarial relationship with Mr. Burton."

She shot him a glare that could etch glass.

"We've got bigger problems right now than this lawsuit," Rutledge said. "Just give me five minutes."

"All right, five minutes."

Parris escorted Rutledge into her cesspool of an office. An odd scent lingered in the air; he couldn't quite place it - a warm, dusty smell.

"Let's get right to it, Ms. Parris, my client is willing to make a settlement offer."

"Why now?"

"Obviously, Chesterfield's murder changes the complexity of this case. My guy wants to extricate himself from this madness."

"How much?"

"Fifty-thousand dollars, and we admit no wrongdoing."

"That doesn't cover my expenses."

"You'll get nothing if we re-litigate."

"Who said anything about a new trial?"

"An assassinated judge is prima facie grounds for a mistrial, wouldn't you say?"

"But the verdict is sealed."

"The verdict is worthless. Besides, the four of us need to distance ourselves from this case."

"Make it $300,000."

"We don't have that kind of money laying around." He blinked rapidly as though he just emerged into strong light. "Seventy-five and that's final."

"You act like it's your money."

"Seventy-five, take it or leave it."

"No."

"Don't you want to consult with your client first?"

"For the family it's not about the money."

"It's always about the money."

"Not this time."

"You're making a big mistake."

"I'll take my chances on the verdict."

"You'll be sorry," he said with a snarl of contempt. "I'll make sure of it."

28

Willoughby, Ohio
6:45 P.M.

Sarah Riehl walked down the hall between the kitchen and dining room, her stocking feet lightly thumping the hardwood floor. She carried a silver candleholder under one arm, a pastel-green tablecloth under the other, and two long-stemmed candles in her hands. Her husband followed, balancing a matching engraved silver tray covered with plates, bowls, and a ceramic soup tureen.

"I still don't see why you invited the old guy over here," Doug said. "He probably wants to be alone."

"He accepted, didn't he?"

She spread the cloth over the table. Doug leaned over and set the tray down. He straightened up and smacked the back of his head against the brass chandelier, causing it to sway over the center of the table.

"Careful, honey," Sarah said.

"My ponytail cushioned the blow." He rubbed the back of his head. "I'll get the wine."

He disappeared down the hall while she set the table. A few moments later he returned with a stainless steel ice bucket and a bottle of red wine.

"I really think you're losing it, Sarah. One minute you're saying the geezer is crazy and should be committed, and the next you're inviting him over for dinner."

"I feel sorry for the man. Is that a crime?" She lifted the lid off the tureen and sprinkled croutons over the cheese soup. "Besides, we need to discuss the case."

"Discuss it during business hours."

"I don't see what you're crying about. You're getting a good meal out of the deal."

"Thank God for small miracles."

"Hey."

"On second thought, maybe I should ask the old boy to move in with us."

The doorbell rang.

"I'll get it," Doug said. "I want to see this guy."

He jogged to the front door and jerked it open. Mead's round, wrinkled face crinkled into a smile as he presented a white pastry box tied with a string.

"I didn't know what your wife was making, so I picked up a chocolate cream pie at Presti's. Chocolate goes with everything."

"I like you already." Doug stepped back and made a sweeping motion with his right arm for Mead to come in.

The old man took careful, deliberate steps through the door. He removed his cream-colored fedora and unbuttoned his overcoat.

"I'll take those." Doug hung the items on a brass coat rack behind the door, then escorted Mead to the dining room where Sarah hovered over the table stirring the soup.

"Professor, so good of you to come."

"No trouble at all."

"You're just in time."

She ladled out a bowl of soup and handed it to him. He lifted it to his nose and took a long, sustained whiff.

"Is that nutmeg?"

"Just a pinch. I'm impressed. Doug wouldn't know if I poured gasoline in it."

"I would if it was on fire."

Mead sipped a spoonful. "Exquisite."

"Thank you."

Doug sat at the head of the table with Sarah to his right and Mead across from her.

"So, tell me, Mr. Mead," Doug said. "What do you think about Sarah's little adventure Friday night?"

"What happened Friday night?"

"Nothing," Sarah said.

"Go ahead and tell him."

She pouted her pretty bottom lip.

"Tell me what?"

"It's no big deal," Sarah said. "A false alarm really."

"Where?"

"King's house."

"Tell him about the dog."

"Doug—"

"But the dog is the best part."

She rolled her eyes. "The surveillance team taped a conversation between King and a hitman."

"A hitman?"

"We thought he planned to kill you."

"He wants to kill me?"

"Don't worry; he wanted the guy to kill his dog."

"To kill his dog. Did you hear that?" Fragments of food ejected from Doug's mouth. "I just laughed my brains out when she first told me. A hitman for a dog - oh man."

"Glad to amuse you, honey."

They finished the soup. Sarah cleared the bowls and replaced them with dinner plates mounded with sauerkraut and sausages.

"This reminds me of the first time my wife tried to cook sausage," Mead said. "She burned them beyond recognition. The house filled with smoke. I laughed, she cried, and we went out to dinner." He settled back in his chair, and his voice dropped to just above a whisper. "I'd give anything to smell those burnt sausages again."

The silence was followed by the tinkling of silverware against china.

"Did you get my email about Booth?" Sarah asked.

"I read it first thing Friday morning. In fact, I spoke to King about it."

"What'd he say?"

"Tell me about your visit with Booth first."

"There's not much to tell. He says King stabbed him while he was sleeping. Sound familiar?"

"Did he say why?"

"He said King was unstable. But he thought it had something to do with him being the ringleader of a bunch of kids who picked on King."

"That's about what King said, with the exception of Booth trying to rape him."

"You've got to be kidding."

"That's what he said."

"Booth didn't strike me as the sexual predator type."

"King was convincing."

"I'm inclined to believe Booth. He has no reason to lie."

"The best lie contains 90 percent truth."

"Yeah, but that works both ways," she said.

"We're talking about a man who couldn't kill his own dog."

"So, he's an animal lover. I'm sure Jack the Ripper loved his cat."

Mead speared a link with his fork and bit off one end. He closed his eyes. An expression of delight encompassed his face. He took a sip of water, then said, "Have you ever seen geese flying south for the winter?"

"What's that got to do with anything?"

"Humor an old man."

"All right. Sure, I've seen them."

"Have you ever noticed that one side of the formation is always longer than the other?"

"Yeah."

"Do you know why that is?"

"Does it have something to do with their instincts or pecking order or something?"

"No. The reason is quite simple - more geese on one side."

Doug snickered. "I like this guy."

"What's your point?"

"Only that sometimes the obvious is exactly what it appears to be."

"I don't buy it. King is a man dealing with a lot of rejection. Living with the idea his own mother wanted him dead has got to be devastating on his psyche."

"I didn't say it wasn't."

"The way I see it, Booth was a bully and got stabbed for his trouble; Chesterfield was a bully and got himself killed. Plain and simple."

"I thought you were convinced Ms. Parris had something to do with it."

"I am."

"So, it's not so plain and simple after all."

"Maybe not." She wrinkled up her forehead. "She's definitely hiding something."

"We've got to know what it is."

"We can have a psychiatric profile developed on her and King."

"I think that's a good idea."

"It may take a little while, but it'll be worth it. These profiles are incredibly accurate. And in the meantime, I'll dig a little deeper into Parris."

"Sounds like a plan." Mead spiked a bite of sauerkraut and jammed it in his mouth. "The food's wonderful."

"Thanks."

"Mr. Riehl, Sarah tells me you're an engineer."

"Metallurgical."

"So, you're pretty good at math?"

"I guess so."

"If it takes three men three days to dig three holes, how long will it take one man to dig half a hole?"

"Half a day."

"You would think so, but there's no such thing as half a hole."

29

E dward Mead walked over to the kitchen window and raised his left hand to shield his eyes from the slanting rays of the rising sun; the glare felt warm upon his face. He looked out across the backyard. Puffy, white clouds dotted the horizon. A leaf tumbled across the blanket of snow, driven by a gust of wind that whistled through the window sash. The inviting aroma of fresh-brewed coffee pervaded the room, along with an overwhelming pang of loneliness. He hated waking up without Victoria.

She was always quiet at daybreak. He thought back over countless mornings spent in this same room. He remembered rambling on and on about his hopes and dreams, and she just nodded or frowned. He really didn't care which, just as long as she was there. Now he missed her silence.

He poured himself a cup of black coffee, spread orange marmalade over slightly burned toast, and began reading the transcript lying open on the table....

The judge entered with rigid dignity, and everybody stood. The bailiff removed the video camera, then ushered in the jury.

"Is the plaintiff ready to call its next witness?" Chesterfield asked.

"We are, Your Honor."

"Proceed."

"The plaintiff calls Joyce Roget to the stand."

An overweight woman stood from behind the plaintiff's table. Mr. King slid his chair back so that she could squeeze past. She strode confidently to the stand, unkempt locks of silver hair bouncing with each step. Pale-blue eyes peered out from under thin, black eyebrows. Deep pucker lines surrounded her mouth and produced a dour expression. She wore black slacks and a black jacket with a picture of Robin pinned to the lapel.

The bailiff issued the oath. The witness laced her fingers together on her lap and turned her gaze directly toward Dr. Baird. Their eyes met for an instant; he dropped his glance to the table and never looked up again. He felt the weight of her stare bearing down on him.

"Please state your name," Parris said.

"Joyce Roget." Her voice was deep and raspy.

"And what is your relationship to the victim?"

"Her mother."

"In your own words, please describe your daughter."

"Robin is... was... a beautiful girl with such a kind and tender heart, maybe a little too tender, too naïve. She developed very early, which didn't help matters any. Her body attracted the wrong kind of men. They took advantage of her, steered her wrong."

"What do you mean by the wrong kind of men?"

"Well, her father left us when she was 8. I never remarried. So, she seemed to latch onto any older guy who gave her the time of day, and with that body of hers, there seemed to be an endless supply of losers. They bought her things and flashed money, and she did whatever they wanted. By the time she turned 16, I couldn't control her. She started dancing in clubs, staying out all night... she broke my heart."

"Do you have any other children?"

"She was all I had."

"Did she have any children?"

"Two."

"Who presently has custody of them?"

"I do."

"I know this is going to be difficult, but I need to ask you some questions about Robin's death. If you need to stop or take a break, just say so."

She nodded.

"Did you know Robin planned to have an abortion?"

"I didn't even know she was pregnant."

"Were you home the evening Robin returned from Dr. Baird's clinic?"

"I was."

"Please describe Robin's condition when she arrived home that night."

"I was sitting in the living room watching Veggie Tales with the kids when she staggered through the door. I thought she had been raped or something. She looked terrible, so pale and weak."

"What did you do?"

"I helped her to the couch and asked what happened. At first, she wouldn't say, then she nodded toward the kids. I sent them outside, and she told me about the abortion."

"How did she look?"

"She looked bloated and pale, and her skin felt clammy. She said her stomach hurt really bad. I told her she needed to go to the hospital. But she said she just wanted to lay down for awhile."

"What did you do?"

"I helped her to bed."

"Would you like a glass of water?" Parris asked.

"I'm all right."

"Are you sure?"

"Let's continue."

"What happened next?"

"The next morning Robin didn't come down for breakfast. I figured she needed her rest, so I let her sleep. I dropped the kids off at day care then went to work. I ran home at lunch to fix Robin something to eat - nothing special, just some grilled cheese sandwiches and tomato soup. I called upstairs for her to come and eat, but she didn't answer. So I went up, and that's when I found her."

"What did you find?"

She closed her eyes and spoke in a monotone. "I opened the door and a putrid smell hit me, like sour milk. Robin lay on the bed perfectly still, white as a ghost. Her eyes were partly open and staring at the ceiling. The sheets were stained with pus and blood from her waist down. I walked over and touched her; she felt cold, so cold. I called her name. Nothing. I shook her. Nothing." Ms. Roget began shaking with sobs, hiding her eyes with her fingers through which tears flowed in a sudden stream. She hammered her forehead, then yelled in another voice, "He killed her! He killed my baby!"

"Objection!"

"He should be in jail!"

Chesterfield pounded the gavel.

"He should be dead!"

"Not another word!" Chesterfield shouted at the witness. "Or I will hold you in contempt. Now get ahold of yourself. The jury will disregard this outburst."

"I have no further questions, Your Honor," Parris said with a smirk. She confidently returned to her seat.

"Does the defense have any questions for the witness?"

"We do, sir," Burton said, while rising to his feet. He coughed a wet, thick cough. He lifted a finger and smiled through the hacking to excuse the nuisance. "Your

Honor, with all due respect for all that Mrs. Roget has been through, I'd like her to be considered a hostile witness."

"Granted." Chesterfield looked at the witness. "Mrs. Roget, you will answer all the defense counsel's questions with a simple yes or no. Do you understand?"

She nodded and wiped her eyes on a balled-up tissue.

"Any additional outburst will land you in jail for the night. Do I make myself clear?"

"Uh huh."

"You may proceed, Mr. Burton."

"Thank you, sir. Mrs. Roget, I only have a couple of questions for you. I'll try to be brief. During the course of raising your daughter, did you ever speak to her about birth control?"

"Yes."

"Did she follow your advice?"

"Objection," Parris said. "Surely the witness isn't privy to her daughter's sexual practices."

"Sustained. Ask another question, Mr. Burton."

"How many children did you say your daughter had?"

"Two."

"Same father?"

"No."

"Did she even know the fathers?"

"Objection!"

"I withdraw the question. How many abortions did she have?"

"One."

"One prior to this incident? Or was this the only one?"

"One prior."

"So at least two that you know of?"

"I guess so."

"You guess or you know?"

"She had two."

"Two. And you said that she could be naïve at times. Would you say she was irresponsible?"

"No more than any other girl her age."

"Yes or no, Mrs. Roget?"

"At times."

"I'll take that as a yes. And you testified earlier that you instructed your daughter to go to the hospital following her latest abortion, is that correct?"

"Yes."

"And she ignored your advice?"

"That's what I said."

"Answer the question with yes or no," Chesterfield said.

She folded her arms. "Yes."

"And Mrs. Roget, do you believe Robin would still be alive if she'd taken your advice and gone to the hospital?"

"Yes."

Burton turned toward the jury. "When this case began, I talked to you about contributory negligence. And I said the law requires each individual to be responsible for his or her own safety. And that ordinary, reasonable steps must be taken to ensure personal care. Obviously, Robin Roget didn't take these steps. She ignored the advice of her mother. She didn't seek medical treatment that would have saved—"

"Objection!" Parris launched to her feet. "Counsel is lecturing the jury, not examining the witness."

"Sustained. Ask a question, Mr. Burton."

"You said you didn't know that your daughter planned to have an abortion, is that correct?"

"Yes."

"Would you have tried to talk her out of it, if she had told you?"

"Yes."

"So, you're opposed to abortion?"

"It's cold-blooded murder."

"Yes or no, Mrs. Roget?"

"Yes."

"And isn't it true that you brought this suit, not because you believe Dr. Baird is responsible for your daughter's death, but because you don't want to accept the truth - that your daughter's own irresponsibility took her life."

"Objection!"

"Sustained."

"I have no further questions."

30

E dward Mead arrived 15 minutes early for his 2:30 meeting with Sarah Riehl. The receptionist directed him up the elevator to the 3rd floor, the first door on the right. He walked into a room that looked more like a command center than a conference room. A rectangular, walnut table stood in the middle of the room surrounded by 14 mauve chairs. A large-screen video conference machine was built into the far wall. A red indicator light flashed Standby in the middle of the screen. Forced air droned through the overhead vents and pumped frigid air into the room. Telecommunications and computer equipment lined the walls.

Sarah Riehl pecked away at one of the computers on the opposite wall and didn't notice him come in.

Mead cleared his throat. "If you called me down here because some of your silverware is missing, it wasn't me."

"Oh, Professor Mead, boy do I have news for you."

"What is it?"

"I thought about what you said, you know, about Parris. In fact, I couldn't get her out of my mind last night. So, I came down here first thing this morning and went back over everything."

"And what did you find?"

"Absolutely nothing. So, I focused on that 18-month gap in her records—"

"And what did you find?"

"Will you let me tell the story?" she said, squinting her eyes at him.

"I'm not interested in the story, give me the bottom line."

"You sound just like my husband."

"I knew there was something I liked about him."

"Do you want to hear what I have to say or not?"

"Of course."

"Well, anyway, I kept going over everything again and again. Then I realized I never ran her Social Security number. I typed it in and bingo, everything popped up."

"Including the missing 18 months?"

"Everything."

"And..."

"She got married."

"Oh."

"To a man named Tom Cassini."

"I see," Mead said. "She used her married name during the gap, then went back to her maiden name after the divorce."

"Only she didn't get divorced. Her husband is dead."

Mead raised his eyebrows. "How did he die?"

"I don't know. All I could get from the Bureau of Statistics was a copy of his death certificate. The coroner ruled it a homicide."

"Was anyone arrested?"

"I don't know. I called the District Attorney's office in New York. The prosecutor who handled the case is no longer with them. But they gave me the name of the detective who handled the case. I've got it written down here somewhere." She rummaged through some papers and yellow sticky notes. "Here it is, Detective Clarence Simpson. I set up a teleconference for 2:30."

"Men in her life have a nasty habit of coming up dead."

"Wouldn't it be something if Chesterfield had been involved in a sex triangle with Parris and her husband? And maybe Chesterfield killed Cassini, so she tracked him down and killed him out of revenge."

"That would make a good plot for a novel, but things aren't so romantic in real life."

"But it's fun to think about."

"We'll know for sure in a few minutes."

Sarah checked her watch then walked over to the conference machine. She picked up the remote control and pressed a few buttons. The screen lit up, and a clock appeared in the upper right-hand corner: 2:29 p.m. She jogged over to the center of the table, grabbed the phone, and dialed the number she had scribbled on her hand. "Ready" blinked across the screen.

"The camera only processes a few frames per second," she said. "It'll look a little choppy."

She pressed a button on the remote control, and the hazy image of an African American male filled the screen; his movements looked mechanical.

"Hello... Can you hear me?" Simpson asked. His lips didn't match the words.

"Loud and clear," Sarah said.

"Good. What can I do for you? You guys aren't investigating me, are you?"

"No, no, it's nothing like that."

"In New York you never can tell. How can I help you?"

"Detective Simpson, do you recall investigating a homicide involving a man named Tom Cassini?" Sarah asked.

"The name's not ringing a bell. About how long ago?"

"Three years. He was married to a woman named Jessica Parris."

"Wait a minute, was the wife a lawyer?"

"Affirmative," Sarah said.

"Yeah, I do remember it now, a stabbing case." Sarah and Mead looked at each other.

"Was the case ever prosecuted?" Mead asked.

"Nope. Charges were never filed."

"Unsolved, huh?"

"Oh no, we know who did it. Got a confession, as a matter of fact."

"Who, who?" Sarah asked.

"The wife confessed."

Mead and Sarah looked at each other again.

"Why wasn't she charged?" Mead asked.

"Good question. She told some cock-and-bull story about her husband attacking her while she peeled carrots. She claimed to have stabbed him in self-defense." He pantomimed the shower scene from *Psycho*. "Then some bleeding-heart neighbors filed affidavits saying the man was abusive, and she feared for her life and that sort of crap. The next thing I know, the Grand Jury threw the case out on the grounds of Spousal Abuse Syndrome. If you ask me, she knew the system and beat it."

"Where did you say she stabbed him?" Sarah asked.

"Got him directly in the throat, buried the blade to the hilt." Mead and Sarah looked at each other again.

"Were there any cuts on his hands or arms?" Mead asked.

"Nope. No self-defense wounds of any kind."

"Obviously no one offers their throat to an angry woman with a knife."

"Where were you a couple years ago?" Simpson sipped a cup of coffee. "Mind telling me why all the interest in the Cassini case after all this time?"

"It's not the Cassini case we're concerned about," Sarah said.

"Parris is a suspect in a murder case here in Cleveland."

"Stabbed another one, did she?"

"How'd you guess?"

"I said she'd do it again if she got the chance."

"Do you still have your file on that case?" Sarah asked.

"It's down in the archives on microfilm."

"Do you mind sending me a copy?"

"Not at all."

"Thank you very much, Detective Simpson," Mead said. "You've been incredibly helpful."

"If there's anything I can do, just holler. I've always wanted to see the Rock and Roll Hall of Fame."

"If we arrest her, we'll be in touch," Mead said.

The screen went blank.

"What do you mean, *'if we arrest her'*?" Sarah said. "We should arrest her right now. We've got probable cause coming out the yin-yang."

"And that's all we've got. I'd rather take a little extra time and get all the facts straight instead of going off half-cocked."

"What're you saying?"

"The fact remains, we don't have any hard evidence, and she's more likely to give us some while out on the street than cooped up in jail."

"You want to give her enough rope to hang herself."

"Exactly, provided she did it."

"What if she runs?"

"She has no reason to, at least not yet." He rubbed his chin. "She may get a little antsy in the morning."

"What happens in the morning?"

"We're going to bring her in for a little visit."

"Good."

"You may want to put a tail on her after that."

"Done."

"If she did it..." He stood up and groaned. "She'll show us."

31

E dward Mead lay on the couch wrapped in a brown and orange afghan. The natural gas furnace kept his home a comfortable 72 degrees, yet his heart felt colder than the Arctic winds rattling against the living room windows. His soul had caught a chill the day Victoria died, and there weren't enough afghans in the world to warm it again. Maybe a cup of tea and a shot of Crown Royal would numb the pain for a little while.

He slid his feet into his slippers and shuffled into the kitchen. He ran some tap water into a mug then placed it in the microwave. He opened the cupboard and found a package of cinnamon Graham crackers sitting in front of the box of Lipton Tea. A pang of grief balled up in his throat.

"They were her favorites."

Never again would she sit next to him on the couch, dunking a cracker into her coffee and watching television. What should he do with the crackers now? Surely, he couldn't throw them away; that would be sacrilegious. He dared not eat them; they belonged to her. He thought back to the first time Victoria snuggled up next to him with her cinnamon crackers and coffee. She dunked a square and romantically lifted it to his lips, but the cracker wilted and dribbled down his chin. They giggled, and she reached up and put her fingers on his lips, then his cheek, and finally around the back of his neck. They kissed. The minutes ticked by the coffee grew cold and...

The doorbell rang.

He mumbled under his breath as he hustled to the front door. He stood on his tiptoes and peered through the peephole. Jonathan Burton rocked from side to side with his hands jammed in his pockets, his breath billowing around his head.

Mead jerked the door open. "What are you doing here?"

"You called me."

"No I didn't."

"I guess it was some other Professor Mead who left a message on my voicemail."

"Oh, that's right." He smacked himself on the forehead. "My mind was somewhere else. Come on in."

"I can't stay long."

"I only need a minute."

The microwave beeped.

"I'll be right back," Mead said, heading off toward the kitchen. "Make yourself comfortable."

Burton unbuttoned his gray, cashmere overcoat and draped it over his arm. He walked over to the baby grand piano in front of the picture window. A bronze bust of Beethoven sat on a lace doily in the center of the instrument. Burton picked up a black and white photo of Victoria in her wedding gown, standing on the marble steps of Severance Hall. She looked so young, so alive. He gently returned the picture to its place and went to sit on the piano bench. He hovered only inches above the cushion when Mead turned the corner.

"Stop!" Mead yelled.

Burton froze.

"Come away from there."

"Is the cushion wet?"

"That's sacred ground."

"What are you talking about?"

"Please. Just sit on the couch."

"Whatever you say. I didn't—" Burton broke into a coughing fit. He held up his index finger until the violent wheezing subsided. "I didn't know."

Burton sat on the end of the couch nearest Mead. A brass lamp on the glass end table between the couch and recliner cast a yellow glow on their faces. Burton's skin looked ashen; his eyes tired.

"Are you all right?" Mead asked. "You don't look too good."

"It's nothing. Probably a touch of bronchitis."

"Sounds more like pneumonia to me."

"You didn't call me over here to ask about my health. So, what's on your mind?"

"Are you still seeing that Parris woman?"

"Professor, we've been through this already."

"I'm not playing, Jonathan."

"Her name is Jessica, and yes I am. Now what?" He threw his hands up in the air. "I suppose you want me to wear a wire."

"I'm not talking to you as a special prosecutor. I'm talking to you as a friend, so please listen to me. I believe your life is in danger."

"Are you insane?" He sprang to his feet.

"Hear me out."

"I don't know what you're trying to pull, but it won't work."

"Sit down and hear me out. I've never steered you wrong before."

"Talk." He dropped back down on the couch.

"This is off the record."

"You don't need the disclaimer with me, Professor. Say your piece."

"I don't know how to say this, so I'm just going to say it. Your little girlfriend is a killer."

"You don't know that for sure."

"I'm not talking about Chesterfield."

"Then who?"

"Her husband."

"What husband?"

"You didn't know she'd been married?"

"What are you talking about?"

"She killed her husband in cold blood."

"Her husband?"

"She skewered his neck, just like Chesterfield." Burton dropped his face into his hands.

"Did you hear what I said?"

"I heard you." He looked up; his face turned a semblance of gray paste. "There must be some mistake."

"No mistake."

"She couldn't... I mean... no way."

"I spoke to the detective this afternoon. She confessed to it."

Silence.

"If it's any consolation," Mead said, "she wasn't indicted. She claimed her husband drove her to it with abuse."

"Yeah, that helps. Let's see, 'Hi John, how ya doing? By the way, you're dating Lizzy Borden. Have a nice day!'"

"In all fairness, she's been a murder suspect for over a week now."

"So am I."

"You're different."

"Why do I feel like we're stuck in a bad Abbott and Costello routine?" He stood up and headed for the door.

"There's a lot you don't know about her."

Burton waved his hands in the air without looking back.

"Walk away from her, John. Do it now."

Burton twisted the knob and cracked the door open. Cold air rushed in. He looked over his shoulder. "I've read about cases like this. It's temporary insanity."

"Do you hear yourself?"

"She's no threat to me," Burton claimed.

"If she's not, your stupidity certainly is."

"I'm a grown man, and I'll live out my days however and with whomever I please." Burton stepped out and slammed the door.

"Foolishness is like bad breath," Mead said, shaking his head. "Everyone knows you've got it but you."

32

Shaker Heights, Ohio
8:50 P.M.

Edward Mead stared at the front door feeling exhausted and dejected. The whole scene seemed surreal, and he couldn't figure out why Jonathan was acting so out of character. He sipped his herbal tea and tried to sort things out. He glanced over at the coffee table where the trial transcripts lay open. Maybe getting back to work would ease his mind. He picked up the loose-leaf pages and started to read....

"Ms. Parris, you may call your next witness," Chesterfield said.

"We have no further witnesses at this time, Your Honor. But the plaintiff respectfully requests the right to call rebuttal witnesses."

"Granted." Chesterfield poured himself another glass of vodka and water. "Is the defense prepared to call its first witness?"

"We are," Burton said.

"Proceed."

Burton walked over to the examiners' podium and said, "The defense calls Paul Alexander."

A tall, thin man stood from about midway back in the gallery then walked toward the front of the room. A close-cropped beard streaked with gray covered his long, angular face. He tripped over his feet climbing the steps to the witness stand. His thick round glasses slid down his nose. He pushed them back up and smoothed his receding black hair.

The bailiff carried the courtroom Bible over to the witness stand. Alexander tentatively placed his right hand on it.

"Do you swear to tell the truth, the whole truth, and nothing but the truth, so help you God?"

"I do."

"You may be seated." The bailiff returned to his post.

"Please state your name for the record," Burton said.

"Paulie Alexander."

"And what is your present occupation?"

"I own a few adult entertainment establishments."

"Strip clubs?"

"Men's clubs."

"And is one of these clubs the Wild Pony?"

"Yeah."

"And have you ever employed a woman named Robin Roget?"

"Yeah."

"And what kind of work did she do for you?"

"She danced."

"Would you care to elaborate on that?"

"She danced real good."

"No, I mean did she dance topless, semi-nude, nude?"

"Oh, she started out dancing topless at the Foxx Trap, another club I own, but we moved her over to the Wild Pony to do the all-nude stuff."

"Why the shift?"

"It's not easy to find hot babes willing to get naked and do private dances. And let's face it, guys ain't going to pay to see some bust-out skeezers."

"For the benefit of the uninitiated on the jury, what precisely is a private dance?"

"That's when one of the girls goes in the back and does a private dance for a client. You know, bumpin' and grindin' kinda stuff."

"And Ms. Roget had no problem making the transition from topless to the more erotic dancing?"

"She took to it like a duck to water. In fact, it was her idea."

"Why would she do that?"

"To make more money."

"Do these lap dances ever include sexual intercourse?"

"Not inside my clubs."

"Mr. Alexander, you're under oath."

"I said not inside my clubs. Now what the girls do with these guys once they leave is their own business, if you know what I mean." He winked at Burton.

"Did Ms. Roget have sex with the patrons outside of your clubs?"

"Objection," Parris said.

"Overruled." Chesterfield nodded toward the witness. "Answer the question."

"The two bouncers I sent with her to the bachelor parties said—"

"Objection!" Parris yelled. "Hearsay."

"Overruled."

"What did the bouncers say?" Burton asked.

"They said, if the men didn't pay her for sex, she'd probably pay them. She was a straight freak."

Mrs. Roget dropped her chin to her chest. Parris patted her on the back and whispered something in her ear.

"Mr. Alexander, do you know if Ms. Roget used drugs during the time she worked for you?"

"Objection, relevance."

"Overruled."

"Yeah, she did."

"What kind of drugs?"

"Crystal-meth, ecstasy, crack. I warned her a couple

times about it. Told her if I caught her bringing the stuff into the club, I'd fire her on the spot. I ain't gettin' my license yanked over some ditzy crackhead."

"Did she stop after you warned her?"

"I don't know if she stopped, but I never caught her with the stuff again."

"So, to encapsulate your testimony, is it fair to say that Ms. Roget was a nude-dancing, drug-using, sex addict?"

"Objection!" Parris nearly kicked over her chair as she jumped to her feet.

"On what grounds?" Burton said. "You heard the testimony, sir. I'm not making this stuff up."

"Overruled."

"But Your Honor—"

"Are you challenging me in my courtroom?"

"No, Your Honor." Parris' gaze impaled him.

"I didn't think so."

"I have no further questions," Burton said and returned to his seat.

"Does the plaintiff wish to cross-examine the witness?"

"You bet I do." Parris then strode to the podium and grabbed it so tightly that her knuckles turned white. "Mr. Alexander, you seem to know a great deal about Robin Roget. Did you know she was a mother?"

"No."

"Oh, you didn't. Now that's surprising. So, you didn't know that when she wasn't exploiting her body to fill your pockets, she was raising a pair of children?"

"The only pair I knew she raised was them long legs, if you know what I mean."

Laughter filled the gallery. Chesterfield snickered.

"Mr. Alexander, did you ever have sex with Ms. Roget?"

"I... ur..."

"Well, did you?"

He looked over at Burton, who shrugged and

sheepishly said, "Objection."

"You've got to be kidding me," Chesterfield said. "This is finally getting good. Answer the question."

"Yeah, I nailed her. So what?"

"Did you use protection?"

"Condoms ain't my bag, if you know what I mean."

"Then it's safe to assume you didn't know she had active cases of gonorrhea and syphilis at the time of her death."

Alexander squirmed in his seat; the color drained from his face.

"Have you had yourself checked lately?"

"I... ur..."

"No further questions."

"The witness may step down." Chesterfield leaned over and slapped Alexander on the back. "She gave you the gift that keeps on giving."

Chesterfield burst into a laugh that showed all his teeth and made his face look like the muzzle of a wolf.

33

Wednesday, February 3
Anthony J. Celebrezze Federal Building
Cleveland, Ohio
8:40 A.M.

E dward Mead stepped into the interrogation room behind Sarah Riehl. An oppressive, airless smell pervaded the tiny cube, a combination of wet dog and old people. Dingy white paint covered the walls. No windows. A square table was bolted to the tile floor; circular brown stains covered the Formica top, no doubt the result of coffee spills from days gone by. A black plastic ashtray filled to the brim sat on the edge of the table closest to the door. Two rusted, metal folding chairs were tucked under opposite sides; a third leaned against the far wall.

"I'm guessing we're here because the subterranean torture chamber was already taken?" Mead said.

"I want to make Parris feel as uncomfortable as possible."

"This should do the trick."

"These basement rooms aren't used very often. Most agents prefer the state-of-the-art studios on the 3rd floor."

"I can see why."

Sarah adjusted the thermostat on the wall near the door. The blower kicked on; a red streamer tied to the overhead vent fluttered to life. The initial gust added a musty tinge to the potpourri.

"Try to keep the first few questions subtle," he said. "I want to disarm her if at all possible."

"You're the boss."

"Thanks again for dinner the other night. I haven't been out since... well, you know."

"Don't mention it. My husband loves you."

Mead slid his hand into his pocket, pulled out a handkerchief, and dusted off the chair before sitting down. He watched Sarah pace about the room, checking her watch, and whispering questions to herself. The closer it got to 9 o'clock, the more flushed her face became.

Someone knocked on the door.

"Come in," Sarah yelled.

Parris strolled in with a leather briefcase in one hand and a tan overcoat in the other.

"Sit down," Sarah said.

Parris calmly obeyed. She crossed her legs and adjusted her black wool skirt over her knee. "Is this when you insert bamboo shoots under my nails?"

"Cut the crap," Sarah said. "Why didn't you tell us you murdered your husband?"

So much for subtlety, Mead thought.

"I guess it slipped my mind."

Sarah slammed both hands on the table and leaned halfway across it. "Don't play with me. You're a slap away from being arrested, and I'll be more than happy to do the slapping."

Parris leaned back in her chair and crossed her arms. A smirk appeared on her face. "Are you threatening me?"

"Why didn't you tell us about your little body count?"

"First of all, I didn't murder my husband; I was never charged, and secondly, I have Fifth Amendment rights."

"So, you admit killing Chesterfield?"

"All I'm saying is if I would've offered unrelated, irrelevant information concerning my husband's death —"

"Both men were stabbed in the throat. I'd say that's relevant."

"See. You've already jumped to the wrong conclusion."

"Why don't you just confess and make this whole thing a lot easier on all of us?"

"Why don't you bite me?"

Thwack! Sarah thumped her fist on the table, every feature in her face twitching.

"Ladies, ladies, please," Mead said. "We're all professionals here. No one is going to slap or bite anyone. Why don't you sit down, Sarah?"

"I'll stand."

"Suit yourself." He paused then dusted the elbow of his coat. "Now, Ms. Parris, why don't we back up here and start with some basic information?"

"Whatever."

"Please describe Judge Chesterfield's office for me."

"You want me to tell you how it was decorated?"

"Just tell me what you remember."

"It was a typical male attempt at a power office." Parris kept her eyes glued on Sarah. "Gold carpet. The lighting was a complete disaster. And he had that copy of *Cleveland Magazine* hanging on the wall, the one with his face on the cover."

"What about the desk?"

"The man was a disorganized swine most of the time."

"Did you happen to notice the letter opener?"

"Of course I noticed it." Her face looked calm, except for an almost imperceptible twitching of her upper lip. "I bought it for him."

"You what?" Sarah asked.

"I gave it to him the first Christmas I worked there."

"An odd gift, don't you think?"

"He was an odd kind of guy."

"Yeah, right." Sarah walked over to the side of the table and looked down on Parris. "Do you expect us to believe it was just a coincidence that Chesterfield got killed with the Christmas gift you bought him?"

"No, it would've been a coincidence if I bought him a gun, and he ended up being shot with it. I bought the man an antique letter opener."

"It's a dagger," Sarah said.

"It's used to open letters. That's why they call it a letter opener."

Sarah backed away from the table and leaned against the wall. She bent one leg under and kicked her shoe, adding another scuff to the collection on the wall.

A banging sound directed everyone's attention to the overhead vent. The streamer went limp. Once the noise subsided, Mead continued. "Ms. Parris, do you think that things are more like they are now than they've ever been?"

"What? I guess so... what was the question?"

"Nothing. How is your law firm doing financially?"

"It's all right."

"How much do you have wrapped up in the Roget case?"

"I couldn't venture to guess."

"With all the filing fees, service fees, discovery, depositions, document preparation, investigation, research, telephone calls, medical experts, etcetera, etcetera, etcetera," Mead said, waving his hand, "you've probably got a small fortune tied up in this case."

"I've probably spent $50,000 so far."

"That's a lot of money."

"You've got to spend money to make money."

"Do you think Chesterfield fixed the case?"

"That's an interesting question." Lines of strain appeared around her eyes. "I can't say for sure, but I'll say this much. His judicial philosophy seemed to be aimed at subverting my case whenever he could."

"Why do you say that?"

"He wouldn't let half of my witnesses testify. I mean they testified, but not in front of the jury. They were pretty much my entire case, and he knew it."

Sarah leaned over Mead's shoulders. "What about the dead husband? I'd like to hear more about that."

"We can talk about it if you want." Her face darkened; a painful look came into her eyes. "Tom abused me for 18 straight months. He made my life a living hell. It wasn't always that way, though. He treated me like a queen when we dated. I thought he loved me; I really thought he loved me. But once we got married, everything changed. He lost his temper all the time, and I couldn't seem to do anything right. He would scream in my face and call me names."

The cadence of her voice quickened. "Then after a while he got rough. He'd slap me if dinner was late. A couple of times I had to take off work until the swelling in my face went down. And the violence carried over into the bedroom too. If I complained, he'd tie me to the bed and have his way with me for hours at a time. He made me do all kinds of degrading things. It turned into rape, straight rape." Her voice quivered; tears glittered on her eyelashes.

"Then one day... I can't get that day out of my mind. He came home from the office drunk as usual. I met him at the door with a smile, and wham, he backhanded me. It felt like my eye exploded. I said, 'What was that for?' He said, 'I'm sure you'll do something to piss me off tonight, so I thought I'd get it out of the way now.' Then he laughed in my face with his stinking Scotch breath. I went over to the sink to finish peeling the carrots. He went through the mail. He found some bill - I don't remember which one - and he went berserk. He charged me. He went for my throat. I didn't mean to. The knife... it... it was self-defense. An accident."

"Which was it?" Sarah asked. "An accident or self-defense?"

"An accident... it happened so fast... maybe both."

"If he was so abusive, why didn't you divorce him?"

"I couldn't. I mean, he wouldn't let me."

"You're an educated, intelligent woman, and that's the best you can do - he wouldn't let you?" Sarah said.

"I don't care if you believe me or not, it's the truth. You weren't there. I can't explain it, but I loved him."

"Do you love Jonathan Burton?" Mead asked.

"What?" Her eyes opened wide. "What kind of question is that?"

"The kind I want an answer to."

"I really don't see the relevance here."

"Answer the question," Mead said.

"I'm not going to articulate for you what I've not yet shared with him."

"So, you do love him?"

"I'm not going to parse my statement."

"Yes or no."

"I said, I'm not going to parse my statement." Parris' eyes darted from Mead to Sarah and back to Mead. She crossed and uncrossed her legs.

"That's all the questions we have for you at this time," Mead said. "Thanks for your cooperation."

"I still have a few questions," Sarah said.

"But those can wait for another day." Mead stood and reached out his hand. "Ms. Parris, you're free to go."

Jessica Parris stood and shook his hand. She straightened her plaid blazer, picked up her briefcase and coat, and headed for the door. She glared at Sarah when she walked past, but Mead thought he noticed the corner of her mouth turn up into a faint smile before she slammed the door behind her.

"How could you just let her walk away?" Sarah said. "We should be slapping cuffs on her."

"On what grounds?"

"She purchased the murder weapon. What more do you want?"

"She bought the thing ten years ago."

"It's a start."

"If we arrest her right now, the entire investigation will be tainted. We'd manipulate the facts to fit our theory."

"You didn't buy that sob story, did you?"

"I'd rather let the facts speak for themselves."

"I think you're making a mistake. The woman's a Black Widow."

The knocking returned. A gush of stale air sent the red streamer fluttering again.

"Sarah, this is what I want you to do. Dig up every shred of financial information you can find on our lovely Ms. Parris. I've got a feeling she's been less than forthcoming."

"I'd rather be wiping the floor up with her smug, little, lying face."

34

Cleveland, Ohio
10:45 A.M.

E dward Mead watched Sarah Riehl walk away, leaving him alone in the tiny room to interrogate his thoughts. He slouched down in the chair, tipped his head back, and focused his attention on the red streamer warring against its tether. It occurred to him that some people were just like that little piece of plastic; they weren't happy unless they were fighting against the very things that gave them stability and meaning. Such people live through years of abandonment and abuse and cycles of profound self-destruction. Sure, they did all right for short stretches of time, but just when it seemed they were about to finally break free from that disastrous prison, the ruinous specter of self-loathing pounced and dragged them back down into the slough of despondency. Reaching out to those people was as dangerous as trying to save a drowning person; they were liable to pull their would-be rescuers down with them. Edward Mead considered Jessica Parris one of these people.

He straightened his neck to the telltale pops and cracks of osteoarthritis. A spasm shot down his left arm, causing his fingers to contract and pulsate. He labored to his feet. Spikes of pain shot through his knees as if broken pieces of glass were embedded in the joints. The discomfort passed nearly unnoticed; pain had become a way of life.

His feet felt weighted as he walked out of the tiny room, his shoes echoing through the sterile hallway. He tried to recall a time when it didn't hurt just to live. But then again, the anatomical distress paled in comparison to the agony of life without Victoria. How do you go on living when your heart is ripped from your chest? How do you withstand the onslaught of days with a sword stuck in your soul? Death is no longer the enemy when it unites instead of divides; it becomes a welcome friend.

Mead pulled open the heavy steel door leading to the parking garage. The wintry air watered his eyes. He squinted and scanned the shadowy concrete deck. His car waited a few spaces to the right. He opened the door, slid into the crushed velvet seat, and twisted the key. The engine sputtered but wouldn't fire. He tried again. Nothing. On the third attempt the engine revved. He put the car in gear and negotiated the winding exit ramp. He caught a glimpse of his reflection in the glass-sided tollbooth. All he could see was the top of his hat and his gloved knuckles on the wheel.

It finally happened, he thought. *I'm the butt of my own jokes.*

For years he loved ribbing the older faculty members about their penchant for riding low and driving slow. And now here he sat with nothing visible to the outside world but a hat and knuckles. Where did the time go?

He steered his car toward the Justice Center and pondered the nature of time. He remembered reading somewhere that time is an irreversible continuum used to measure the duration of moving bodies in space. And because the continuum can be divided into smaller, identifiable segments - like minutes and seconds - time must be constant. But that didn't seem to fit his own experience. In fact, time didn't seem to be constant at all. When he was a kid, a 20-minute activity, like a trip to the grocery store with his mother, seemed to take about three hours. But now at age 77 the same 20 minutes flew by in an instant. *Could it be that a child's mind, with its rapidly growing number of untainted brain cells, is capable of processing vastly higher numbers of thoughts per second so that time appears to creep along? Whereas the antiquated mind, with its neurological network worn down from years of activity, is only capable of processing a few thoughts per second, therefore leading to the perception of time ticking away much faster? If consciousness is held constant, then time itself is a variable that changes at the rate of thoughts per second.*

"That's pretty good," he said out loud. "I should write that down before I forget."

He searched the front seat for a piece of scrap paper and looked up in time to see the Justice Center up ahead on the right. He parked the car and went inside to pick up the day's transcription, only to discover it had already been sent to his office at the law school. He climbed back into his car and headed for University Circle. Twenty minutes later he parked in his reserved spot off Bellflower Road near the Peter B. Lewis Building. While the university touted the building as an architectural gem, he thought it looked like a metallic bow tie that clashed with the surrounding neighborhood. He walked past the eyesore to the law school next door.

The temperature had climbed to a balmy 32 degrees, and the wind had all but vanished. He found his office empty and figured the staff must be out to lunch. The bundle from the courthouse jutted from his mail tray. Since the weather looked so nice, and he needed the exercise, he tucked the brown envelope under his arm and headed off to Sears Library on foot.

The sidewalks were clear behind the law school but turned icy on the narrow path leading to the rear of the student center. The fresh salt sounded like Rice Krispies in milk as it ate through the layers of ice. He crossed Euclid Avenue in front of Severance Hall, and his stomach rumbled.

He checked his watch. It had been over 16 hours since his last meal. He followed a group of students along the sidewalk until he reached the main entrance to University Hospital. He figured the cafeteria would be a good place to read the transcript, and a bowl of vegetable soup would hit the spot.

He dawdled along the corridors deep in thought, oblivious to the rush of activity surrounding him. He navigated the maze-like halls as if on autopilot, until he found himself in the Ireland Cancer Center, where Victoria suffered through so many experimental treatments. He turned around and stared at the sign above the door, wondering how he got there, when he heard a familiar bronchial, asthmatic, hacking cough.

Mead turned toward the sound, his line of sight obscured by a group of nurses huddled in front of the receptionist's desk. He stretched his neck over the group and made out the faint outline of a gray cashmere overcoat, and he thought he could see the man holding up an index finger.

"Can I help you, sir?" a reedy voice asked.

He felt a touch on the elbow and turned to see a young Candy Striper smiling at him.

"I'm on my way to the cafeteria."

"It's on the other side of the building. I can show you the way, if you like."

"I know where it is." He turned back around.

The group of nurses had dispersed, and the cougher was gone.

35

Cleveland, Ohio
12:55 P.M.

E dward Mead looked around at the teeming humanity in the University Hospital cafeteria and decided to get his soup to go.

He trudged across the slush-covered Adelbert Road en route to his comfortable hideaway in Sears Library. Instead of his usual table overlooking the brick-paved quad, he sat on the Martin Luther King Jr. Drive side of the building. He spread open the transcript on the table and turned his attention to his lunch. He lifted the Styrofoam bowl to his lips and slurped a gulp of vegetable broth. He wiped his mouth, then began to read....

"Is the defense ready to call its next witness?" Chesterfield asked.

"We are, Your Honor," Rutledge said.

"Proceed."

"Thank you, Your Honor." Rutledge stood and buttoned his glen plaid sport coat, then walked to the examiners' podium carrying a manila folder. He adjusted his glasses, blinked a few times, and cracked his knuckles.

"The defense calls Dr. Kathleen Zigler."

A thin, middle-aged woman walked to the front of the room wearing a black pinstriped skirt, matching blazer, and a forest green turtleneck. Her coarse, almost black

196

hair curled like lamb's wool and formed a huge cap on her head. Her small, mean, pursed-up lips were coated with an ample dose of red lipstick. She nodded to the judge before taking her seat. The bailiff administered the oath and returned to his position near the door.

"State your name, please," Rutledge said.

"Dr. Kathleen Zigler, that's Z-I-G-L-E-R."

"And your occupation?"

"I'm the director of the Abortion Surveillance Branch of the Centers for Disease Control."

"Is that a part of the federal Department of Health and Human Services?"

"It is."

"How long have you held that position?"

"Fifteen years."

"And what is your role at the Abortion Surveillance Branch of the CDC?"

"We classify and investigate reported claims of abortion abuse, and we assess the preventability of abortion-related deaths."

"Have you had the opportunity to review the autopsy and postmortem data in the Roget case?"

"I have."

"Do you recall the coroner's ruling in that case?"

"I believe he ruled the cause of death to be septicemia due to incomplete abortion."

"And in your expert opinion, is that ruling correct?"

"No."

"What do you believe the correct ruling should have been?"

"Cardiac arrest caused by an acute combination of bacterium Neisseria gonorrhoeae and bacterium Treponema pallidum in the bloodstream."

"And for the benefit of the jury, could you explain that in layman's terms?"

"Certainly. Bacterium Neisseria gonorrhoeae is the

clinical term for gonorrhea. Bacterium Treponema pallidum is syphilis. Both are incredibly dangerous bacterium, and if left untreated are lethal."

"What are some of the symptoms for the infection?"

"The symptoms vary. In some women, gonorrhea causes frequent and painful urination, along with pus-like discharge from the vagina or urethra. The disease can spread through the bloodstream to cause infection in other parts of the body."

"Did Ms. Roget display these symptoms?"

"She did, but hers were negligible. Some women only experience a slight increase in vaginal discharge and some inflammation, and many aren't aware they have the disease."

"But you said her case was severe."

"Severe indeed. However, the seriousness of symptoms doesn't always correlate with the severity of the case. Her bloodstream revealed an acute case."

"And the syphilis?"

"Syphilis is a complex disease. The organism gains access to the body through a minor cut or abrasion in the skin or mucous membranes. Early treatment is vital. In the primary stage, sores appear on the genitals and rectum. Rash and lesions develop during the second stage. After a latent, hidden stage, the final stage brings with it numerous complications in all parts of the body - and can include blindness, mental disorders, nerve and heart problems, and death."

"The coroner testified Ms. Roget suffered from stage one syphilis. Do you agree?"

"No."

"Please explain."

"Sometimes the infection goes through intermediate periods when no symptoms are present. But the bacterium continues to spread through the body. These "remissions" occur between the first and fourth stages.

Based on the blood tests and the autopsy photos, I would say that Ms. Roget had just come out of the latent stage, and sores were beginning to reemerge in the final stage."

"Could this latent period account for the variance between your ruling and that of the coroner?"

"I believe so. I'm sure the presence of sepsis in the bloodstream probably masked the presence of the other pathogens. Someone not thoroughly trained in the field of infectious disease could easily overlook something like this."

"Allow me to shift your attention to the events surrounding Ms. Roget's abortion. Dr. Zigler, is it standard protocol for women seeking abortions to fill out a medical history questionnaire?"

"It is."

"And have you had the opportunity to review Ms. Roget's questionnaire?"

"I have."

"Your Honor, the defense would like to submit a copy of the questionnaire as defense exhibit A."

"Granted," Chesterfield said with a yawn.

Rutledge produced two copies of the questionnaire from the manila file on the podium. He walked over and handed a copy to the bailiff and the other to the witness.

"Dr. Zigler, I'd like to direct your attention to question number seven. Do you see the question I'm referring to?"

"I do."

"Please read the question and the answer Ms. Roget gave."

"The question reads: Do you presently have or have you ever received treatment for any sexually transmitted diseases? Ms. Roget answered no."

"That's curious, yet she suffered from both gonorrhea and syphilis. Why do you think she lied?"

"Objection!" Parris shouted.

"Sustained. Ask another question."

"Yes, Your Honor. Dr. Zigler, given Ms. Roget's answers on the questionnaire and the mildness of her symptoms, would Dr. Baird - or any other prudent physician - have reason to suspect the presence of such diseases?"

"Physicians routinely rely on their patients being truthful. So, to answer your question, no, he'd have no reason to suspect she was anything but truthful."

"I see," Rutledge said. "And in your expert opinion, did Ms. Roget's intentional misrepresentation ultimately contribute to her death?"

"Objection," Parris said. "Conjecture."

"Overruled."

"By withholding such vital information from her physician," Dr. Zigler said, "Ms. Roget certainly contributed to her own death. Yes."

"I have no further questions, Your Honor."

Rutledge scanned the jury before returning to his seat. Some faces looked attentive, some disinterested, and some were sound asleep.

"The witness is yours, Ms. Parris," Chesterfield said.

"Thank you, Your Honor." She strode to the podium, her black pumps tapping on the hardwood floor. "Dr. Zigler, I don't have the benefit of a medical education, so please bear with me."

The witness nodded.

"Dr. Zigler, when did the Center for Disease Control get involved in the Roget case?"

"A few months ago. Mr. Burton contacted me."

"So, you didn't investigate the case on your own?"

"No, we didn't."

"But I thought you said it's your responsibility to investigate all abortion-related deaths. How is it this case slipped through your fingers?"

"Nothing slipped by us."

"Then why didn't you investigate it on your own?"

"Because it's not an abortion-related death."

"Excuse me." Parris gripped the sides of the podium. "Did you say Robin's death was not abortion-related?"

"That's correct. She died of complications from gonorrhea and—"

"Yeah, I know, and syphilis. I heard you the first ten times. But the official report said it was abortion-related."

"The autopsy was wrong."

"But you couldn't have known that before you investigated. Or did you just guess the autopsy was wrong when it came across your desk in Atlanta?"

"Objection," Rutledge said.

"I withdraw the question."

Zigler crossed her arms.

"Dr. Zigler, are syphilis and gonorrhea curable?"

"If caught and treated early enough."

"What's the standard treatment?"

"Penicillin and antibiotic therapy."

"Did the autopsy show the presence of antibiotics?"

"I don't think so, no."

"Isn't that odd?"

"I don't understand the question."

"Well, if she knew that she had these diseases, why wouldn't she seek treatment?"

"Objection," Rutledge said. "The witness can't speak for the deceased."

"Sustained."

"Well, Dr. Zigler, I'll rephrase the question. Is it possible that Robin Roget didn't know she had these diseases, and therefore didn't know to get treatment?"

"It's conceivable, but unlikely. We're talking about pus-like discharges and itching sores. She'd have to be a complete moron not to know something was wrong."

"But you said the symptoms could be so mild that many women don't realize they have the infections."

"Hers wasn't a mild case."

"But it is possible that Robin didn't know she was

infected?"

"Possible but not plausible."

"Nevertheless, if she didn't know she was infected, then she couldn't have lied on the questionnaire. Therefore, she couldn't have knowingly contributed to her own death."

"Objection!" Rutledge leapt to his feet, blinking both eyes. "Counsel is lecturing the witness, not examining her."

"Sustained."

Parris reviewed her notes. "Dr. Zigler, are you a member of the American Abortion Rights Action League?"

"I am."

"And you work for the Abortion Surveillance Branch of the Center for Disease Control?"

"I do."

"Isn't that a conflict of interest?"

"No."

"You don't believe that promoting abortion on the one hand, and policing it on the other is a conflict?"

"Objection," Rutledge said. "The witness has already answered the question."

"Sustained."

"Dr. Zigler, would it be a conflict of interest for the president of a tobacco company to be assigned the task of determining if cigarette smoke is a danger to public health?"

"I... I don't see a conflict. Professionals can look past personal interest in the performance of their duties."

"Yeah, right." Parris rolled her eyes.

"It's true, I say."

"Getting back to the Roget abortion. You testified earlier that you reviewed the autopsy issued by the Cuyahoga County Coroner, did you not?"

"I did."

"So, you're aware..." Parris shuffled through some papers until finding the autopsy report. "That Dr. McCorkle found a large rupture at the base of Robin's uterus?"

"I am."

"And you're aware that Dr. Baird pulled approximately 14 inches of small intestine into Robin's vaginal cavity?"

"I am."

"And you're aware that Dr. McCorkle found the head and torso of the aborted baby thrust inside her abdominal cavity?"

"I am."

"And yet you claim this... this... wholesale slaughter didn't lead to Robin's death?"

"Objection," Rutledge said. "Argumentative."

"Overruled," Chesterfield said. "The witness will answer the question."

"I believe a woman with a healthy immune system would have survived such post-surgical trauma." Dr. Zigler crossed her arms, bumping the microphone in the process. "In Ms. Roget's case it didn't matter if the perforation was the size of a pin or a pear, the gonorrhea and syphilis gained direct access to her bloodstream and attacked her heart, lungs and kidneys."

"Are you certain of this diagnosis?"

"I'm confident that—"

"We can have the body exhumed."

"You asked my opinion."

"And in your opinion, is Dr. Baird guilty of medical malpractice?"

"In my opinion—"

Rutledge cleared his throat.

Zigler looked over at him, then said, "The evidence is inconclusive."

"You've got to be kidding me."

"I gave you my answer."

"Dr. Zigler, have you ever performed an abortion?"

"I have."

"Do you consider yourself one of the country's premier abortionists?"

"No."

"But you are competent?"

"I am."

"Have you ever perforated the uterus of one of your patients?"

"No."

"Is it medical malpractice for an abortionist to perforate a patient's uterus?"

"Perforations are a common side effect. In fact, I read a recent study from India that found one of every 250 abortions performed in a hospital ended with a perforated uterus."

"But is it malpractice?"

"In my opinion, no, it isn't."

"Is it malpractice for a doctor to pull over a dozen inches of intestine into his patient's vaginal cavity then release her without notifying her or advising her to seek emergency treatment?"

Zigler's lips moved; she cast a glance at Rutledge. He shook his head.

"No, it isn't," she said.

"Is it malpractice for a doctor to perform abortions while drunk or high on drugs?"

"Objection."

"Sustained."

"What if a doctor cuts open his patient's chest and eats her heart. I suppose that wouldn't be malpractice in your opinion, either?"

"Objection!" Rutledge shouted. "She's badgering the witness."

"Sustained," Chesterfield said. "Another question like that will land you in jail."

"Your Honor, the witness is responsible for abortion oversight, yet she's clearly attempting to mislead the jury."

"Examine the witness or sit down."

"Yes, Your Honor." Parris stood with her hands on her hips, her nostrils flaring. "Dr. Zigler, I have one final question. If you were pregnant and wanted an abortion, would you allow Dr. Baird to operate on you?"

"I believe he's competent."

"But would you let him operate on you?"

The witness paused.

"Dr. Zigler?"

"Sure, why not?"

Parris shook her head, and with a tone of disgust said, "I have no further questions, Your Honor."

36

Sarah Riehl stopped at the vending machines in the Sears Library lobby and bought a Diet Coke and a bag of Doritos. She walked past the circulation desk and boarded the elevator. As the doors closed, the can slipped from her hand and thumped on the floor near her feet. She picked it up and wiped it on her pants. A few moments later the doors opened on the top floor. A dank, musty scent soured her face. She felt a sneeze coming on.

The dust mites must be having a field day up here, she thought.

Floor-to-ceiling bookshelves stood in precise rows like overgrown dominoes. She stepped off the elevator, made a left around the corner and proceeded to the table where she had last found Professor Mead.

"He's not here," she said. "That's odd."

She looked out the window at the bundled–up students milling around from building to building with backpacks slung over their shoulders. She sat down, ripped open the Doritos and popped one in her mouth. She chewed slowly while staring across the quad at the Physics building. She groped around the table for the Diet Coke. Her fingers found the cold, wet aluminum and pulled the tab. A geyser of carbonated water and saccharin erupted.

"Shoot!"

She rummaged through her bag for something to mop up the mess.

A fisted hand reached over her shoulder and offered a handkerchief.

"Here you go," the male voice said.

She turned to see the smiling face of Edward Mead.

"Where'd you come from?"

"Over there."

"I thought this was your table." She took the handkerchief and sopped up the foaming puddle until the white cloth turned brown.

"I've sat at this table for over 20 years," he said. "But today I felt like I needed a fresh perspective."

"Sorry about your hanky."

"Don't worry about it. I've got a drawer full of them." He eased himself into the chair across from her.

"I've got the financial information you wanted on Parris." Sarah pulled a brown envelope from her bag. "She's practically bankrupt. Every penny to her name is wrapped up in the Roget case. And get this, a week before Chesterfield bought the farm, she took out a personal loan to pay her office lease."

"That's what I thought."

"I smell motive."

"That's probably my breath. I had some for lunch."

"You had what for lunch?"

"Mushrooms."

"I said motive. I smell motive!"

"Oh. Hearing's not what it used to be."

"I think you do that on purpose."

"What?"

"Act confused."

"You're perceptive." He lifted an amused eyebrow. "Now, let's hear your motive theory."

"The way I see it, Parris put all her eggs in one basket,

and Chesterfield smashed them. She believes he fixed the case - a case she literally can't afford to lose - so she kills him. The case is declared a mistrial, and she keeps her head above water until a new judge is assigned to the case."

"That sounds about right, with one tiny exception."

"What's that?" she asked.

"That's not her M.O."

"Why isn't it?"

"She killed her husband out of desperation and self-defense."

"If you believe her story."

"Her story is—"

"Personally, I don't."

"Whether she killed her husband in cold blood or in self-defense, she acted out of passion to stop being abused. The Chesterfield murder is completely different."

Sarah picked up the bag of Doritos and tossed a couple in her mouth. She crunched for awhile then said, "It's not different at all. Chesterfield abused her by fixing the case. He made her feel helpless and trapped, so she lashed out."

"Judicial abuse is a far cry from sexual abuse."

"Yeah, but don't forget Parris had a sexual relationship with Chesterfield. Who knows what kind of sadistic things he did to her?"

"She said he wasn't abusive."

"She's a liar."

"Even liars tell the truth when it serves them best." Mead rubbed his thumb and forefinger over his eyes. An eyelash fell and stuck to his chin. "How much do you suppose Ms. Parris weighs?"

"There you go again."

"I'm serious."

"I don't know... 120 maybe."

"I'd guess about 117. I could always guess Victoria's weight within a pound."

"And your point is?"

"Parris is a small woman, not really athletically built either. She may not be physically capable of committing this crime. Do you have any idea how much force it takes to drive a letter opener through a man's neck and pin him to a chair?"

"The throat is pretty soft tissue." She pressed her fingers over the side of her windpipe. "And the blade didn't hit any bone. With her adrenalin flowing, she could easily have done it."

"Perhaps."

"Are you leaning toward King again? He's got to weigh 300 pounds."

"It's not his M.O. either. King snapped out of fear."

"Again, if you believe him."

"Chesterfield's murder was an act of aggression."

"Maybe King is passive-aggressive."

"He very well may be," Mead said.

"Well, if you don't think Parris or King did it, who did? Your buddy Burton?"

"I'm not ruling anyone out at this point. What I want is some hard evidence."

"The profilers tell me the psych workups on Parris and King are almost complete. We could have them as early as tomorrow."

"Good, very good."

"Those things are so accurate it's creepy. When I was at the academy, we studied the Ted Bundy profile. They even predicted the kind of food he liked."

"The profiles definitely should shed some light." His eyebrows furrowed together.

"Something on your mind, Professor?"

"Yeah, have you ever noticed the word *verb* is actually a noun?"

37

Cleveland, Ohio
3:35 P.M.

E dward Mead strolled out the front door of Sears Library and instantly regretted his earlier decision to walk over from his office. The sun glowed deceptively bright, but the temperature had plummeted throughout the afternoon. Strong wind gusts picked up tiny ice crystals from the blanket of snow and blew them in horizontal sheets. Mead tucked his chin and heard the frozen pellets rattle off his fedora.

He cut across the quad and followed the winding sidewalk around Yost Hall to Adelbert Road. A hot dog vendor nodded to him, then slid open the lid on his cart, allowing the tart scent of sauerkraut to escape with the billowing steam. Mead took a big whiff, then stepped off the curb between two parked cars.

Beep! Beep!

He stumbled back.

Jonathan Burton waved from behind the steering wheel of his black Mercedes Benz and motioned for Mead to swing around to the passenger side door. Mead obeyed, opened the passenger door and climbed in.

"What are you trying to do, give me a heart attack?" Mead said.

"Where you going? I'll give you a lift."

"My office."

Burton pulled out behind a green van and followed it to the Euclid Avenue intersection. The light turned red, and a stream of students flooded across the walkway. Burton rippled his gloved fingers on the walnut steering wheel.

"Mind if we take the scenic route?" Burton asked. "I've got something to talk to you about."

"I'm in no hurry."

Burton adjusted the heater, then said, "Do you remember the time we put that bathroom in your basement?"

"About 15 years ago, wasn't it?"

"You spray painted the overhead pipes while I sanded the drywall joints."

"Boy, what a mess," Mead said.

"The dust mixed with the black paint and got all in your hair and eyebrows."

"Victoria said I looked 20 years younger."

"You looked like Moses coming down the mountain."

"I remember you convinced me not to hire a plumber, because you said you could install the toilet yourself."

"I got it in, didn't I?"

"The thing tilted back so far I didn't know if I should rip it out or buy a set of handlebars for it."

Burton laughed, winced, then placed his right hand on his side. "We've shared some good times."

The light turned green. They made a left on Euclid, then a quick right on Martin Luther King Jr. Drive. The former Mount Sinai Hospital with its gaudy purple exterior sat on the hill to the left.

"You wanted to talk to me about my plumbing?" Mead asked.

"Not exactly."

"What's on your mind, Jonathan?"

"This is friend to friend, off the record?"

"Sure."

"Promise me you won't act on anything I say, at least not for 24 hours."

"What is it?"

"Do I have your word?"

"You have my word."

Burton took a deep breath. "This has been heavy on my heart for awhile now. I've wanted to tell you - I really did - but you've been through so much."

"What is it?"

"I haven't been completely honest with you."

"About what?"

"Lots of things."

"Like..."

"Well, for starters, do you remember the reason I told you I missed Victoria's funeral?"

"You said you were out of town on business."

"Yeah, well, that's only partially true. I was in Philadelphia, just not on business. I went for some experimental treatments, frog eggs injected with herpes virus. They—"

"Whoa there. Experimental treatments for what?"

"I thought you knew."

"Knew what?"

"How could you not know? You followed me today."

"What are you talking about?"

"Today at the Cancer Center. You followed me."

"I didn't."

"Then why were you there?"

"I was on my way to the cafeteria and just ended up there. My mind was somewhere else."

"Then you don't know."

"I'm getting a little tired of this."

"Professor, six months ago I was diagnosed with malignant pleural mesothelioma."

"Cancer?"

"From asbestos."

"Good Lord." A look of pain covered Mead's face. He leaned back, his body rigid. "Why didn't you tell me?"

"You had your hands full with Victoria."

"How did you get exposed to asbestos?"

"I worked in the shipyards during the summers when I was in college. They had me mixing asbestos in big plastic buckets and lining the boiler pipes with it by hand. No masks, no respirators, nothing. Who knew?"

"What are the doctors saying?"

"Let me put it this way. Life expectancy is about 12 months after diagnosis. The tumor encapsulates the lungs; they fill with fluid. It's completely inoperable."

"Can they slow it?"

"Maybe a little. They've packed my lungs with a medicated powder. It seems to have helped, but I still have to go in and have my lungs tapped every few weeks. That's why I was at the hospital today."

"I can't believe it, Jonathan. I don't know what to say."

"There's nothing to say."

"How long do you have?"

"Maybe six months... maybe. I used to pray for a miracle; now I pray it won't be too painful."

Silence filled the car as it weaved along the winding road past the snow-covered Cultural Gardens. Mead felt nauseous. He thought about the day Victoria gave him the tragic news. Something surged up from his heart; his soul quivered; he wanted to sob. Cancer had struck again; it was happening again. A shiver ran up his spine like a hand of ice had squeezed his heart.

Burton slowed the car to a near halt, checked both ways, then made a U-turn. Mead gave him a funny look.

"What are they going to do, give me a ticket? I won't live to pay it."

"You've got to have hope. Victoria didn't give up. You never know what tomorrow may bring."

"Believe me, I have a pretty good idea of what

tomorrow's going to bring."

Another long silence followed. They didn't speak for nearly a minute as the car passed through the ornamental, arched underpasses built from Depression-era brick. They made a left on Chester, a left on Euclid, and continued on solemnly until they reached Severance Hall.

"I don't know what Tony was thinking to get me involved in this case," Mead said.

"He thought it would be good for you."

"How do you know?"

"I called him last week."

"I didn't think you and the Attorney General were on speaking terms these days."

"What can I say? I've been burying a few hatchets. Anyway, he wanted to give you a reason to get out of the house. Plus, he thought I'd help you if I could."

"Remind me to slap him the next time I see him."

"So, tell me, Mr. Special Prosecutor, do you know who did it?"

"I've known since the first night."

"That's what I thought. I just can't figure out why you haven't arrested anyone yet."

"Soon, maybe tomorrow."

"So, you don't need my help?"

"This isn't that tough."

"Do you mind sharing a little with me? We're still off the record, aren't we?"

"I don't see how it could hurt. Besides, if you repeat anything I say, I'll deny it."

"And the 24-hour rule is still in effect?"

"I just said there won't be any arrests at least until tomorrow."

"All right, so give me the scoop. Which one of us had the brains to pull it off?"

"If it was simply a matter of brains, I would have to put my money on you."

"Me?"

"Of all the suspects, you've got the most stable disposition. You keep your head under fire, nothing rattles you. And you've got a logical and analytical mind. The others couldn't get into Mensa if they added their IQs together."

"Thanks, I think."

"It's a compliment." Mead slapped him on the back. "I teach all my first-year students that for any premeditated crime to be successful, every single detail must be carefully planned - no contingencies, nothing left to chance."

"I remember that speech."

"The way I see it, the other three couldn't execute a plan to save their lives. Rutledge would blow it; he can't think on his feet. King wouldn't do it; basically, the man's a coward. Now your girlfriend, she's a different story. There's no doubt in my mind she could kill; she already has. But she's too impetuous and would probably slip up at crunch time. Now you, on the other hand, suffer from none of these deficiencies."

"Are you trying to say I did it?"

"No, no, nothing of the kind."

"But you just said—"

"What I said applies to a premeditated crime."

"You don't think Chesterfield's murder was planned?"

"It was clearly a crime of opportunity. A flash of rage caused someone to lose their head and snap. This isn't your kind of crime. It doesn't fit your personality."

"You sound quite certain."

"I've known you for a long time."

Burton slowed the car and turned into the parking lot outside the law school and parked.

"Thanks for the ride."

"Don't mention it."

Mead opened the door and stepped out.

"So, let me get this straight," Burton said. "You don't think it was premeditated?"

"Nope."

"So, it must have been a spur-of-the-moment thing."

"Precisely."

"And since my personality doesn't lend itself to impetuous behavior, you're convinced I couldn't have done it."

"Correct."

"That's interesting," Burton said as he shifted the car in reverse. "Yet I killed him."

38

Edward Mead stood in the parking lot watching the tail lights of Jonathan Burton's car merge into traffic. Mead's chest heaved as if a wild animal was trapped inside, kicking itself free. Jonathan's words rang in his ears. Tiny sparkles danced before his eyes. How could this be? It didn't make sense. He stood speechless until the Mercedes disappeared around the corner. He tried to walk, but his knees buckled then stiffened. He staggered over to a concrete parking barrier and sat down. He needed to think.

How could Jonathan have killed Chesterfield? Mead must have missed something, but what? Maybe there was something in the remaining transcription that would unravel this Gordian knot. He took a couple deep breaths, struggled to his feet, and then spurred his aching legs into a semi-trot toward the law school. He burst into his office, looked at his secretary and tried to speak, but his tongue refused to obey.

"What is it?" she asked.

"Today's transcription, where is it?"

"Don't go anywhere."

She swiveled around, pulled open the top drawer of her desk, and grabbed a large white envelope. "Here you go. Mr. Thompson delivered this for you personally."

"The Clerk of Courts came here?"

"He wanted to discuss those transcripts I just gave you. He said they include some information you may find vital to your investigation."

"I'll get on them as soon as I can."

"Also, Jonathan Burton just called."

"How long ago?"

"Just before you walked in."

"What'd he say?"

"He wanted to apologize for rushing off like he did, and he wants to get together tonight. He said you'd understand."

"Yeah, I understand." He turned toward his office door once again.

"There's one more thing."

"I don't think I can stand one more thing."

"Agent Riehl is waiting for you in your office."

"She's in there now?"

"Yes sir. She got here about five minutes ago."

"What does she want?"

"She said it was imperative she see you as soon as possible, so I told her she could wait in your office. She also said that I should be expecting a fax."

"What a day," he said with a sigh.

He opened the door to his rectangular-shaped office. His desk, meticulously organized, sat in front of the solitary window. Bookshelves lined the other three walls and were covered with volumes of every size and color. Sarah Riehl sat in the wooden chair next to his desk. She stood when he walked in.

"You don't look too good, Professor."

"Didn't I just leave you at the library?"

"Deja-vu."

He tossed the envelope on the desk.

"I got a call on my way back downtown," she said. "The psych profiles are finished. I'm having them faxed over."

He dropped heavily into his chair and rubbed his knuckles into the fleshy bags surrounding his eyes. "I must be trapped in the Twilight Zone."

They sat quietly for a few moments. Edward Mead struggled to clear his mind. He needed to focus. He would deal with Jonathan later. Sarah's lips moved, but he could scarcely hear what she said for the throbbing of his temples.

"I'm sorry, could you repeat that?"

"I said, do you mind if I ask you a personal question?"

"Go ahead."

"In all the years you were married, did you ever think about getting a divorce?"

He thought a moment. "Just once."

"Only once?"

"We got into a real humdinger of a fight a few months after we were married. I don't remember what the fight was about. I think she bought a purse or something we didn't need and drained our checking account. But whatever it was, the fight got vicious, and we both said things we shouldn't have said. When I got to the point where I wanted to shake her, I went upstairs and started packing my suitcase. I figured if marriage was going to be this tough, it wasn't for me. I about had my suitcase filled when Victoria came upstairs and did the only thing that could have saved our marriage."

"What did she do?"

"She grabbed her suitcase, threw it on the bed, and started packing too."

"I don't get it."

"Neither did I, but what she said stopped me from ever thinking about divorce again."

"What did she say?"

A smile stretched across his face. "She said we were no good without each other, so if I was leaving her, she was coming with me."

He chuckled. "Can you imagine that? What a woman."

"She must have been."

"Why'd you ask? Having some problems at home?"

"A little rougher than—"

A knock on the door.

They both turned to see his secretary walking in with a bundle of fax pages.

"Here you go, sir, hot off the press." She handed the papers to Mead then scurried out, closing the door behind her.

"Which one do you want first?" he asked.

"Give me Parris. I've been wanting to get inside her head for awhile now."

He handed her the report then began reading King's profile. He read slowly. His mind cleared and quickly absorbed the information.

Ten minutes later he looked up to see Sarah staring at him.

"What do you think?" she asked.

"I'd like to read the other profile first."

"Fair enough."

They swapped reports. He read each line deliberately, occasionally mumbling under his breath.

"Well?" she said.

"Absolutely frightening."

"I know, Parris is one sick puppy. Although it doesn't surprise me. I knew she was sociopathic before I read the report."

"No, I mean it is frightening how thorough this is. Every shred of information from kindergarten report cards to MMPI tests has been compiled, tabulated, and crunched into this." He held up the report.

"Yeah, cool, isn't it?"

"Eerie," he said.

"I'm a little shocked King is so normal."

"You sound disappointed."

"I expected some kind of odd pathology. And I'm a little stunned his IQ is so high. I guess I pegged him wrong."

"Looks can be deceiving."

"You can say that again. From all appearances Parris is an attractive, intelligent professional. All the while, just below the surface, she's a ticking time bomb waiting to explode."

"Just because her profile is disturbing, doesn't mean she's guilty."

"With all due respect, Professor, you must be out of your mind. The computer says she's likely to use lethal force if she feels trapped. Her husband trapped her; she killed him. Chesterfield trapped her; she killed him. What more do you want, video footage of her plunging the dagger into Chesterfield's neck?"

"I've got my reasons."

"Is there something you're not telling me?"

"Call it discernment."

"I don't see why we don't arrest her right now."

"Just one more day."

"Professor, she could kill again."

He leaned back in his chair, lost in gloomy speculation.

"What is it?"

"Nothing," he said rising to his feet. "I've got a few things to look into tonight. After that we'll make our move."

39

Cleveland, Ohio
5:05 P.M.

E dward Mead lay back in his chair and propped his feet up on the credenza in Chesterfield fashion. He closed his eyes and imagined himself in the judge's chambers just before the murder. One by one he envisioned each suspect creeping into the room, stealthily picking up the letter opener, then standing over the victim poised to plunge the dagger into the waiting throat. Each time he pictured Chesterfield's eyes spring open as the cold steel punctured his skin. His arms flinched then fell limp as the blade severed the spine.

One by one he saw the would-be assassins make their retreat. First Parris coolly walking away, checking her dress for speckles of blood. Then King limped out with sweat rolling off his face and neck. Next, Dr. Rutledge rushed out in near panic, blinking incessantly. And lastly, Jonathan Burton stoically strolled away, stopping short of the door to have a coughing fit.

"Just what I thought," he said, opening his eyes. "Now let's see if I can confirm it."

Feeling invigorated, he tore open the white envelope, pulled out the transcripts and began to read....

"Does the defense wish to call another witness?" Chesterfield asked.

"No, Your Honor," Burton said. "The defense rests."

"Very well, does the plaintiff wish to call any rebuttal witnesses?"

"We do, Your Honor," Parris said.

"Proceed."

"Your Honor, the plaintiff calls the defendant, Dr. Thomas Baird, to the stand."

"Objection!" Burton shouted.

Chesterfield's face flushed. "Court's in recess! Counsel in my chambers, now!" He slammed the gavel on the bench, stormed down the steps, and bolted into his chambers.

The attorneys bickered among themselves in front of Chesterfield's desk. As soon as King, who trailed the others, made it into the chambers, Chesterfield lit into his most discourteous tirade yet. He peppered his profanity with such vulgar, sacrilegious, and odious epitaphs that Burton cocked an eye to see if the paint was peeling off the walls.

When Chesterfield finished, he belted back a snort of vodka, belched, wiped his mouth on his sleeve and said, "Will someone explain to me how you cretins passed the bar?"

"I can explain," Parris said.

"That was a rhetorical question, you jitbag."

"No, I mean I can explain why I called Baird."

"You have ten seconds." Chesterfield plunged into his chair, turned his back on the uneasy group, and flung his feet upon the marble-topped credenza.

"Your Honor, I've researched this. Under Ohio's Adverse Witness Statute, the plaintiff may call a physician-defendant and examine him as an expert."

"I'm listening."

"The statute authorizes the plaintiff to elicit testimony from the physician-defendant as if he were under cross-examination."

"That's got to be a violation of the Fifth Amendment," Rutledge said. "I'd like to see some case law on that."

"Silence, punk!" Chesterfield shouted. "I own you."

Rutledge's face twisted into a scowl.

"I have a case," Parris said. *"Oleksiw vs. Weidener.* I don't remember the exact citation, but it's in the Annotated Revised Code, section 2317.07, I believe."

"Hey, King," Chesterfield said. "Gimp over to the bookshelf and bring me Title 23."

"Excuse me, sir, but—"

"I don't hear those pasty-white thighs chafing."

King moped over to the bookshelf like a dog that had been beaten too much. Perspiration formed on his brow. He retrieved the volume and placed it on the desk. His elbow knocked over the letter opener as he withdrew his hand. He propped it back up as Chesterfield spun around and picked up the book.

"Let me see here. Yeah, here it is. Surprisingly enough, Little Miss Paring Knife is right."

Parris stared at him open-mouthed.

"Yeah, I know all about your exploits in New York. Lucky for me I dumped you when I did," he said with a sarcastic note. "I do my homework. Burton, it looks like your drunken butcher will be taking the stand."

"Sir, could the defense have a 24-hour continuance to prepare my client?"

"What are you, stupid?"

"Your Honor—"

"Did I stutter? We're finishing this trial today. You idiots have squandered enough of my time." He slammed his fist on the desk. "And I'm telling you now, if we have to come in these chambers one more time, I'm bolting the door and slapping snot bubbles out of all four of you. If you think I'm playing, ask Parris. Do I make myself clear?"

"Yes, Your Honor," they said in unison.

"Good. And when this is over, I've got a little surprise

planned for you. Now get back in there, and let's get this circus over with."

The group reassembled. Dr. Baird took the stand. He unbuttoned his navy suit jacket and sat down. He seemed not more than 35, yet he was bald with a few gray locks about his temples. Deep furrows lined his high, broad forehead. His pale blue eyes darted back and forth between Parris and the jury. A thin sheen of perspiration bloomed on his upper lip. He looked tired and bloated.

Parris took her place at the podium and began the questioning. "Please state your name for the jury."

"Thomas Baird. Doctor Thomas Baird."

"And how do you make your living?"

"I'm a gynecologist and obstetrician."

"I didn't ask what you studied in medical school, I asked how you make your living."

"Excuse me?"

"Are you an abortionist?"

"Yes, I am."

"And you make a good living at it?"

"You say it like it's something I aspired to out of medical school. I can assure you I did not. Doctors don't start out as abortionists; it's something they end up as. For me, it started out as a means to supplement my income. I didn't exactly finish tops in my class, so the hospitals were not beating my door down with offers. My loans were due, so I did a couple abortions. No one told me that once I entered the abortion field, my medical career - for all intents and purposes - was effectively over."

"Nevertheless, you do get rich from killing babies."

"Objection," Burton said, half-standing.

"Sustained."

"I'll rephrase the question. Do you ever feel guilty about killing babies?"

"When I finish a procedure, I feel a fleeting gratification that I've done an efficient job, nothing more."

"That's hard to believe."

"I swear I have no feelings aside from the sense of accomplishment, the pride of expertise. On inspecting the contents of the bag, I feel only the satisfaction of knowing that I've done a thorough job. I'll admit it wasn't always so easy."

"What do you mean by that?"

His Adam's apple bobbed up and down. "Well, I took the Hippocratic Oath, which says you're not supposed to do abortions. I took the Maimonides Oath, which says you're not supposed to do abortions. But the law says it's okay, so here I am." He looked down at his hands. "It's strange. There are times I get downright angry at myself for feeling good about grasping the head of the fetus, for feeling good about doing a technically good procedure. I guess when success is measured by how well you destroy a life, it causes turmoil somewhere down deep inside. But for the most part, I don't feel anything. I do my job."

"Has this turmoil ever caused you to abuse your patients?"

"Objection!" Burton shouted, then coughed behind his hand.

"Overruled."

"I don't think there's anyone out there doing abortions who hasn't wished at some point that the situation creating the demand for these things would just go away. There have been plenty of times when I've been at the end of my rope." He looked at Parris. "I admit feeling anger toward my patients for their sexual irresponsibility."

"But have you ever abused your patients?"

"If you're asking me if I've ever intentionally committed medical malpractice, no."

"I'm asking you if you've ever abused your patients."

"I may not have always been as gentle as I could have been, but I wouldn't call it abuse. I give these women what they want."

"Doctor, do you have a substance abuse problem?"

"No."

"Have you ever checked yourself into a detox clinic?"

"I have."

"Do people without substance abuse problems typically check themselves into rehab centers?"

"I don't know, maybe they do."

"Probably for the jigsaw puzzles, huh?"

"Objection."

"Withdrawn. So, you don't believe that you have a problem?"

"It's under control."

"Have you ever been intoxicated while performing abortions?"

"I sometimes have a few drinks over lunch to settle my nerves, but I've never been drunk."

"Have you performed abortions while under the influence of narcotics?"

"Objection," Burton said.

"Overruled. The good doctor will answer the question," Chesterfield said with an odd smirk.

"I've medicated myself at times."

"Since when did cocaine become a prescription drug?"

"Objection!"

"I withdraw the question," Parris said. "Do you recall performing an abortion on Robin Roget?"

"Vaguely."

"Vaguely! You nearly killed the woman."

"Objection, Your Honor."

"Cut the grandstanding," Chesterfield said.

"Yes, Your Honor. Dr. Baird, could you pick Robin Roget out of a line-up?"

"I literally do hundreds and hundreds of abortions a year, and to be honest with you, from my vantage point most of my patients look alike." He chuckled nervously.

"A little joke. Yes, I remember her."

"Were you self-medicated on the day you performed Robin's abortion?"

"I don't recall."

"Were you drinking that day?"

"I don't recall."

Her eyes narrowed. "Do you recall ripping a foot of her intestines through her vagina?"

"Objection."

"I'll bet that doesn't happen every day?"

"Objection," Burton said, raising his voice.

"Sustained."

"I'll rephrase the question. Do you recall any medical complication in Robin's case?"

Baird's eyes shifted from the jury to Burton to the jury to Parris. "I don't recall."

"You have no explanation for the injuries she sustained?"

"I can't say with any certainty."

"But you have read the postmortem reports?"

"I have."

"So, I don't need to repeat the litany of injuries she suffered?"

"No."

"Well, let's say you were testifying as an expert in another case where a patient suffered similar trauma. What do you think would cause such injuries, injuries such as those experienced by Robin?"

"Hypothetically?"

"Yes."

"Hypothetically speaking, a doctor may have difficulties locating the fetus. It's all done by feel, you know, in the blind. You just poke around until you find the little bugger. Sometimes the curettage slips and punctures—"

"Excuse me, a curettage is?"

"A surgical scoop with sharp edges. We use it to scrape inside the cervical cavity." He made a twisting motion with his right hand. "It dismembers the fetus."

"Please continue."

"As I was saying, sometimes it's possible to puncture the soft tissue and cause holes in the uterus, cervix, or vagina. It is possible - hypothetically speaking, of course - that the curettage penetrated the abdominal wall, and the suction tube might have caught on the small intestine and inadvertently pulled it into the vaginal cavity."

"You did all that to Robin, and you don't consider it malpractice?"

"I was speaking hypothetically. But as I recall, Ms. Roget's abortion was typical. Her post-operative condition appeared normal. I specifically remember telling her to see a physician if she experienced any excessive bleeding."

"You don't recall if you were drunk or high on that day. You don't remember any complications, but you specifically remember instructing her to see a doctor if her bleeding persisted."

"Uh huh."

"That's convenient. And how do you explain the head and torso of her baby being thrust into her abdominal cavity?"

"The pathology lab examines the fetal remains to ensure that all the pieces have been removed. If a large portion is missing, we typically call the patient back in for a follow-up procedure. Most of the time the retained material passes on its own."

"Are you saying this is not unusual?"

"The Medical Review Board has routinely found that even if a physician knowingly sends a woman home with retained fetal material, he hasn't violated the acceptable standard of care. Some abortionists routinely leave the fetal skulls in their patients. It's no big deal."

Parris walked over to the plaintiff table and picked up two documents. "Doctor, do you belong to the American Abortion Rights Action League?"

"I do."

"Have you ever participated in any Risk Management seminars sponsored by the League?"

"I have."

"I'm going to read you part of a statement presented at one of these seminars, and I want you to tell me if you're familiar with it. All right?" He nodded.

"The document reads, 'We do have bad practitioners, and it's affecting all of us. We have been reluctant to do anything or say anything about it because of the physician shortage. We don't want the bad press, but when something happens, under our breath we say, 'Well, it was just a matter of time.' We all know this stuff is going on, and it's going to get worse unless we do something about it. I want to know what we're doing to control this.'"

She walked over to the stand and handed him the paper.

"Are you familiar with this statement?"

He examined it carefully. "No."

"Are you sure? Take your time."

"I'm quite sure."

"Do you agree with the statement?"

"I don't believe so, no."

"That's a shame," Parris said as she returned to the podium.

"Because you wrote it 12 years ago."

Murmuring rippled through the jury box and gallery.

"I'm now holding in my hand a flier distributed at a recent seminar," she said. "It lists a half-dozen or so recommendations for new abortion clinic start-ups, and I quote, 'Keep clinic records as vague as possible; keep written records to a bare minimum; keep employees from knowing too much so if they quit they can't testify in a malpractice action; get Crisis Pregnancy Centers out of the phone book so women won't know who to call if they get injured; and harass attorneys who represent injured women.' Are you familiar with this document, Dr. Baird?"

"Yes, I am."

"And why is that?"

"I wrote it."

"How long ago?"

"I don't know for sure, probably last year sometime."

"It was last year, about a month after I filed this suit. Come a long way, haven't you, Doctor? I have no further questions."

She returned to her seat and whispered something into King's ear. He nodded and scribbled down a note on his yellow legal pad.

"Would you like to redirect the witness, Mr. Burton?" Chesterfield asked.

"I would."

"Proceed."

"Thank you, sir."

Burton stood slowly. His charcoal suit hung loosely on his lanky frame. He looked emaciated, like someone had scooped the stuffing out of him.

"Do you remember the first abortion you witnessed?"

"Yeah... yeah I do." His palms felt sweaty. He wiped them on his pants. "During medical school I had to observe a few abortions. At one point they had me identify the fetal parts to make sure all the pieces had been removed." He shook his head. "A tiny arm, some ribs, a chunk of leg."

"How did the experience affect you?"

"It was disturbing. All the political rhetoric doesn't prepare you for the gory reality."

"But you do believe in a woman's right to choose?"

"There's a big difference between intellectually

supporting a woman's choice and actually cutting up the babies. I know, because I'm the one getting rid of the bodies. Abortion may be legal, but I don't think anyone who is actually performing them can say it's not killing. The question becomes, 'Is this kind of killing justifiable?' In my own mind... well, it's how I make my living."

"Dr. Baird, do you recall any visible signs of venereal diseases when you examined Ms. Roget before her abortion?"

"No."

"Did you inform her to seek medical treatment if she experienced any complications after surgery?"

"I did."

"Did she sign a consent form?"

"Yes, she did."

"Did she sign a waiver?"

"She did."

"One last question, doctor. You testified earlier that once you became an abortionist your medical career was over. Do you still feel trapped in this profession?"

"When a doctor heals someone or brings a new life into the world, he's the hero. But no one ever says 'Thank you' to an abortionist. Just one time I'd like one of my patients to be happy to see me." He looked down at his shoes. "Working in an abortion clinic is not something... well, my choice at this point is to remain an abortionist or get out of medicine altogether." He looked at the jury. "I'm like a caged rat - no longer interested in the cheese, only looking for a way out."

"No further questions, Your Honor."

40

Shaker Heights, Ohio
9:05 P.M.

E dward Mead gazed out the living room picture window. All was still on Van Aken Boulevard except for a man out walking his black Labrador Retriever. The twinkling stars in the cloudless sky meant sub-zero overnight temperatures, but at least there would be no snow in the morning to sweep off the sidewalks. A gas lamp stood at the end of the driveway; its flame flickered in the wind, sending shadows dancing across the unbroken carpet of snow on the grass.

Still no sign of Jonathan Burton.

Mead returned to his recliner. The enticing scent of buttered microwave popcorn filled the room. The half-empty bag lay on the coffee table along with a can of Cotton Club Root Beer and an opened bottle of Tylenol.

The Drew Carey Show blared from the television in the background. His mind scrambled to sift and piece the data together. His heartbeat hammered at his temples. The top of his head throbbed. Feelings of resentment welled up in his heart. The case had been a headache from the beginning; now it turned into a migraine. He could strangle Jonathan for being involved in this mess. A despairing sense of futility mingled with his pain as he thought of the nights he missed visiting Victoria because of this case. At least it would all be over soon, and his life could return to normal - whatever that was.

The doorbell rang. His feet found his black leather slippers, and he shuffled to the door.

"Good evening, Professor." Burton flashed a lifeless smile.

"If I was 20 years younger I'd knock you out."

"I know, I know. I will explain everything." Burton stepped over the threshold, removed his coat and hung it on the coatrack behind the door. "Let's sit down. This could take awhile."

They took their usual seats, Mead in the overstuffed recliner and Burton on the couch.

"Start talking," Mead said.

"Ninety-nine percent of the people on this planet have absolutely no idea when they'll die."

"So."

"I, on the other hand, have a pretty good idea. It's rather liberating."

"What's that got to do with you killing Chesterfield?"

"It has everything to do with it. Probably everyone has hated someone enough to kill him at some point in their lives."

"I'm feeling that way right now."

"Only two things stop them - moral restraint or fear of the consequences. Morals have never been high on my priority list, and since I won't live to face the consequences, I was free to do society a favor."

"I'm surprised to hear you say that."

"Sometimes you need to thin the herd."

"That doesn't sound like you."

"Having your life cut short by 30 years has a way of changing a man."

Mead examined Burton's face. His hairline receded noticeably over the last few months. He had lost a great deal of weight, and his face looked gaunt and jaundiced.

"Do you mind if I turn down the TV?" Burton asked.

"I'm having a hard time hearing you."

"Go ahead."

"Where's the remote?"

"I haven't seen it since Victoria died. She used to think it was funny to hide it from me." He smiled. "She probably took it with her."

The television sat in an oak entertainment console to the right of the baby grand piano. Burton rambled across the room, pressed the mute button, and then returned to his seat.

"I noticed you're not coughing tonight," Mead said.

"I do pretty good for a few days after they tap my lung. My side just hurts like you can't believe when they're done."

"Were you having your lung tapped during the trial?"

"No."

"That's what I thought." He settled back in his chair. "I've been reading through the trial transcripts."

"That's what you said."

"I'm up to Baird's testimony, and I've got to commend you. You handled the trial well."

"I learned from the master."

"You even managed to throw some sympathetic light on old Dr. Mengele."

"Baird's not a bad guy. He started off trying to do the right thing. The work jaded him."

"He should lose his license."

"He probably should, but that's not up to me. My job was to provide him with the best defense his money could buy. I think I did that."

"I can't figure out how Chesterfield hasn't been disbarred for his unprofessional behavior. It's all on the record as plain as day."

"He usually sanitizes the record," Burton said.

"Sanitizes it?"

"He's got his stenographer trained to skip over

the nasty stuff. It's common knowledge around the courthouse. Besides, he was on the judicial review board for the State Bar. He had himself protected."

"I can't believe the things he said to Parris and King."

"Kinda funny in a sadistic sort of way."

"Do you think you won the verdict?"

"I think I made the best case."

"Having Chesterfield in Rutledge's pocket didn't hurt either."

"I didn't notice any unusual influence."

"Most of his calls went your way."

"That's because I was right most of the time."

"But that's what got me stumped. Why would you kill a guy who was tough on your opponent?"

"I hated the man."

"Then it was premeditated."

"It wasn't."

"You're too analytical to take a chance like that. It's not your way."

"Maybe I'm not as predictable as you think."

"Yes you are."

"I'm not."

"Jonathan, it takes you two weeks to decide which pair of shoes you're going to buy."

"I'm telling you I had no idea I was going to kill him until I walked in his office," he said in a loud voice, almost shouting, yet stammering at every word. "I... I went into his chambers to use the restroom. I... the pompous ass was all stretched out, his feet up, that dagger-thing sitting right out there just begging me to pick it up. My blood started boiling. I... I had nothing to lose, so I stabbed him. He had it coming."

"If you thought you won, why risk a mistrial? Why blow a sure victory?"

"Objection, Counselor. That's a compound question."

"I'm not playing."

"Look, next week isn't promised, at least not for me. I didn't stop and think about it. If I did, I probably wouldn't have killed him. But the opportunity presented itself, so I took it."

"I'm not buying it."

Burton shrugged. "It's the truth."

"Why confess now? You were getting away with it."

"I could see you guys closing in on the wrong person. I couldn't go to my grave knowing someone else would spend the rest of her life in prison because of me."

"Very chivalrous of you."

"I should've come forward earlier."

"I appreciate your integrity, Jonathan."

"Tomorrow morning I'll give a full statement and turn myself in."

"That won't be necessary."

"Why not?"

"Because first thing in the morning I'm going to have Agent Riehl arrest your girlfriend."

"What?!" Burton leapt to his feet, his arms outstretched, his fingers spread like claws. "Why?"

"Because you're lying."

"I'm not."

"Then admit you planned it."

"I didn't."

"I don't believe you."

"All right, I planned the whole thing."

"You're lying again."

"What do you want from me?" Burton said, his voice filled with emotion.

"Say you didn't do it."

"But I did."

"The only thing I can't figure out is why you're so sure she's guilty."

"She didn't do it."

"You must be certain, or you wouldn't be willing to

sacrifice yourself for her."

"That's not true."

"Why are you so sure?"

"I swear."

"Look Jonathan, I know you didn't do it, and I know you believe she did. What I don't know is what makes you so sure?"

Burton collapsed back on the couch and covered his face with his hands, his breathing audible.

"It's over, Jonathan, all you can do is help her." Mead leaned over and placed his hand on Burton's shoulder. "Tell me how you know?"

Burton looked up, his eyes bloodshot, his face twitching. "I saw her do it."

41

"Y̶ou what!?" Mead yelled.

"I saw her do it."

"How?"

"The... I... the..."

"What are you babbling about?"

"If you give me a chance, I'll explain."

"Go ahead."

"I saw her staggering back from behind Chesterfield's desk with a crazed look on her face."

"Stop right there!" Mead shouted. "Take a breath and start at the beginning."

"All right, do you remember the first night you interviewed me?"

"Of course."

"And I said I spent the morning with Jessica at the conference table, and she got up to use the restroom."

"Yeah."

"Well, what I didn't say was that after she got up, I followed her. I wasn't trying to spy on her, I just really had to go. I mean, the longer she lingered back there, the more I thought of all the coffee I drank and the bottles of water

239

and—"

"I get the picture."

"I went back there to hurry her along, but she wasn't there. No sign of her."

"Go on."

"The restroom is situated in that little L-shaped hall between the conference room and Chesterfield's office. It's in a blind spot. So, I took a couple steps around the corner and there she was, backpedaling from behind the desk with her hand stretched out toward the blade with that ghastly, contorted look on her face." He closed his eyes and shuddered. "Man, it's disturbing. I can still see her standing there."

"Which hand did she use?"

"I don't know."

"Think man, which hand?"

"I... I guess... her right."

"Don't guess."

"Her right hand, I'm sure of it. I couldn't see the left side of her body. The chair was in the way."

"She's left-handed."

"Does it matter? I saw her do it!"

They locked eyes then both looked away.

"Jonathan, I got a look at her psych profile today, and it's not good. She's profoundly disturbed."

"Who are you telling? I saw her firsthand."

"Does she have any idea you saw her?"

"I don't think so."

"She will kill if she feels trapped."

"I don't see how she could've seen me. I slipped into the restroom and locked the door."

"Has she asked any probing questions?"

"Nothing."

"Hinted at anything?"

"No."

"If she suspects anything..." Mead braced his hands

against the armrests and boosted himself up. He paced the length of the room shaking his head. "Where is she now?"

"How should I know?"

"You're supposed to see her tonight?"

"No."

"What were you thinking?"

Burton shook his head.

"You believe you're a witness to a murder, so what do you do? You obstruct justice and date the assailant. I can't wait to see what you'll do for an encore."

Burton's lips moved, but he made no sound.

"What were you thinking?"

"Do you want to know?"

"Yeah, I want to know."

"Do you really want to know?"

"Spit it out."

"I don't want to die alone. There. Are you happy? I don't want to die alone."

"Well, guess what, Jonathan," Mead said sarcastically. "Neither do I."

"But you're old."

"Do you think that makes a difference?"

"I didn't mean it like that. I—" Burton doubled over, moaning in pain. His face went pale.

"What is it?"

"My side."

"What happened?"

"The medication must be wearing off."

"Is there anything I can do?"

"I need to lie down."

"Maybe I should call your doctor."

"No. This happens all the time."

"Here, lie on the couch."

"No. I need my medication." He winced and wobbled to his feet. "I left it at home."

"Do you want me to drive you?"

"The pain is easing up. I'll be okay."

"I'd better follow you in my car."

"No need. I'll be fine in a minute." Burton walked over to the coatrack with his left arm tucked against his side.

Mead walked beside him, then helped him on with his coat. "Are you sure you're going to be all right?"

"I'll be fine in the morning. If you want me to make a formal statement I will."

"We'll talk about it tomorrow."

Burton turned to face Mead with a grave look, his voice quivering, "I'm sorry I've disappointed you. You've been like a father to me."

"Don't worry about that. It'll be over soon."

Burton blurted out a wracking cough. He jerked open the door and a whoosh of frigid air rushed in.

"Call me when you get home," Mead said, "so I know you made it safely."

"Good-bye, Professor, and thanks again for everything you've done for me."

"Call me."

Burton nodded and pressed his lips tightly together as if trying to hold back his emotion. He turned quickly and took irregular strides toward his car. Mead watched his longtime protégé get in the car and drive away.

A man born of women is of few days and full of trouble.

He closed the door, then dragged his feet through the living room not knowing how to feel. He needed to do something to stop the world from spinning.

Jonathan didn't look good; he's not going to be around for much longer.

He mindlessly picked up the half-empty bag of popcorn as he passed by the coffee table, deep in thought.

Carrying that secret around must've been tearing him up inside.

He carried the popcorn bag up the hardwood steps,

down the hall, and into the master bedroom. He didn't realize he had the bag in his hand until he sat on Victoria's side of the bed.

"Where did this come from?" He crumpled the bag and tossed it in the wastebasket near the oak dresser. "I must be losing my mind."

He gently peeled back the covers to expose Victoria's pillow. He reverently picked it up like a sacred vestige and cradled it in his arms.

"I miss you, Angel."

He rocked the pillow tenderly. "Life down here gets harder every day. I'm eager for my last breath. It can't come soon enough."

He closed his eyes and pressed his nose against the pillowcase. He sat without moving for a long time and unconsciously dozed off. For an instant Victoria was back in his arms again. She snuggled up against him on the couch. He felt the weight of her face on his shoulder, and he nuzzled against her. She looked so young; her skin felt smooth and soft. Her warm breath made the hair on his neck stand on edge. He puckered his lips to kiss her on the cheek.

The phone rang.

He opened his eyes.

She vanished.

42

E dward Mead fumbled with the phone, then pressed the receiver to his ear. "Hello... hello." A dial tone buzzed. "Jonathan must've made it home."

He pushed the callback button on his phone, and Jonathan Burton's number flashed across the LED screen, but the line was busy. A noise at the window startled him. Something tapped against the glass. He reached over and pulled back the curtain. An ice-covered branch from the magnolia tree bumped against the window with each gust of wind.

"Boy, that's annoying."

He walked over to the nightstand, turned on the Bose Wave stereo, and the mellow tones of the Cleveland Orchestra filled the room. He kept the radio perpetually tuned to WCLV 104.9 FM, the area's premier Classical music station. He adjusted the volume until the tapping at the window was completely drowned out.

He took off his robe, turned off the light, and climbed under the covers. The minutes ticked away. His body wanted to sleep, but his mind wouldn't let it, racing from thought to thought. He replayed the events of the day and conjured up a thousand questions he should have asked Jonathan. Pressure built at his temples. He felt a nagging sensation in the pit of his stomach that something was left undone. He flipped on the light and saw the final bundle of transcripts laying on the nightstand. They were stuffed in his mailbox when he returned from the office. Maybe a little work would relax his mind. So he picked up the papers and started to read....

"The plaintiff may proceed with closing remarks," Chesterfield said.

"Thank you, Your Honor."

Parris pushed back her chair and walked around the plaintiff's table to the jury box on the right side of the courtroom. The box jutted out from the wall and contained three rows of four chairs, each row slightly staggered and elevated. The overhead fluorescent lights reflected off the decorative brass railing that lined the box.

"A medical license is no guarantee of skill," she began. "And skill is no safeguard against cruelty. Patients are completely vulnerable to the mental health of their health care providers. Ladies and gentlemen of the jury, this is not a movie or a television show. This is a real-life trial. And the outcome of this trial, your verdict, will impact the lives of people for years to come. The State of Ohio is asking you to make a monumental decision today. You are to determine not only if Dr. Baird is responsible for Robin Roget's death, but if you find that he is, you must then put a price tag on Robin's life.

"We, the Plaintiff, are not only asking you to hold Dr. Baird accountable for his heinous actions, but to send a message to any other sadistic abortionist waiting in the wings. And how do you send this message? You send it through punitive damages; you hit them in the pocket. After all, money seems to be the only language people like the defendant understand. And maybe, just maybe, your verdict will save someone's life."

Parris paced along the box, running her French-manicured fingers along the brass railing, once again making eye contact with each juror as she went.

"The defense has offered a wonderful array of smoke and mirrors. They would have you believe that somehow Dr. Baird is the victim here. They want you to excuse his horrendous malpractice because Robin lived a somewhat promiscuous lifestyle. I realize that Mr. Burton didn't say it in so many words, but I'm sure you picked up the implication. But such an argument is no different than attempting to excuse a drunk driver by claiming the person he killed shouldn't have been on the highway in the first place. Furthermore, the defense wants you to ignore the mutilation, overlook the neglect, forget about the malpractice and believe Robin's failure to disclose her sexually transmitted diseases led to her death. Personally, I find such a contention insulting to your intelligence. Even the defense expert conceded the possibility that Robin didn't know she was infected. And you heard the testimony of Dr. McCorkle, the county coroner; he was quite certain Robin died of septicemia due to incomplete abortion. Unlike the defense expert who seemed more interested in defending the abortion industry, Mr. McCorkle rendered a fair and impartial decision based on the forensic evidence. He had no axe to grind." She paused and leaned forward.

"There are two ways for a plaintiff to win a medical malpractice case. The first is to present clear, direct evidence of physician negligence. I believe I've done that through the coroner's testimony and oddly enough, directly from Dr. Baird's own mouth. You heard him admit to drinking on the job and to drug use... excuse me... self-medication. And I think the autopsy report said it all. Dr. Baird screwed up, and a beautiful young woman lost her life.

"The second way for a plaintiff to prevail in a malpractice case is by using the doctrine of *res ipsa loquitur* - the thing speaks for itself. To win under this second method, all the plaintiff has to do is stack up the circumstantial evidence and allow the jury to decide for themselves what happened. In the case at hand, you simply have to answer the question, 'Would Robin Roget be alive today if Dr. Baird never touched her?' And let's be honest, the question isn't that hard. A perfectly healthy young woman walks into his clinic, and a few hours later she limps out mutilated and butchered. The next day she's found dead. I trust you will sift through all the misdirection and confusion the defense injected into this trial and see that the evidence speaks for itself. You must find Dr. Baird responsible for Robin's death. It's truly the only just option you have. Her children are depending on you." She bowed her head. "Thank you."

Jessica Parris returned to her seat with an unusual air of confidence as a sort of subdued hum passed through the courtroom.

"The defense may proceed with closing remarks," Chesterfield said, as he drained the last of the vodka and water into his glass.

"Thank you, Your Honor," Burton said. He walked over to the jury box and stood with his legs wide apart, his hands clasped behind his back.

"Ladies and gentlemen, when this trial began, I asked you to wait patiently and not jump to conclusions until all the cards were on the table. I told you things are not always as they first appear. You've heard the witnesses, you have examined the evidence, and now it's up to you.

"Let's not beat around the bush, Dr. Baird is an abortionist. I'll be the first to admit that he performs a nasty, despicable task. But that task happens to be legal in our country at present. Now I know some of you are opposed to abortion, and that's okay. To be honest with you, I happen to be pro-life myself. But right now, that doesn't matter. I took an oath to zealously defend my client, and you took an oath to look past personal convictions and bring back a verdict based on the evidence.

"I know this may come as a shock to some of you, but abortionists are people just like you and me. And all the political rhetoric in the world can't insulate these people from the soul-numbing work they do. Physicians like Dr. Baird are trapped between two extremes. On the one hand, they have a job to do and a responsibility to their patients. On the other hand, they have to get rid of the tiny bodies. This duality exacts an incredible toll, and the defense openly admits Dr. Baird has paid a high emotional price. But facts are stubborn things, and facts are what your verdict must be based upon.

"Let's take a few moments to review the facts. Fact: Ms. Roget withheld vital information from her doctor. This omission caused Dr. Baird to follow a course of medical action that he otherwise would not have taken. Gonorrhea and syphilis are serious, life-threatening diseases. And by withholding this critical information from her doctor, Ms. Roget became guilty of contributory negligence.

"Fact: she did not seek medical treatment following the abortion. Dr. Baird specifically instructed her to do so. Her mother implored her to do so. But Ms. Roget carelessly and recklessly disregarded her own responsibility. And unfortunately, she suffered the consequences. Even if you choose to believe Dr. McCorkle's assertion of the cause of death, you cannot deny that Ms. Roget's failure to seek medical attention was the proximate cause of death."

Burton fought back a wince as a sharp pain shot through his rib cage and clawed at his lungs.

"Fact: most importantly, Ms. Roget signed a consent form and a waiver. I know this may sound like a technicality, and it may not seem fair, but it's the law. Allow me to give you an example. A 14-year-old boy, who survived a botched abortion, filed suit for assault and battery against the doctor. The unsuccessful abortion left the boy with hearing loss and brain damage. He lives every day of his life knowing his own mother wanted him dead, and he carries on his body the scars to remind him of that rejection. A tragic story. But the judge was forced to throw out the suit because the mother signed a waiver. In the eyes of the law, she assumed the risk. Case closed. And the same applies to Ms. Roget. When she signed her name on the dotted line, she became legally responsible for everything that followed. It may sound cruel and heartless, but it's the law.

"A few minutes ago, Ms. Parris tossed out an impressive-sounding Latin phrase *res ipsa loquitur*. And everything she said about this doctrine is true. However, just like so many things during the trial, she left out a few essential details. And these details make all the difference in the world.

"For instance, she didn't tell you that in order for a plaintiff to prevail under this doctrine, three elements must be met. First, the plaintiff must prove the injuries in question could not have occurred in the absence of clear negligence. Dr. Zigler's testimony decisively refutes this point.

"Secondly, the injuries must have resulted from an action under the exclusive control of the attending physician. Dr. Baird never had exclusive control over any part of the abortion, because Ms. Roget withheld vital information from him.

"And lastly, the injuries must not have resulted from any voluntary act of negligence on the part of the patient. When Ms. Roget willfully refused to seek medical treatment, she became the negligent party. So now that you've heard the rest of the story, as Paul Harvey would say, how many of these three essential points has the plaintiff proven? That's right, zero."

Burton cleared his throat; his speech became increasingly labored.

"Now I know a little Latin myself. And unlike the plaintiff, the phrase I'm going to share with you actually applies to this case. It's the doctrine of *volenti non fit injuria*. This concept simply states that a plaintiff may not recover for injuries that she voluntarily exposed herself to. In a nutshell, if she assents to a known and appreciated danger, she cannot recover damages. Plain and simple.

"Ladies and gentlemen, Ms. Parris says you have a difficult job, but I don't see it that way. When you weigh the evidence and look at the facts, it seems to me your decision is cut and dried. The plaintiff has tugged on your heartstrings, and I admit this is an emotional case. But I'm asking you to look at the facts, vote with your head, and uphold the law. Thank you."

43

Thursday, February 4
University Heights, Ohio
8:20 A.M.

Edward Mead parked his car in the circular driveway in front of Jonathan Burton's two-story colonial, its red brick blackened with age. He opened the door and shivered. The steady current that had been blowing early that morning rose again. A fine dry snow began falling, but it didn't stay on the ground. The wind whirled and blew it across the lawn. Burton had purchased the home after his second wife kicked him out of their Lakewood condominium.

Apparently, his affair with the Italian stewardess hadn't gone over well. He'd quickly bought this majestic, turn-of-the-century home, though at first the five bedrooms seemed a little excessive. But they came in handy when wife number three moved in with her three teenaged daughters. The marriage fizzled after two years, and Gloria took the kids and a sizeable alimony and moved to Florida. So, at the age of 50, Burton found himself alone in a house too big for an aging bachelor. And while he vowed never to marry again, he couldn't bring himself to move.

Edward Mead ambled along the slate sidewalk, then climbed the brick steps leading to the portico. Four white pillars supported the semicircle overhang. Tiny icicles dangled from the gutter's lip.

Mead rapped on the double doors with the brass knocker.

No answer.

He waited a few seconds then pressed the doorbell.

No answer.

He reached for the knocker again. Two black sedans sped up the drive and screeched to a stop a few inches behind his car. Sarah Riehl jumped out of the passenger door of the first car and ran toward him. Three men in dark suits followed close behind.

"Professor, I'm glad you're here," Sarah said, panting. "I called you a dozen times. Thank God you checked your email."

"I never check my email."

"Then you don't know?"

"Know what?"

"About the confession."

"What are you talking about? I came here to take Jonathan's statement."

"So, you do know."

"Speak English."

"We came to arrest Burton."

"Says who?" A crease appeared between Mead's brows.

"Professor, Burton confessed to the murder."

"Impossible. When?"

"He sent emails to everyone."

"That can't be."

"I'm afraid so."

"There must be some mistake."

"No mistake. He gave a full confession, detailed the crime, and even apologized to the other suspects."

"No... no..."

Mead pounded on the door with his fist.

No answer.

"He'll explain, you'll see," Mead said, turning toward

Sarah. "He's not feeling well."

"Flu?" Sarah asked.

"Lung cancer."

"Oh, I had no idea." Mead beat on the door again.

No answer.

"Maybe we should knock the door down," one of the young agents said as he took off his mirrored sunglasses.

"Why don't we try the door first?" Sarah said and twisted the knob. The door pushed open. "Does he usually leave his house unlocked?"

"Never."

"Maybe he's expecting us."

They walked into the two-story great room, with its high-paneled wainscoting of olive-stained oak. The cream-colored ceiling was riddled with intricate plasterwork. Oriental rugs covered the floor. Two hardbacked Victorian chairs faced the red brick fireplace; several ornamental china jars were arranged on the mantel. In the far corner a statuette of Rodin's *The Thinker* stood on a satinwood table.

"Anybody home?" Sarah yelled, with her hands cupped around her mouth.

No answer.

"Jonathan!" Mead shouted.

"Maybe he changed his mind about turning himself in," the young agent said.

"Hartlieb, you and Foster check the basement," Sarah said. "Atkinson, you check the first floor, and Professor Mead and I will check upstairs."

The group split up. Mead and Sarah climbed the creaking arched stairway. Mead felt increasingly uneasy with each step. None of this made sense.

"Where's his bedroom?" she asked.

"It's the last door on the right."

"What exactly did he say last night?"

"He tried to convince me he killed Chesterfield."

"What!?" She stopped short of the top step. "He confessed, and you didn't tell me?"

"He was lying. I knew it, and he knew I knew it."

"But he confessed."

"When I pressed him, he admitted seeing Parris do it."

"No way."

"That's what he said."

"And you didn't tell me?"

"You'd have been the first to know as soon as I had it in writing."

She pressed her lips together and shook her head. "No special treatment, huh?"

"The man's dying."

"If he saw her do it, why'd he confess?"

"To take the fall for her."

"Would he do that?"

"Before I found out about the cancer, I would've said definitely not. But a desperate man is liable to do desperate things."

"This whole thing is bizarre."

The hardwood floor in the narrow hall showed signs of wear. Three inlaid walnut doors lined each side of the hall, and all were open except the master bedroom. They examined each room as they went and found no sign of Burton. They cautiously approached the master bedroom. Mead reached for the knob. Apprehension gripped his heart.

"Don't touch that," Sarah said. "Fingerprints."

"Jonathan," he yelled. "Are you in there?"

No answer.

Sarah squatted down and carefully placed her purse on the floor. She dug in and found a pair of rubber gloves and an FBI evidence bag. She left the purse where it was, stood up, and grabbed the knob with her fingertips. The door swung open.

The queen size bed was rumpled and unmade. A pair

of black wingtips sat neatly on the Oriental rug under the bed. A white lace lampshade glowed atop a blue ceramic lamp on the nightstand; its dim bulb seemed oddly out of place as the bright morning light poured through the windows. Sarah walked over to the computer console in the far corner of the room. Mead followed close behind. A serpent-like screensaver wiggled across the monitor and twisted into impossible geometric contortions. She clicked the mouse. The screen cleared, and a few lines of text appeared.

"Here's the email," she said, "it definitely originated from here."

"But where's he at?"

"He's not here."

"His Mercedes is in the drive."

"Does he have another car?"

"No."

"Maybe he called a cab."

"Or an ambulance," Mead said, with a hint of concern in his voice. "He had some sharp pains last night. What time did his email arrive?"

"Around 8 o'clock this morning."

Mead looked at his gold watch, the one Victoria gave him on their 50th anniversary. "It's only 8:30 now."

"He couldn't have gotten far. We'll head downtown and coordinate the manhunt from there. We'll bring in Parris, we'll get his statement, and we'll wrap this up today." She looked around. "But I've got to make a pit stop first. Is there a powder room around here?"

"In the corner by the closet." Mead pointed to a door slightly open with the toilet in plain view.

"Thanks. I'll only be a minute."

She headed off for the door while Mead sat on the edge of the bed. He allowed himself to relax; his shoulders drooped and he took a deep breath. He noticed a layer of perspiration covered his face. He mopped his brow with his handkerchief.

"Professor!"

The frenzied sound of her voice spurred him to action. He rushed across the room as fast as his 77-year-old legs would go. He dashed into the bathroom and stumbled over a pile of clothes. He planted his right foot on the wet tile and slipped. Sarah caught him by the right arm. His left hand dangled into the cold bath water. He looked down and his face contorted in horror.

Jonathan Burton lay under 8 inches of water, his steel blue eyes partly open. His legs were bent; his knees jutted out of the water. His head and torso were submerged, his skin a pale purplish-blue. He was completely nude except for a stainless steel wristwatch.

44

Anthony J. Celebrezze Federal Building
Cleveland, Ohio
5:10 P.M.

Sarah Riehl paced along the wall of windows in the 5th floor conference room, and mindlessly looked out over Lake Erie. She allowed the day's events to replay in her mind. The Burton investigation took priority, so she'd pulled the surveillance team off Parris and had them cordon off Burton's property. The forensic task force arrived at the scene a little past noon and set to work sweeping the house. She instructed the team leader, Jimmy Graham, to check in with her every few hours throughout the day. On the way back downtown, she stopped by the morgue to expedite the autopsy. A sinking feeling gripped the pit of her stomach as she saw the only material witness to the Chesterfield murder stretched out on a marble slab with a toe tag hanging off his foot. She knew if the pathologist ruled the cause of death a suicide, Parris would slip away.

She looked across the table at Professor Mead. Saggy blue-black bags of flesh encircled his eyes. He looked exhausted and hadn't said much since morning. She didn't push him. She knew he needed to be alone with his thoughts. What a nightmare these past two months must have been for him.

Someone knocked on the door.

"Come in," she said.

A delivery boy from Bo Loong entered carrying a large white bag.

"Is there an agent Riehl here?"

"That's me. Just set the bag on the table."

He complied, smiled, and held out his hand. "Fourteen ninety-five, please."

"Hold on a second." She looked around the room but didn't see her purse. She moved the mauve chair and searched under the table, but it wasn't there either.

"I seemed to have misplaced my purse."

"I'll pay for it." Mead reached for his wallet. "How much did you say it was?"

"Fourteen ninety-five," the delivery boy said.

Mead handed him a twenty. "Keep the change."

"Thank you, sir." The boy turned and walked out, closing the door behind him.

"I can't believe I lost my purse."

"It's got to be somewhere."

"It's probably in my car."

She opened the bag and pulled out two white cartons and handed one to Mead. They sat across from each other. He opened his carton and lowered his nose to take a whiff.

"This smells delicious."

"Shrimp stir fry."

"Good choice."

They ate quietly for a few minutes. Mead's face appeared to brighten.

"What're you thinking about?" Sarah asked.

"I was wondering if you ever checked to see who our suspects called from Chesterfield's conference room the day of the murder. As I remember they each made at least one call before the verdict came in."

"No, I didn't, but I'll have the boys downstairs get right on it."

She picked up the phone at the center of the table,

pressed a few buttons, then asked for phone records on every call that came in and out of Chesterfield's conference room during the hours in question. She hung up, pulled a couple of egg rolls from the bag and handed one to Mead.

"Any word from the morgue?" he asked.

"Not yet."

"What's the holdup?"

"Sometimes it's hard to distinguish between an accident and suicide."

"Suicide! Never. Jonathan wanted every day he had coming."

"They've got to look at all the options."

"He probably fell asleep and slipped under the water."

"Probably. But in light of how everything turned out, the way he worded his confession takes on a little more significance."

"I haven't seen it yet. Do you have a copy handy?"

"Here it is."

She reached into her front pocket, pulled out a folded piece of paper, and handed it to him. He unfolded it and read it out loud.

I can no longer carry the guilt and shame that has plagued me since that fateful day when I killed Judge Samuel Chesterfield. I slipped into his office during the deliberation and stabbed him in the larynx while he slept in his chair. I accept full responsibility for my actions, and I'd like to make a formal apology to my fellow attorneys: Rutledge, King and Parris. I'm sorry for the embarrassment I've brought to you and your families. I will not allow my actions to ruin the careers and lives of the innocent. I will, therefore, do the honorable thing.

Mead bit down on his bottom lip and handed the paper back to Sarah. "And you thought the honorable thing meant turning himself in?"

"Wouldn't you?"

"No."

"In all fairness, at the time I didn't know he was terminally ill, and I certainly didn't know he saw Parris commit the crime."

"It looks like he set himself up as a lightning rod."

"You mean to divert the attention away from Parris?" she said.

"It's a pretty good plan really. If he confesses then kills himself, there's no way to recant. Case closed."

"And she goes free."

"One problem with that scenario though," Mead said.

"What's that?"

"I don't believe he cared enough about her to ruin his reputation. And I really don't think he wrote that confession."

"What makes you say that?"

"I've known the man for over 25 years, and I've read a lot of his writing, from homework assignments to legal briefs. That's not the way he writes."

"A man planning a suicide may not have been thinking about the quality of his prose."

The phone rang.

She picked it up. "Agent Riehl here... uh huh... uh huh... send him right in." She hung up the phone. "A tech from the lab is here with the preliminary postmortem results."

A few moments later, a tall, broad-faced, square shouldered man entered with a manila folder tucked under his arm.

"Agent Riehl?"

"That's me."

"We're not quite finished, but I wanted to give you what we found so far." He handed her the report. "A few anomalies popped up."

"Like what?" Mead asked.

"For starters, his body was riddled with cancer."

"We knew that."

"Also, the estimated time of death based on the email is a bit off."

"How so?" she asked.

"Based on the degree of rigor mortis, the deceased expired sometime between midnight and 3 o'clock."

"That's odd."

"But here's the kicker, he didn't drown."

"How could that be?"

"He didn't have any water in his lungs."

"But we found him underwater," she said.

"Dead before he hit the water."

"You sure he didn't drown?" Mead asked.

"Yep."

"Then how'd he die?"

"We don't know yet, and probably won't till tomorrow morning."

"What's the holdup?"

"These things take time. I'll let you know as soon as we have a definitive finding."

The technician turned toward the door.

"Before you go," Mead said. "What happened to his watch?"

"It's bagged and tagged."

"Could I see it?"

"Sure. Stop by on your way out."

The tech walked away. Mead picked up the carton and shoveled a heap of rice into his mouth. "We can rule out suicide."

"I don't think we can rule anything out at this point. Maybe he poisoned himself."

"But why jump in the tub?"

"To make it look like an accident."

"Why do that?"

"For the insurance money."

"He didn't have any children to leave the money to."

She shrugged.

"And why program the computer to send a confession at 8 o'clock in the morning, hours after his death?"

"Maybe he didn't want anyone to rush over there to revive him." She picked up an egg roll. "Sort of like Cortez burning his ships, you know, no turning back."

"But I really can't see him taking his life for Parris. She meant nothing to him."

"Maybe he didn't want a slow, painful death."

"Or maybe he didn't kill himself at all." The phone rang.

She picked up the receiver, placed it on her shoulder, and bit off the end of the egg roll. "Graham, this is Riehl. Hold on, I'll put you on the speaker. I've got Professor Mead here with me." She pressed a button. "Hello. Can you hear me?"

No reply.

She pressed another button. "Hello, can you hear me?"

"Loud and clear."

"Good. How's it going over there?"

"We're still sifting through a lot of data, but we'll be done shortly."

"What do you have so far?"

"The computer guys confirmed the email originated from Burton's computer. They say he logged on at 12:12 a.m. and logged off at 12:21 a.m. They're lifting the prints off the keyboard right now."

"Good."

"Also, we've lifted the most recent prints off the bathroom, bedroom and the living room doorknobs, and they all match. And get this, they belong to Jessica Parris."

"She was the last one on the scene?" Mead asked.

"It sure looks like it."

"I knew it," Sarah said.

"The bedroom and bathroom are loaded with her skin and hair fibers."

"I knew it."

"That's all we got so far."

"Good work, Jimmy. I'll be in touch." She hung up and looked at Mead. "I knew it. She killed her husband, she killed Chesterfield, and now she's killed Burton."

"You don't know that."

"Professor!"

He looked down, waited a few seconds and raising his head, said, "All right, bring her in."

She made a fist and jerked her elbow down. "Yes!"

"Just be careful."

"Don't worry. I'll send the boys to arrest her. Besides, I've got to hunt down my purse."

She dug in the bag and tossed Mead a fortune cookie. "Here you go."

"Thanks."

"What's it say?"

He broke it in half and pulled out the tiny slip of paper.

"A man must be ready when his time comes." He shoved half the cookie in his mouth.

"Let me see what mine says."

She grabbed her cookie and broke it in half. "Champions don't become champions in the ring, they are merely recognized there."

45

Sarah Riehl drove her hunter-green Saturn south on Ontario and made a left on Euclid Avenue as the last vestiges of sunlight dipped below the skyline, marking the end of a crazy day. No doubt tomorrow would prove to be even more eventful with Jessica Parris in custody. But before Sarah could concentrate on Parris, she first needed to find her purse. She relived the day in her mind. The purse hung from her shoulder when she left the house in the morning, and she remembered digging through it at Burton's house. But did she have it when she left? *No. It must be there.*

She turned right on East 55th Street and then left on Carnegie Avenue. She would swing by Burton's on the way home. At first, she was annoyed at the thought of driving 20 minutes out of her way, but then again going home didn't sound too inviting at the moment. She and Doug had argued at least once a week during their entire 15 years of marriage, but this morning's blowout had turned unexpectedly vicious. It was her fault, and she knew it. She hated it when Doug got the upper hand, and whenever that happened, she had to go for the jugular. It was her nature. And now she kicked herself for being so mean.

Twenty minutes later Sarah arrived at Burton's home

in University Heights. She parked on the street then ducked under the yellow police tape twisting in the wind. She trudged across the frozen yard toward the portico, each step crunching through the thin layer of ice covering the snow. She climbed the brick steps. A large padlock fastened a chain that looped around the doorknob. She fuddled with the keys Agent Foster gave her before leaving the Federal Building. She tried several keys before the right one slid in. The padlock sprang open, and she unwrapped the chain.

She pushed open the door. Every light in the place burned brightly. The rhythmic ticking of the grandfather clock from the far corner sounded unusually loud against the backdrop of silence. She retraced her steps through the great room, past the couch, over by the fireplace and back to the antique desk.

No purse.

She climbed the arched stairway, each step creaking underfoot. A search of each second floor room proved fruitless. She stood still for a few moments before easing open the door to the master bedroom and stepping in. It looked so much different with the room illuminated by artificial light. She tiptoed over and around small numbered arrows on the carpet and furniture identifying locations where evidence samples had been collected. The computer had been removed, and something else was conspicuously missing... her purse.

Sarah crept toward the bathroom. A tiny voice from the childhood recesses of her mind told her not to go in there. Images of Burton's naked, bloated body flashed before her eyes. *What a way to go, alone in a bathroom. It seems so undignified. Surely the end of a human's life should be more sacred than that.* She reached for the bathroom door. She hesitated. Her own mortality pressed down on her. She touched the knob.

Thwack!

She startled, spun around, and drew her pistol.

Thwack!

The noise came from the window. A black bird smacked headlong into the glass then tumbled to the ground.

She shuddered.

An overwhelming sensation to flee filled her heart. She turned and walked toward the door, then broke into a dead sprint when she reached the hall as if something was chasing her. She raced down the steps and burst through the door. The oppression lifted when the frigid air hit her face. She lashed the chain around the doorknob and fastened the padlock with the speed and dexterity of a master magician. She quick-stepped across the yard, repeatedly looking over her shoulder at the front door.

She hopped in her car, locked the doors, then cranked the engine. She took a few deep breaths and suddenly felt foolish.

"Some tough FBI agent," she said. "Chased out of an empty house by a goofy bird."

She drove off, and the closer the car got to Willoughby the more she realized the argument this morning had been Doug's fault. *After all, he was the one who brought up the money thing. A few pair of shoes and a purse here and there certainly doesn't break the budget. Admittedly, bringing up his mother may have been a low blow, but she did drink too much.*

"He can get more of the same tonight," she said as she turned onto Mentor Avenue. "The ball's in his court."

The street lights bathed the neighborhood in a pale incandescent glow. The bare trees and telephone lines cast shifting shadows of blue and gray and pink on the snow-covered lawns. She pulled into the driveway behind Doug's Dodge Intrepid.

"If he wants to fight about money, that car will be good for at least a half-hour's worth. He needed that car like a hole in the head."

She walked along the sidewalk toward the front door and braced herself for battle. She stopped at the mailbox next to the front door.

"Would it break his back to grab the mail every once in a while?"

She pulled off her gloves, tucked them under her arm, and then rifled through the stack of bills.

"Uh-oh, the Talbot's bill. I'd better hold on to that one. He doesn't need the ammunition."

She stashed the bill in her coat pocket and opened the front door. The living room was dark. Three flickering lights emanated from the coffee table. Candles. Her eyes crinkled, and a smile stretched across her face.

Either he's trying to make up, or the power got turned off.

She set the mail on the drop-leaf table in the corner of the foyer, then took off her coat. She walked over to the coffee table and picked up a note that was tucked under the center candle. It simply read, "I'm sorry." A trail of *Hershey's Kisses* looped around the living room and down the hall where a line of white candles stood like sentinels on saucer-plates about three feet apart leading to the bedroom.

Her resentment vanished. Doug might be hardheaded at times, but underneath that gruff exterior beat the heart of a hopeless romantic. She loved that about him. This was going to be a good night after all. She strolled down the hall unbuttoning her blouse.

She slowly opened the bedroom door. The lights were off, and the blinds were closed.

"Honey, I'm home," she said, each word dripping with seduction.

No reply.

"I said, Honey, I'm home."

Silence.

"Doug, if you fell asleep, you're in big trouble."

No answer.

She flipped on the lights and staggered back. Doug lay unconscious on the floor at the foot of the bed, face down with a white power cord wrapped around his ankles. His arms were bound behind his back with a leather belt. Blood covered his arms and pooled on the hardwood floor at his side. A jagged gash ran from his right elbow to his wrist. A pair of pantyhose were tied as a tourniquet around his bicep. Blood trickled from a cut above his right eye.

Jessica Parris straddled his back, one hand gripping his ponytail and pulling his head backward, the other hand clenching a serrated steak knife. Her nostrils flared like a dog picking up the scent.

Shivers raced up and down Sarah's spine.

"You shouldn't leave your purse lying around," Parris said in a voice that set Sarah's teeth on edge. "You never know who might find it."

"Please... I'll do anything."

"You bet you will. Pop the clip out of that gun... no... use your left hand."

Sarah reached under her blazer, released the snap on the shoulder holster, and pressed a button on the handle of the 9 millimeter. The clip ejected and thudded on the floor.

"Now take your thumb and forefinger on your left hand and pinch the butt of your gun... good... now throw it out in the hallway."

Sarah tossed the gun. It clattered down the hall and crashed into one of the candles and broke the plate.

"Put your hands up," Parris said.

"Why are you doing this?"

"You ruined my life. I figured I'd return the favor."

"I'm just doing my job."

"And that makes it right?" She jerked Doug's head back. His mouth opened. A faint moan slipped out.

"Please, he needs a doctor."

"You're breaking my heart."

"Whatever you want I can get for you."

"Can you bring Jonathan back?"

Sarah stuttered.

"I didn't think so." Parris slashed the knife across the back of his head.

"Nooo!" Sarah screamed.

His limp body collapsed to the floor face first.

"My compliments on your cutlery." Parris held up his ponytail with a patch of scalp attached at the base. "Quite sharp."

Sarah stepped forward.

"Stop right there."

"He's bleeding to death. Let me help him."

"Oh no. We're going to have a little fun first."

"Please—"

The fire alarm in the hall squealed.

Parris flinched.

Sarah lunged.

They tumbled over Doug's limp body and slammed into the nightstand. Parris slashed the blade at Sarah's face. Sarah weaved her head and deflected the knife with a quick backhand, the point missing her eye by less than an inch.

Sarah snatched Parris by the throat and squeezed with all her might. Parris gasped for air and desperately jabbed the knife deep into Sarah's shoulder. The steel penetrated to the bone. Sarah shrieked and released the choke. Parris jerked the knife free. Sarah rolled back over Doug and sprang to her feet.

Smoke rolled into the bedroom through the top of the doorframe.

Parris bellowed and charged with the knife thrust out in front of her. Sarah jumped back and to the left. The knife missed her. Their bodies collided. They stumbled through the doorway and landed in the hall. Parris leapt on top of Sarah, hacking wildly with a crazed look on her face. Blood poured from Sarah's palms as she flailed her hands in defense. Sarah curled her left leg up high enough to kick Parris in the chest and drove her back.

Sarah looked over her shoulder. A white candle lay on its side midway down the hall, igniting the wallpaper. Flames climbed the wall and scorched the ceiling. The pistol lay a foot behind the candle surrounded by broken bits of plate. Sarah crab-walked back toward the gun. Parris surged forward and dove at Sarah's legs, driving the knife into Sarah's thigh.

Sarah howled.

Parris drew back the knife, a demonic expression contorting her mouth. Sarah kicked her left leg and drove her heel into Parris' face, smashing her nose and squirting blood across her face. The blow sent Parris reeling.

The alarm in the bedroom blared to life. Fire spread across the ceiling. Intense heat engulfed the hall.

Sarah crabbed toward the fire and the gun. She stretched back her right hand, the gun inches away. Parris pounced. She drove her knees into Sarah's chest and knocked the wind out of her. The blade slashed. Sarah caught her by the wrist, the tip inches from her nose, blood trickling from the knifepoint and onto Sarah's cheek.

They struggled. Deadlocked. Sarah shoved with all her remaining strength. Parris stumbled back. Sarah stretched her right hand and grabbed the gun. Parris rushed forward, holding the knife above her head with both hands. Sarah swung the gun around and pressed the barrel directly against Parris' forehead.

Parris drew back the knife.

Sarah cocked the hammer.

"There's... no... clip... in... that... gun," Parris said

between exhausted breaths.

"One... in... the... chamber."

"You're bluffing."

"Drop... the... knife."

"I'll... drop... it," Parris said, "in your heart."

Parris plunged the knife.

Sarah squeezed the trigger.

The hammer struck the firing pin. A single, 9 millimeter bullet erupted from the barrel, entered Parris' forehead, and exploded out the back of her head, spraying brain matter against the burning wall. The impact of the bullet flung Parris' body back into the flames.

Sarah froze, horrified at the scene. The living room fire alarm added its warning to the others. Time was running out. Sarah limped down the hall and climbed over Parris. The flames chewed through the walls. Smoke billowed along the ceiling. The heat was unbearable. She dashed into the bedroom. Doug lay motionless.

"The house is on fire!" she shouted, shaking his shoulders.

His eyes opened slightly. He struggled against his bonds.

"Untie my legs."

She feverishly worked at the power cord wrapped around his ankles. It came loose. She started on the belt on his wrists.

The alarms continued to scream. Flames engulfed the bedroom door. "I can't get it," she said.

"Forget it. Help me up."

"Can you walk?"

"I'll have to."

Sarah laced her hand under his left armpit and helped him up. His legs were rubbery, but he stood. She kissed him on the lips.

They rushed into the hall leaning on one another. The putrid stench of burning flesh filled the hall. Jessica

Parris' body smoldered and sizzled on the floor. They raced through the gauntlet of flames, through the living room and out the front door. They collapsed on the snow-covered lawn.

"We made it," Sarah said.

No response.

"Honey?"

His eyes glazed over, his face ashen.

She rolled him on his side. The tourniquet had come loose, and blood pulsated from the huge gash. She cinched the panty hose tightly around his arm. The bleeding slowed to a trickle. She unfastened the belt and cradled him in her arms as the sound of sirens rent the air. A few moments later the fire trucks and paramedics dashed to the scene.

46

Edward Mead stopped by the University Hospital gift shop and purchased a Pick-Me-Up Bouquet and a box of chocolate-covered cherries. He broke the stem off a small daisy and tucked it in the lapel of his beige wool overcoat. He felt a little apprehensive about seeing Sarah. Maybe she wouldn't want to see him. Maybe she blamed him for this disaster since he'd dragged his feet on arresting Parris. Why not? He blamed himself.

He checked the room number written on the palm of his hand, then asked an orderly for directions. He took the elevator to the 4th floor then walked the length of the antiseptic-smelling hall to the last room on the right. Sarah sat up in bed reading the *Cleveland Plain Dealer*. She didn't see him at first. He quietly examined her battle-marked face, her eyebrows singed, her left eye swollen; a multitude of scratches and cuts riddled her face and neck. He stood by the door until she looked up.

"Professor!"

"How're you feeling?" he asked.

"I've been better."

"I bought these for you."

"You shouldn't have."

"It's the least I can do." He placed the gifts on the stand

beside her bed and sat down in the blue vinyl chair. "I read your statement. That must've been a nightmare."

"Let's just say I could use a vacation." She adjusted the IV pole with her bandaged hands.

"How's your husband?"

"It was touch-and-go there for a while. He lost a lot of blood. They grafted some veins from his leg into his arm." She looked over at the empty bed. "He's down in therapy right now. I knew that he was feeling better this morning when he started whining about his ponytail."

"His ponytail?"

"Parris scalped him."

"Ouch."

"I'd been after him to get rid of that thing for years. I guess she did me a favor."

"You know the only recorded haircut in the Bible caused a man to lose his eyes."

"I guess I'll have to start calling him Sampson."

Mead, feeling nervous, smiled and looked at the floor. "I'm really sorry about all this, Sarah."

"Sorry for what?"

"For everything you've been through."

"It's part of the job."

"But I feel responsible."

"It's not your fault."

"I drove by your house on the way over," he said, shifting his weight.

"The paper said it burned to the ground."

"There's nothing left."

"What a mess."

"Have you got a place to stay?"

"Yeah, we'll end up either at my sister's or his mother's."

"If there is anything I can do...."

"Everything is insured." She gave a crooked, rather pathetic smile. "I'm just glad it's over."

"Just about. There's still a couple of loose ends to tie up."

"Like what?"

"I've got to go to the morgue and sign the release on Parris' body."

"Somebody actually wants it?"

"The foster mother."

"She must be a saint."

"On the phone she sounds like she's in her 90s." He paused, then said in a more tender voice, "The woman actually apologized to me for what Parris did, like it was her fault."

"Wow."

"Then I've got to stop by the lab. The boys are still processing a mound of forensic evidence from Jonathan's house. In fact, they're headed back over there again today to follow up on something I overlooked. Sometimes I just don't know where my mind goes."

"What did you forget?"

"I promised your doctor I wouldn't talk shop with you. He says you need your rest. Don't worry about it. Everything will be wrapped up by the end of the day. Only one thing remaining."

"What's that?"

"Read the verdict."

"I thought it was sealed."

"I spoke to Justice Sudberry an hour ago. He's going to unseal the verdict tomorrow morning. I've already notified King and Rutledge."

"Where at? Can I come?'

"At the Federal Building. It'll be a closed-door session in Judge D'Andrea's chambers at 9 o'clock. If you're up to it, I think I can arrange to have you read the verdict."

"Me?"

"Now that you're a hero and all."

"I'm not a hero."

"You are to me."

"Come here." She motioned with her hand.

"What?"

"Bend over."

He complied, and she kissed him on the cheek. "I'll be there."

He straightened and pressed his hand to the spot where her lips touched; a faint flush crept under his pale skin. "What was that for?"

"For being you."

47

Edward Mead sat alone at the far end of the conference table in Judge Frank D'Andrea's spacious chambers with a single manila file in front of him. Three high-backed oak chairs lined both sides of the polished table, with two additional chairs at the ends. A warm mellow glow radiated from the chandelier suspended by black chains from the vaulted ceiling. Every aspect of the room from the decorative plaster walls to the thick-pile, scarlet carpet projected an aura of power and elegance.

Mead sipped his hazelnut coffee as Walter King limped in with Mrs. Roget. King nodded to Mead, pulled out a chair for Mrs. Roget, then sat next to her in the middle seat. A few moments later Dr. Rutledge strolled in, talking on his cellular phone and looking pretentious in a three-piece, navy blue, wool-and-silk suit. He laid his tan leather briefcase on the table and sat across from King. He turned his back slightly away from Mead, ignoring him, and continued chatting in a hushed whisper.

Just before 9 o'clock Sarah Riehl hobbled in, obviously still in pain. She wore an elegant, white-wool coat with a black leather belt tied around the waist.

"Good morning," Mead said. "You're looking rather overdressed this morning."

"Don't start. Underneath this coat is a Carolina Herrera halter gown."

"The hiking boots are a nice touch."

"Thanks for noticing. These clothes are all I've got left. Luckily they were at the cleaners."

"How're you feeling?"

"Better. My hands are a little stiff, though." She held up her palms, still wrapped in white gauze.

Dr. Baird wandered in, looking tired and hungover. His eyes were sunken with blue marks under them. As soon as he saw Rutledge, he made a beeline for the chair beside him. He avoided eye contact with everyone.

"How's your husband?" Mead asked Sarah.

"He's already itching to get out of there."

"Good."

"But the doctors said he may need additional surgery if the dexterity in his fingers doesn't return."

"I'll keep him in my prayers."

"Thanks. Looks like it's show time."

Judge Frank D'Andrea entered flanked by two federal marshals. The judge was short with a powerful build and shiny bald head. He sat at the head of the table opposite Mead. The marshals took positions by the door.

"I'm assuming you all know why you are here this morning," D'Andrea said. "So, let's get right to it. Special Prosecutor Mead has requested Agent Riehl read the verdict, and in light of the heroic personal sacrifices she's made in bringing this case to its lawful conclusion, I'm inclined to concur, unless either counsel objects."

"No, Your Honor," King and Rutledge said in unison.

"Very good." He reached inside his sport coat and pulled out a white envelope with a crested seal attached to the back. "Pass this down to Agent Riehl."

He handed the envelope to Dr. Baird, who cradled it

for a few moments before passing it to Rutledge, who handed it to Sarah without looking at her. Sarah took the envelope, weighed it in her hand, and then stood. She broke the seal and pulled out a thick, matted document. Mead glanced around the table: Rutledge blinked twice, then dabbed at his nose; Baird stared at the table; Mrs. Roget sat stone-faced; and King broke into a sweat.

"In the case of Roget versus Baird," Sarah began, "we the jury being first duly and lawfully sworn, do find the following: as to the count of medical malpractice, we the jury find the defendant guilty as charged."

Rutledge squinted his eyes tightly shut. The veins on his forehead and neck swelled and beat as if they would burst. King smiled; a sigh escaped him.

"And as to the count of wrongful death, we the jury find the defendant guilty as charged."

Baird dropped his head. Mrs. Roget looked rigid and impassive, as if she had not heard the verdict.

"As to the compensatory damages, we the jury award the estate of Robin Roget the amount of two million dollars. And as to punitive damages, we further award the Roget estate an additional 30 million dollars."

King pumped his fist and giggled. Tears welled up in Mrs. Roget's eyes and spilled onto her cheeks.

"Your Honor," Rutledge said. "The defense wishes to appeal both the verdict and the damages."

"So noted."

Sarah went to sit down. Mead stopped her.

"I believe there's something else in that envelope."

She stretched open the top, looked down inside, then fished out a folded square of yellow paper and examined it.

"Hey, my signature is right here. I remember this." She glanced at Mead. "How did you manage—"

"Open it," Mead said.

She unfolded the paper.

"What's it say?" King asked.

"It says, 'Dr. Rutledge, you are under arrest for the murder of Judge Samuel Chesterfield.'"

"What?!" Rutledge bolted upright in his chair, blinking like a strobe light. "Burton already confessed. This is ridiculous."

"You have the right to remain silent," Mead said.

"I know my rights."

"Are you waiving your rights?"

"You have no grounds to arrest me."

"I have to disagree with you there. The evidence is overwhelming."

"You've got nothing."

"You see, that's where you're wrong. A couple of days ago I asked Agent Riehl to track down the phone records for all the calls our suspects made from Chesterfield's conference room on the day of the murder. And just yesterday the FBI sent me an interesting report. It seems you received a series of calls from a Mr. Robert Prescott during the breaks in the jury deliberation."

"Who's that?" Sarah asked.

"Mr. Prescott is also known as Juror Number 8 from Baird's trial. Mr. Prescott signed an affidavit last night admitting he was offered $10,000 dollars in cash by Dr. Rutledge here to fix the case in Baird's favor."

"That's absurd," Rutledge said.

"Prescott stated that when he called you during the final break and said the deal was off, you were quite agitated. In fact, he said you threatened him."

"You've lost it, old man."

"When you knew the case was lost you crept in and killed Chesterfield. Personally, I think he knew about your arrangement with Prescott and was holding it over your head. So, by killing Chesterfield you freed yourself from potential intimidation, blackmail and abuse. A lethal objection."

"I don't have to sit here and take this." Rutledge stood. The marshals drew their weapons.

"Have a seat," Mead said. "I'm not quite finished yet."

Rutledge plopped back down.

"The forensic lab also made an interesting discovery yesterday. When they examined Jonathan's computer, they found microscopic white powder on some of the keys. In fact, the residue only showed up on the exact keys used to type Jonathan's confession. As it turned out the powder is used to lubricate rubber surgical gloves. Now, why do you suppose Jonathan would strap on a pair of surgical gloves before typing a confession?"

"How should I know?" Rutledge said, his voice so unexpectedly loud that it made King flinch.

"Well, the lab boys got an enterprising idea and decided to recheck the weapon used to kill Chesterfield, and you know what they found? That's right, traces of the same white powder on the handle. Isn't that a funny coincidence? Now where do you suppose Jonathan got surgical gloves, Doctor Rutledge?"

"I don't see what this has to do with anything. So what if Burton wore rubber gloves? I'm sure a lot of criminals do."

"But we didn't find any gloves at his house. And if he typed the message before he died, the gloves should've been somewhere."

"Burton confessed, then killed himself. It's as simple as that."

"See, you're wrong again there. The coroner ruled Jonathan's death a homicide."

"But the newspaper said he drowned."

"That's what the killer wanted us to think. The autopsy showed Jonathan died of cardiac arrest from a massive potassium overdose. A tiny fiber from his pants ended up buried in his buttocks, tainted with potassium, so we know he was injected through his pants."

"If he didn't kill himself, it must have been Parris."

"That occurred to me."

"Of course." Rutledge thought a moment, then a curious smile played over his face. "Why else would that psycho try to kill Agent Riehl?"

"I was ready to accept that, especially in light of the fact Jonathan was ready to testify that he saw her kill Chesterfield."

"Of course, it makes perfect sense. Parris did it."

"See, you're wrong again," Mead said. "The morning we found Jonathan dead, his front door was unlocked. Something really out of character for a guy who was so security conscious. That night, as I lay in bed thinking about it, I remembered a conversation he and I had a few years ago. He had been toying with the idea of having security cameras installed around the house. You know, the kind people use to spy on their baby-sitters? Apparently, some cash had come up missing, and he didn't trust the cleaning service. I tossed and turned all night thinking about it, so yesterday I sent a few agents back over to Jonathan's, and you'll never guess what they found. That's right, security cameras everywhere. We reviewed the tapes from the night Jonathan died, and we got some excellent footage of your car pulling up in the drive just before midnight."

"I went to discuss this case," he said, turning a shade paler. "Colleagues confer all the time."

"You may have conferred for awhile. The video showed Jonathan answering the door, and you stepping into the living room. The conversation looked cordial until Jonathan had one of his coughing fits. Just the break you were looking for. You needed a fall guy, and Jonathan was an easy target. You knew he was sick; any trained eye could pick up on his symptoms. He may have even discussed his condition with you. Maybe he sought free medical advice, not knowing that all the while you were looking for some way to implicate him. And what better way than securing a written confession from a dead man. So, while he was coughing and fighting for breath, you drove your knee into his stomach—"

"I didn't."

"It's on tape," Mead said, taking a breath between each word. He paused to regain his composure. "While Jonathan, my friend, writhed around on the ground like some animal, you pulled out your trusty syringe, the one you loaded at home with malice and premeditation, and injected him with a lethal dose of potassium. You knew it would stop his heart and leave no telltale signs... unless someone was looking for it. You carried him upstairs, stripped him naked, put him in the tub and ran the water. You typed in the confession and programmed it to be sent in the morning, so you'd be sure to have an alibi. But the only flaw in the plan was those pesky little nanny-cams hidden all over the place."

Rutledge stammered.

"You listen to what I'm about to say, because I'm only going to say it once." Mead pronounced each word deliberately, as though chiseling out each one separately.

"But... but..."

"But nothing. What you're going to do is make a full confession, and I mean now, within the next 30 seconds. And in exchange, I will not have you executed. But so help me God, if you force me to take you to trial for double homicide - the murder of Burton and Chesterfield - I won't rest until I personally strap your body into the electric chair and smell your putrid flesh fry." Mead looked at his watch. "You now have 20 seconds."

Rutledge sat rubbing his thighs with both hands, nodding, patting himself on the knees.

"Ten seconds."

Rutledge's face twitched and contorted.

"Time's up," Mead said with a gleam in his eye. "Now

I'll give you the same mercy you gave Jonathan."

"No, wait, wait."

"Time's up."

"All right, all right," he said in a breaking voice, a cold sweat glistening on his forehead. "I did it."

48

Edward Mead sat in his recliner listening to the finale of Beethoven's "Moonlight Sonata," his Bible spread open across his lap. Over the course of his life, he had probably read First Thessalonians two dozen times, but for some reason today it seemed brand new. He got excited reading about the Lord's return. He thought about how awesome it would be if Jesus came back while he was visiting Victoria so that he could see her rise from the dead. A chill raced up his spine. What a day that would be. He wondered what she would say.

The doorbell chimed.

He placed the Bible on the coffee table, pulled the handle on the side of the La-Z-Boy to lower the footrest, then shuffled over and opened the door.

"Sarah, what a pleasant surprise."

"I hope you don't mind me stopping by unannounced."

"No... no."

"If you're busy, I can come back later."

"No, not at all. I was just sitting around wondering why the word phonetic isn't spelled the way it sounds." Sarah smiled.

"Come right in."

285

She stepped over the threshold, and the floral scent of her perfume blew in along with a gust of frigid air. He closed the door and gave her the once-over. The cuts and bruises on her face were beginning to fade. She unfastened the black belt of her white wool coat revealing a stiff, new pair of jeans and lavender sweater. He noticed her hands were no longer bandaged, and that made him feel good. He directed her to the couch, then eased back down into his chair.

"To what do I owe this unexpected pleasure?"

"Would you believe I happened to be in the neighborhood and decided to drop by?"

"No."

"In that case, I came by to pick your brain."

"Don't pick too much, I don't have any to spare."

"Yeah right," she said, smiling at him with delight. "After the hearing yesterday, I stopped by the office to see the footage from those hidden cameras you talked about. And you know what? Jimmy Graham and the boys from forensics looked at me like I was crazy. They hadn't a clue what I was talking about."

"Imagine that," he said with a knowing grin.

"You made it up?"

"I bluffed a little."

"A little?"

"Okay, maybe a lot."

"You had me going."

"That's the idea."

"But how did you know it was Rutledge?"

"The potassium and the residue from the surgical gloves tied him right to it."

"No, I mean, how did you know from the very beginning?"

"He confessed the first night."

"No he didn't."

"He did."

"I was sitting right there."

"You weren't listening."

"Sure I was."

"Then you didn't pay attention to the detail."

"I took notes."

"Do you remember me having each of the suspects describe what the others were doing throughout the day?"

"Yeah."

"Jonathan, Parris, and King all had something in common. Do you know what that was?"

"No."

"They all recalled things with the same degree of clarity in the morning as well as in the afternoon."

"What?"

"I'm not saying they all remembered the same things. But they were consistent with themselves."

"I don't understand what you're trying to say."

"Let me put it this way: Rutledge only vaguely remembered the major events of the morning, but he had total recall of everything that happened in the afternoon. That showed he was preoccupied in the morning, deep in thought. He schemed, he planned, he weighed his options. But in the afternoon, he remembered everything in vivid, precise detail. His adrenaline was pumping. He just killed a man and had no way of escape. He had to watch everything and everyone. He made it a point to remember that King was the last one to use the restroom. In fact, the restroom was probably his undoing."

"What about the restroom?"

"In the morning Rutledge used the restroom several times. He went back there so often that everyone noticed and mentioned it. He scouted things out. He had to be sure his plan would work. But then in the afternoon, he didn't go to the restroom a single time. He made sure it couldn't be said he was the last one back there. He wanted to stay above suspicion. And I'm sure that by 5 o'clock his bladder was ready to bust."

"How did you put all that together?"

"As I said, the answers are always in the details. Do you remember me asking what each of them had for lunch?"

"Yeah, I thought you were crazy."

"Everyone had something to eat except Rutledge. He ordered lunch with the rest of them - before the murder - but couldn't manage to get a single bite down afterwards. His nerves were shot."

"Oooh..."

"But probably the most telltale piece of evidence was the murder itself."

"The weapon?"

"No, the way it was carried out. If someone stabs another person out of spontaneous rage, the victim is usually poked full of holes like Swiss cheese. But what did we find?"

"One cut."

"One surgically precise cut. So precise, in fact, that it pierced the larynx and severed the spine without so much as nicking a single vertebra, rending old Chesterfield paralyzed and mute. Simply put, it was the work of a surgeon."

"But Burton said he saw Parris do it. Why would he lie?"

"He didn't lie. He truly believed she did."

"That doesn't make any sense."

"Sure it does. Parris probably went back into Chesterfield's office to give him a piece of her mind or maybe she went back there to kill him, who knows? But whyever she was back there, Jonathan walked in just in time to see her reaction to finding her former lover pinned to his chair by a dagger - a dagger she'd bought for him. I'm sure it was a disturbing sight, even for a woman who had once stabbed her husband."

"That would explain why she acted so tense during the interview. But why not just tell us what she saw?"

"Would you have believed her?"

"Probably not."

"There you have it."

She shook her head. "I still don't see how she blamed me for Burton's death."

"That's easy. You were the hunter. In her mind you were the one who pushed him over the edge."

"That's a strange kind of love."

"That's a hysterical kind of love, more from wounded pride than from the heart."

"Hey, I just thought of something. If you knew Rutledge did it from the beginning, why did you have me waste all that time investigating the other three?"

"I had to be sure the evidence led back to Rutledge, and there might have been some kind of conspiracy going on, or..."

"Or what?"

"Or I could have been wrong." He winked at her with a playful smile.

"How're you holding up, Professor?"

"I'm feeling fine."

"I mean about Burton. I know you two were close."

"I'm all right. He didn't have much time left, and, besides, at my age you learn to hold onto the things you love loosely."

"But don't you get angry?"

"I learned a long time ago that hardening of the heart will kill you faster than hardening of the arteries."

"You're a remarkable man." She looked at her watch, then stood up. "I've got to run. They're releasing Doug in about an hour."

"And you have a place to stay?"

"His mother's. The woman hates me."

"I find that hard to believe." He stood slowly with a

groan and stretched out his hand. "Don't be a stranger."

"I won't." She shook his hand then gave him a hug. "And thanks."

"For what?" he asked.

"Just thanks."

Lake View Cemetery
3:15 P.M.

Edward Mead closed the door of his car and trudged across the frozen ground to Victoria's mausoleum. Something in the clear, pine-scented air invigorated him. Crisp frost clung to the bronze door like dried salt; he pressed it open, and reverently stepped in. He stood for several moments staring at Victoria's nameplate, tracing his finger over the letters.

"I found the remote control today," he said, his voice barely audible. "Very clever of you to hide it in the oven. Of course, I'll have to buy a new one now. It took me forever to get that burned plastic smell out of the kitchen."

Silence.

"Well, the case is finally over. You would've been proud of me. I did well. And as much as I hate to admit it, getting involved was a good thing. It helped me be me again, if that makes any sense."

Silence.

"The trial showed that everyone suffers from abortion. Without a choice, the baby suffers. With choice, the mother and the abortion providers suffer. Deep down, everyone knows life starts at conception. Taking that life has consequences."

Silence.

"I went to church today, first time since you left. It wasn't easy sitting in the pew without you, but I got through it. The message was good, from Acts Chapter 20:

repentance of sin and faith in Christ for salvation.

"I guess it's time for me to accept the fact that I may be down here for a while without you. Don't get me wrong. I miss you like crazy, and you can't imagine how much I look forward to seeing you again. But there may be a few things left down here for me to do. And with the Lord's help, I'm going to find out what they are and do them. He will call me home when He's ready. Until then I'll come and see you tomorrow and the day after that and the day after that and... well you get the idea."

He kissed his index finger and pressed it against her name.

"I love you."

He turned around and examined the vault that would someday hold his remains. He raised his eyebrows, smiled, then walked away. As he trudged across the crunching snow, he instinctively reached for his handkerchief to wipe his eyes, then realized he wasn't crying.

The End

Please Enjoy The Following Excerpt From:

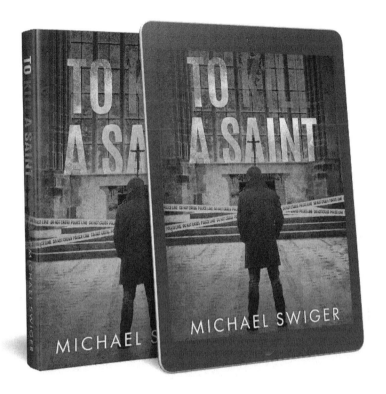

1

Saturday, October 14
Clifton Park, 6 miles west of Cleveland
Lakewood, Ohio
2:04 A.M.

Cuyahoga County Prosecutor, Peter Saul, fumbled for the phone on the nightstand beside his bed.

"Who is this?"

"April Denholm. Sorry to wake you, sir, but we've stumbled onto a pretty gruesome scene a few blocks from your house."

Peter Saul looked over at his sleeping wife, Marilyn, her red hair draped across her face. He spoke in a hushed whisper.

"What'd you find?"

"A woman called the station a few hours ago to report a peeping Tom over at St. Andrew's Church. We didn't get here until a few minutes ago."

"Why the delay?"

"She's notorious for false alarms, so the local police didn't take her seriously."

"Go on."

"When the patrolman arrived, the front door was open, so they walked in and found a corpse stabbed to death on the altar. It's pretty messy."

"Did you call Jimmy Graham?"

"He's already here snapping pictures."

"I'll be right over."

"There's more."

"What?"

"The pastor is all scratched up, and he isn't talking."

"I'll be there in ten minutes."

Saul hung up the phone then turned on the lamp on the nightstand. He slung his legs over the side of the bed and fished his feet around for his slippers. He shuffled over to the closet and pulled a pair of jeans over his pajama bottoms. He tugged on an Ohio State sweatshirt, a pair of wingtips, and grabbed his tan overcoat. He walked around the other side of the bed, leaned over, then kissed his wife on the cheek. She opened her eyes.

"What time is it?"

"It's very late."

"Where are you going?"

"They found someone murdered over at St. Andrew's."

"That's just down the street."

"Don't worry, everything is fine."

"Check on Jason before you go."

"I'm sure he's okay."

"Just look in on him."

"I will. Go back to sleep."

He kissed her on the forehead; she closed her eyes. He walked down the hall and noticed light reflecting on the hardwood floor under his stepson's bedroom door.

That kid will be the ruin of me.

He trudged down the arched stairway, across the great room with its vaulted ceiling, and into the attached garage. A few minutes later he parked his black BMW on the street outside St. Andrew's Church. Yellow police tape, strung from tree to tree, fluttered in the breeze and surrounded the white-sided building. The steeple's silhouette reached into the moonlit sky. Lights blazed through the windows. Saul walked up the uneven sidewalk and nodded to the uniformed patrolman standing near the front door.

Lieutenant April Denholm met him inside the vestibule, her

bright blue eyes looking surprisingly alert for this time of the night. Wheat-gold ringlets dangled around her oval face and partially covered her milk-white neck and narrow shoulders.

"Give me the scoop," Saul said.

"The deceased is a blonde female approximately 25 years old. No ID. She was stabbed repeatedly, dozens of times actually."

"Does the pastor know her?" Saul asked.

"If he does, he's not saying. You want to talk to him? We've got him in the office."

"Not yet, I want to look around first."

They walked down the center aisle; the sound of their shoes echoed through the cavernous room and mingled with the rapid clicking of a camera shutter. As they approached the sanctuary, a sickish-sweet scent of blood mingled with a tinge of sage permeated the air. The victim came into view, tied to the altar. She lay with her arms and head hanging off one end of the altar, her blonde hair spilling back toward the floor. The pink blouse was ripped open and saturated with blood. Her bra was hiked up around her throat. Ample breasts were cut to ribbons. Punctures and slashes riddled a taut abdomen. White lace panties hung from her left ankle. Coagulated blood blanketed the altar, and puddled on the floor in an irregular, black pool. A gray skirt lay crumpled in a ball on the floor.

Jimmy Graham stopped snapping close-ups and turned toward Saul.

"Howdy, Pete. How's this for a little late-night excitement?"

"I could do without it, Jimmy. What's your take?"

"Well, it looks to me like one of the first blows must've hit a lung. You see how this fine mist of blood covers everything like red spray paint?"

"Uh huh."

"If you look close you can see it emanates from this one diagonal wound here to the right of her sternum, right here, between the ribs." He pointed with his finger. "Blood in the lung must've mixed with air and sprayed everywhere."

"You're a regular Sherlock Holmes," Denholm said.

"You got any better explanations?"

"Lose the attitude people," Saul said. "We all have a long night ahead of us. Jimmy, I want pictures of everything."

"I'm on it."

"Any sign of rape?"

"It's hard to tell."

"We'll probably have to wait on the autopsy for that one."

Saul turned toward Lt. Denholm. "What about this peeping Tom?"

"Detective Myles is talking to the neighbor right now."

"Good."

"Also, we found some footprints near that window over there."

"What?" Saul's curious eyes opened wide. "What are you talking about?"

"We found footprints."

"Why didn't you say so?"

"We found them since I called you."

Saul's forehead wrinkled. "Let's go have a look."

They walked toward the side door to the right of the sanctuary. A uniformed officer stood in the doorway, his blue eyes blazing; he stepped aside. Around the side of the building, two lights mounted on tripods illuminated a large patch of ground.

"What did you find?" Saul asked.

"We've got a pretty good set of impressions," Lt. Denholm said. "They look fresh but a little indistinct."

"What do you mean, indistinct?"

"Whoever stood here didn't stand still, almost like he was dancing in place."

"Can you lift the impressions?"

"I'll be able to get a couple good casts. There may be more footprints around here. I'm keeping everyone off the grounds until daylight."

"Good, good."

"You think the perp staked out the scene before he went in and took care of his business?" Graham asked.

"Maybe."

"Or a lookout," Denholm said.

"Or maybe a witness." Saul patted her on the back. "Take your time, these prints are critical."

"Now do you want to see the good pastor?"

"Yeah, I guess it's time."

The group walked back around the church. Crickets chirped in the cool air.

"You know," Saul said. "It's been my experience that most homicides that get solved are done so within the first 48 hours."

"Why's that?" Denholm asked.

"Any witnesses who haven't stepped forward within the first couple days probably won't appear at all. And usually new clues don't surface after the initial investigation."

"That makes sense."

"So, we need to take our time and make these first hours count. Sun Tzu says, 'That which depends on me, I can do; that which depends on the enemy cannot be certain.'"

"That's interesting."

"What's this guy's name?"

"Jamison. Pastor Howard Jamison."

They walked back in the side door then crossed the front of the church. A uniformed officer tied a plastic bag over the victim's left hand. On the lefthand side of the sanctuary two uniformed officers stood with their back against a door; they stepped aside. Saul and Denholm walked in and closed the door behind them. Off in the corner of the small rectangular office sat a chubby, bloody, middle-aged man with his face buried in his hands. Thin hair lay plastered to his balding scalp by a layer of sweat, like strands of brown seaweed. He wore a light blue shirt with the sleeves rolled up to the elbows and a pair of pleated, tan Dockers.

"Pastor... Jamison," Saul said.

The man looked up. Three deep gouges ran from the center of his high forehead and down his left cheek. Dry, crusted blood ringed the nostrils of his beak-like nose. His puckered eyelids quivered as a pair of vacant gray eyes darted around the room.

"Pastor Jamison." Saul threw a leg over the edge of the desk and bumped a book – a Satanic Bible. "I need you to tell me what happened."

Jamison started to say something, checked himself, then dropped his head.

"What did you do?"

Silence.

"Pastor Jamison, it would really be helpful if you told us what happened here tonight."

No response.

"Do you know who that girl is?"

Jamison looked up; his face went white to the lips.

"Pastor, it's quite late," Saul said, his voice rising at each word. "And there's a dead girl in that room over there, on the altar for Christ's sake, and I want to know how she ended up with a chest full of holes."

Tears welled up in Jamison's eyes, brimmed over his lashes, then ran down his cheeks. His thin lips trembled; he spoke in a breaking voice.

"I'd like to talk to an attorney."

Saul didn't speak for a long moment, then a wolfish smile spread across his face.

"In that case, you have the right to remain silent..."

Don't Miss These Best Sellers by
Michael Swiger

Racism. Romance. Revenge.

A crusading congressional candidate, Marcus Blanchard, is framed for an election-night murder. Three powerful foes - his entrenched opponent, a drug lord, and a racist political boss – all want him dead. Accused of killing the woman hired to kill him, Marcus turns to the only man he can trust.

Brilliant but struggling with the ravages of age, Edward Mead takes the case while nursing his wife through Stage 4 breast cancer. Mead is thrust headlong into Cleveland's gritty underbelly. He collides with drug dealers and thugs, race riots and protests, and an all-pervasive political corruption that enslaves its citizens in poverty while sowing the seeds of division and hatred.

John Grisham meets Agatha Christie in this fast-paced, legal thriller murder mystery that grapples with the urban unrest in communities across the country. This book will leave you exhilarated and entertained, but most of all it will make you think.

A corpse on an altar. A witness who isn't talking. An ancient vow of secrecy.

It's 2 a.m. when County Prosecutor Peter Saul arrives at the scene of a grisly murder at St. Andrew's Church in an affluent suburb of Cleveland, Ohio. Pastor Howard Jamison is covered with the victim's blood, and there's a Satanic Bible on his desk.

Attorney Hunter St. James has spent a lifetime fighting his father's disgraceful legacy. With his career in shambles and his socialite girlfriend pregnant, St. James is assigned a pro bono case he knows he can't win. His atheist beliefs have not prepared him for a Bible-believing client and a subsequent crusade for truth that hurls him headlong into the dark, supernatural world of the occult.

Psychologist Faith McGuire, recently divorced with a special-needs son, longs for a second chance at romance. A confluence of deadly events thrust her into the epicenter of this whirlwind thriller, threatening everything she loves.

The physical and spiritual worlds collide in this high-suspense thriller that pierces the veil of secret societies and conspiracy theories and will leave you struggling to put it down.

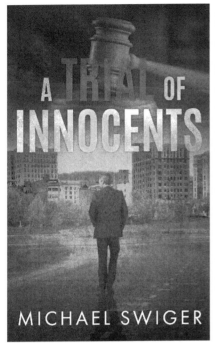

A pregnant woman is savagely beaten, leaving her unborn baby dead, and the would-be mother clinging to life in a coma. A special-needs man, who can't or won't talk, is arrested. The sensational crime draws national media to a quiet Ohio Valley community crying for vengeance.

Prosecuting attorney Lori Franks, beautiful and ruthless, will stop at nothing to advance her career. Having sought an abortion years before, she now seeks the death penalty against a handicapped man accused of killing an unborn baby. When a chance meeting followed by a DNA test confirms her baby was switched at birth, she sues to gain custody of the little girl she once tried to kill.

Defense attorney Danial Solomon is drawn into both cases. Sparks and attraction fly as he and Franks clash both inside and outside of the courtroom. Solomon's crusade for truth catapults him headlong into a lethal labyrinth of conspiracy and corruption that may cost him his life.

This fast-paced, faith-based, legal suspense thriller races from the life-and-death decisions of the operating room to the tension-packed fireworks of a murder trial with the unique mix of legal intrigue and page-turning suspense that catapulted John Grisham to the Best Seller list.

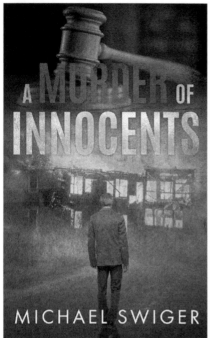

A terrorist explosion rocks a peaceful Ohio community and triggers a nationwide manhunt. A teenage girl is accused of concealing her pregnancy then killing her newborn baby. A Machiavellian political operative will stop at nothing in his quest for power.

Defense attorney Danial Solomon must unravel the divergent strands snatched from today's headlines before it costs him his life.

With one client dead and another's life hanging in the balance, Solomon's blossoming romance with Lori Franks swirls into a lethal vortex of crime, conspiracy and corruption.

In this masterful sequel to *A Trial of Innocents*, Michael Swiger once again entwines the reader in a tense, twisty legal thriller and fast-paced, faith-filled journey until the final page. Swiger proves once again that no reader can outguess a master storyteller.

ACKNOWLEDGEMENT

A special thanks:

... to Dr. James Dobson, whose 20 years of influence on my life has profoundly impacted the contents of these pages;

... to Edward DiGiannantonio, Esquire, for vetting the courtroom scenes;

... to Ann Collett at the Helen Rees Literary Agency, whose thoughtful suggestions have vastly improved this book;

... to my editor, Ramona Tucker, whose penetrating insights and impeccable sensibilities have smoothed off some of the rougher edges of my prose;

... to my proofreader and copy editor, Mike Jackoboice, whose tireless efforts, keen eye, and quest for perfection have resulted in a book that I am very proud of;

... to my wife, Susan, whose collaboration is indispensable to everything I write; and

... to my Lord and Savior Jesus Christ, in whom I live and move and have my being.

Printed in Great Britain
by Amazon

28300779R00175